MI

Mike Grist is the British/American author of the Chris Wren and Girl Zero thrillers. Born and brought up in the UK, he has lived and worked in the USA, Japan and Korea as a teacher, photographer and writer. He enjoys Ultimate Frisbee, 5k runs and spending time with his wife and son.

Christopher Wren (thrillers)

Saint Justice
No Mercy
Make Them Pay
False Flag
Firestorm
Enemy of the People
Backlash
Never Forgive
War of Choice
Hammer of God

Girl Zero (thrillers)

Girl Zero
Zero Day
Kill Zero

The Last Mayor (post-apocalypse)

The Last
The Lost
The Least
The Loss
The List

The Laws
The Lash
The Lies
The Light

NEVER FORGIVE

A CHRISTOPHER WREN THRILLER
BOOK 8

MIKE GRIST

SHOTGUN
BOOKS

SHOTGUN BOOKS

www.shotgunbooks.com

Paperback ISBN - 978-1-7398496-2-7

1

DELAWARE

Deep in the woods of Delaware, Christopher Wren raised a twelve-pound maul high overhead, savoring the weight and the balance.

It was evening, maybe coming on for 8 p.m., and a late summer breeze drifted through the dense woods of sassafras, silver maple and sand hickory, carrying the sweet scent of sap. Wren stood in the center of his thirty-acre 'farm', twenty miles south of the little town of Frederica.

Not a soul within at least five miles, as far as he knew.

He took a deep, lung-filling breath.

He felt better than he had in years. The maul felt good, poised upright against the graying sky. It was a composite log-splitter with a 27" fiberglass shaft and a drop-forged steel blade; a tool every bit as suited for its job as a Sig Sauer .45.

Wren brought it down, arcing gracefully to strike the wood flush in the center, splitting it with an almighty crack. Twin halves spun away like ejected shotgun shells. The shaft's fiberglass design numbed the shock up Wren's arms, but the ringing sensation still reverberated into his core, as satisfying as a slug of cold beer.

Wren let out a satisfied sigh. This was the life.

He picked another log from the scrap pile and set it on the stump, raised the maul again, then the first bullet ripped through the calm forest air.

The slug whipped by barely a yard away and buried itself in the log cabin wall with a solid smack, chased by a resounding muzzle blast. Wren barely had time to register it before a second bullet came fast on its heels, slitting a shallow line across his bicep as the maul blade fell.

Twenty years of special operations experience kicked in and Wren dropped where he stood, just as the forest opened up in a storm of automatic gunfire.

He hit the ground hard, three hundred pounds of solid muscle against the clearing's pounded sand. His mind began to spin instantly, and he tucked in close to the heap of scrap wood as the onslaught thickened, assessing the enemy threat. Heavy sniper rounds drilled into the thick logs like bass drum strikes. Lighter automatic shells shattered dried-out branches and slapped against the cabin's wall.

At least five assailants, Wren figured, maybe more, as he worked a tactical map of the farm. There was the cabin at his back, its open door only five yards away and looming invitingly. His Sig Sauer .45 and Benelli tactical shotgun were inside, but that was a non-starter. If he did somehow get in and hole up with the guns, they wouldn't help much when the attackers tossed in gasoline and a match.

Ahead lay the circular clearing, thirty yards in diameter, with his attackers most likely under tree cover on the far side. No way for Wren to mount an assault against them armed only with a maul. That left the flanks. If Wren was in their position, he'd have a guy creeping up right now on either side. As if in confirmation, a spray of bullets abruptly chewed through a corner of the log pile, almost hitting Wren's legs.

A burst of adrenaline dumped into his system and he embraced a third option. Retreat then attack.

He took a breath, waited for a brief lull in the firing, then surged into a sprint for the rear of the cabin.

"He's out!" someone shouted, then Wren circled under cover at the rear of the cabin. He sent a quick thanks to the heavens that no fresh flood of bullets met him here, which meant they hadn't encircled him. Not full professionals, then; knowing that shifted his calculus.

It was time to attack.

He jumped up, grabbed the cabin's low gable and pulled himself smoothly onto the sloping tarpaper roof. Only two weeks back he'd been up here tacking the paper into place. Now he flattened himself out and went very still.

From the clearing the salvo of gunfire subsided, replaced by shouted orders.

"Squad one go south, squad two north!"

Wren used the covering sound of their movement to belly-crawl up to the roof's crest and peer over. With the sun sinking off to the right, his profile wouldn't be easy to pick out against the darkening skies in back.

As he watched, a mob of attackers streamed out of the tree cover and split into two squads of four: figures in dark green and brown camo gear, all carrying matt-black AR-15 rifles. They didn't look like federal soldiers to Wren, or cartel enforcers, but you never could tell.

The squads folded around either side of the cabin. Wren counted three more in the clearing; looked like a captain advancing in the center. He was an older guy carrying a pistol with a thick Nathan Bedford Forrest goatee. Two younger guys with rifles padded either side of him, their eyes roving the woods.

"Clear south side!" squad one shouted, somewhere behind Wren now.

"North side clear!" shouted the other, meeting in the middle. "No sign of where he went."

"Find him," the goatee captain ordered.

"I don't see him in the woods," the first voice answered. "There's no trail at all."

The captain came closer still. He looked up.

"Maybe he went-"

Wren rose to his feet, crossed the roof's crest in three big strides and leaped, covering fifteen feet of lateral distance and ten vertical in less than three seconds. Three hundred pounds of solid muscle and bone fell from the sky, bringing the maul arcing with him.

The drop-forged blade hit the captain's head with a crack and split it like year-old sassafras, right down to the beard. Wren hit the clearing hard, burying his momentum in a shoulder roll that dragged the maul from his grip.

He came up fast: the captain was on his knees, wild eyes divorced from each other by the maul, the two guards just staring in shock. Wren lurched up, snatched the nearest man's AR-15 and fired into the other point-blank.

The man he was holding screamed. Wren broke his neck and sprinted to the woods.

Gunfire erupted behind him but the bullets flew wild; there was no chance they'd strike accurately while running themselves. Wren reached the clearing's edge in seconds and dropped into shadow, flat to his belly like a sniper, the guard's rifle butted hard against his shoulder.

The four members of squad one sprinted halfway across the clearing. Wren racked the AR-15's slide and picked them off like mayflies, teaching them the errors of their impatience. He hit the last guy with a headshot when he was still five yards off; utter economy of ammunition, just like he'd been taught in the Corps.

The man dropped to the sand and the clearing fell silent.

Far off a cluster of birds took raucous flight.

Wren lay flat and still, surveying the scene. The captain was down for the count, along with his guards and four other men. That left five, who must have retreated behind the cabin.

Wren rose to his feet. It was already getting dark. No time

like the present; he circled through the woods until he had them flanked.

They were panicking; shouting at each other in too-loud whispers, peering around the cabin at their dead friends. These weren't special operators or cartel sicarios. They were amateurs, and Wren almost felt like letting them go.

Then dark thoughts entered his mind, about what could have happened if these men had come in a few days' time, when Jake and Quinn were here for their very first sleepover on the farm.

That thought set a cold fury burning in Wren's chest.

For that crime, they all had to die.

2

FORGIVE

Wren watched the body of one last survivor.

The others were all dead. It had been easy; belly-crawl around the clearing then snipe them with head shots. They hadn't stood a chance. One man remained, slumped against the cabin wall, breathing fast and shallow thanks to the bullet Wren had put into his gut. Every now and then he whimpered a few words.

Wren was already thinking about disposal.

The trucks they must've come in would look bad if anyone saw them, but if he disappeared the bodies, the trucks wouldn't matter. Any story would work, absent evidence. Maybe these men had just come out to go camp and got lost.

Wren looked past the dying man to his cabin. It had taken a month to build. At first he'd struggled to get the huge cabers into position, even with the help of an A-frame, as each weighed in excess of four hundred pounds. Every night he headed over to one of the truckers' roadhouses along the Interstate for huge calorie-replenishing meals; a litany of burgers and steak and pancakes and bacon and chicken with fries on repeat, before passing out exhausted in a hammock beneath the stars.

He'd put on mass like a bull calf on growth hormones,

bulking up his 6' 3" frame. His chest, back and thighs had grown as thick as the logs he hauled around the site. One night his hammock snapped, unable to bear his ballooning weight. He reinforced it with steel cables and kept right on.

He got the roof up in a week, brought in beds for his kids Jake and Quinn, furniture, kitchen units; he rigged a septic tank, water tank and gas generator to power lights and heat. At two months he started to look further afield, and began chain-sawing outward into the forest. He shared sketches with Jake and Quinn, letting them chime in on the design of the BMX trails he was going to blaze, the assault course, the treehouse maze. Every addition seemed to require another addition to maximize it.

An archery range, Quinn had suggested, and why not? There was room. A canoe to ride up and down the creek in? Sure, Wren could build a canoe, probably. Then he had to make a jetty, too, and a shed to keep life jackets and other safety gear in. Then some huts around the clearing, for Jake and Quinn's friends to stay at. Then some high wires, linking the tree houses. On and on it went.

Wren had savored every moment.

He still did. If everything went as planned now, his ex-wife Loralei never needed to find out any of this had happened. Nobody needed to find out. He'd keep his visitation, keep his kids.

Wren collected two high-powered LED lanterns from the cabin. He set one down atop the splitting stump, where it cast a white glow across the clearing. Everywhere blood spread from dead bodies. At a minimum, he'd have to turn all this earth over. Nobody was moving now, though, and that was a blessing. All bled out.

With the other lantern in hand, he walked back to the sole survivor.

He was big, maybe 6' 5" or more, but terror and pain had shrank him, pressed up against the log cabin wall. His skin was pasty pale and he was shaking uncontrollably. The air was rank and stank of vomit.

"Please," he said.

Wren set the lantern down and dropped into a squat. Getting on the guy's level. A fresh flop sweat broke down his face. His dark collar was already rimed with stains. Close up, Wren saw the small dark X symbols stitched into the breast of his tactical uniform.

"You're with X," Wren said in his low, rumbling bass.

X. The homegrown terror group Wren's father had created before he died, that outlived him far enough to throw Texas into chaos.

"I'm not anymore," the man said, the words coming too fast and tripping over each other. "I swear it. I'm through with X. Really through."

Wren said nothing. The rage was gone now, buried back in the clearing. All that remained was necessity.

"Please, give me a break," the man said. "You can be merciful. Just let me go. I'll never come back, I swear."

Wren only looked at him. "What's your name?"

"W-Walton. Walton Meeks."

"Walton," Wren said, sounding out the name. "You have kids?"

"Uh, yessir! Two kids. Daughter's a teen, boy's in marching band."

Wren figured that was a lie. No point trying to call it out, though. "And you know I have kids, right? They could've been here. They will be, in a couple of days." He took a slow breath. "Did you check if they'd be here, before you came out to kill me?"

Walton's eyes flared wide, like this was a trick question he had to figure out. It took him five long seconds. "Yes! We checked. We knew it was clear!"

That was obviously a lie, too.

"No you didn't. You came here to kill me, and you could've

killed my kids in the crossfire. Maybe you hoped to. Now you ask for mercy, but how much mercy were you going to show me?"

Walton's eyes spun around the dark woods like he could spy some way out. "Listen, Mr. Wren. You know all about brainwashing, right? That's what happened to me. I was brainwashed, but I'm better now, I swear."

Wren liked this part least. "Tell me who sent you."

The man gulped air. "Who sent me?"

"This is your shot. I can find them and shut them down. Maybe you go free."

"I don't, uh..." Walton trailed off. "There's nobody. Nobody sent us."

Wren considered. That didn't sound like a lie. "What do you mean, nobody sent you? Eleven men. You all have equipment. You're all wearing an X uniform. You've clearly trained together, worked together. So who sent you?"

"We're not... uh. We're a militia. Ammenites of Texas, we're called. Out of DeWitt County. Nobody sent us. We sent ourselves, I guess. We've been training together for years. Only took to X late and I wish I never had. I'd take it all back. But sent us? I guess it was just the captain, and he's dead now."

Wren tried to absorb that. It didn't seem to make sense. There was always somebody further up the chain, dictating the flows.

"I don't believe you."

"It's true!" Walton insisted, and a heat like genuine anger came to his cheeks. "You know what happened in Texas. You think anyone's going to organize at scale there now? It's not worth the risk. There's no bigger organization." He sucked in a hot breath. "So we just sent ourselves. That's it."

Wren rocked back on his heels.

Sent themselves.

It was the worst answer possible. It meant there was no head of a new organization, which meant no single strike could stop attacks like this. If these Ammenites could find him, then others could too.

How did you stop that?

"I never wanted to go to Texas," Wren said. More to himself now than anything. "But your people dragged me in."

Walton shook his head earnestly. "I understand. Anything for a quiet life, right?" He gulped. "I'm the same way, from now on. I won't hold a grudge, I swear it. I'm gut-shot, but if you call an ambulance right now, I'll heal. Please. Forgive and forget, I say."

Forgive and forget. But Wren could see the truth stretching out ahead. It wasn't going to stop. Idiots would keep coming, and if he let this man go? They'd come all the faster.

Wren retrieved the Sig from his back waistband.

Walton's eyes bugged. "Wait, you don't have to do this! I forgive you! Can't you forgive me too?"

The gunshot rang out through the night.

3

AFTERMATH

"Christopher!"

Wren jerked awake in his hammock with his name echoing in his ears.

Trees stretched up above him, filtering the bright afternoon sunlight. It was hot and his whole body ached. He smelled ash and old smoke on the wind. Flashes came back to him of the long, wearying night he'd spent, burning all eleven bodies down to dust.

"Christopher Wren!"

It was a female voice. Now he sensed people in the woods around him, engines rumbling not far off, and rolled out of the hammock and onto his feet.

His eyes stung and he squinted against the brightness, running his blurry gaze over the dusty sand of the clearing, seeking out any sign of bloodstains and bullet shells. He'd searched for hours by lantern light through the night, turning over soil and collecting spent cartridges, but it had been dark and he'd hardly been at his best.

Gratifyingly, though, he saw no signs of evidence now.

He raised grimy hands to rub his dry eyes and staggered out into the light.

"Ma'am, he's here!" came a voice.

A young man in a gray suit stood at the north side of the clearing, right hand on the gun holstered at his hip, left hand holding a tablet computer.

"Who are you?" Wren growled. His voice came like a thirty-year smoker's, rough and husky. "What are you doing on my land?"

The guy didn't answer, just regarded Wren coolly. Others came into view then, melting out of the woods. Four figures. Six. All with their hands on their weapons. Wren swept his gaze over them until he saw a familiar figure entering the clearing.

She had blond hair pulled back so tight it had to hurt, a solid bodybuilder's frame with broad shoulders and thick thighs, but a pretty face boasting sharp blue eyes and prominent cheekbones, wearing a dark FBI jacket with a satchel slung over her shoulder.

"Hi, Boss," she said.

"Sally?"

Wren and agent Sally Rogers had a long history together. Once Wren's lieutenant, Rogers had headed up his team when they took down the Blue Fairy darknet ring. There'd been ups and downs since then, but they'd come out on the same side.

Now she emerged from the thick drifts of ash where Wren's cabin had once stood. Gray dust feathered her black pants up to the waist.

"Looks like you had a big fire last night, Chris."

Wren said nothing.

Seen in the cold light of day, the absence of the cabin was a blow. He'd made the decision in the small hours, then ferried the bodies inside, poured gallons of gasoline inside and lit a match, but still the gap it left came as a shock. At least the fire seemed to have done its job, erasing every last shred of evidence.

At least, he hoped.

"I fought it," he said, holding out his hands. "The fire." His arms were covered in red burn marks and black soot, so it seemed a good cover. Even now the stench of smoke coming off his clothes made his eyes water. "Back and forth to the creek all night, tossing buckets, but I couldn't stop it."

Sally Rogers strode toward him, passing patches where he'd turned and watered the sand, draining bloodstains into the earth. She didn't seem to notice, and the other members of her team went back to their business. Wren watched them with half an eye. If he had to make a guess, he'd say they were scouring the trees for shell casings.

Evidence of a mass firefight.

Had he got them all?

"It must have been quite the battle," Sally Rogers said, noticing the way he watched her team. "The fire, I mean. Especially when all those Texan X followers turned up in the middle. What were they, Ammenites?"

Wren affected a slight frown. "I don't know what you're talking about."

Rogers cocked her head. "No? They didn't come here, have themselves another Alamo? The trees around here are blistered with gunfire, and-"

"I do target practice," Wren interrupted. "All the time. Yesterday evening I must've misfired somehow, and that's how the cabin got lit up. My own fault. I didn't notice until it was too late."

Rogers stopped in front of him. For a long moment she sized him up, lingering on his arms, chest and legs, all swollen from three months of strenuous physical labor. The biggest he'd ever been, he figured. He had a clear foot on her, weighed a hundred-fifty more, but she was plainly unintimidated. A hard charger herself, she was hard charging still.

"You got fat."

"It's nice to see you too, Sally."

"If I'd known you'd come out here like a cow to fatten in the pasture, I might've visited earlier."

"I didn't tell anyone for a reason. But you'd be welcome for a visit. Your team, though..." He let that hang for a second. No need to talk about warrants and jurisdiction. "What are you doing here?"

She set her jaw. "The Ammenites. Eleven men, Chris, in some kind of X cell. An AI threat matrix fired on their behavior patterns, targeted at you. Seems they came here last night. I scrambled a team as soon as I knew. We found their trucks a few miles up the trail, but no sign of them. Now here we are." She spread her arms in a faint shrug. "Still no sign."

Wren nodded slowly. "Well, I appreciate you looking out. Seems I got lucky they didn't find me."

Sally smiled, but there was no warmth in it. "Seems so. It is odd you had such a fire last night. Given the gasoline stench still hanging in the air, I'm thinking you kept around twenty gallons inside the cabin?" Her tone turned mock-chiding. "You should know better than that. The temperature could've hit fifteen-hundred degrees. Easily hot enough to incinerate flesh. Crumble bone, too. Destroy everything but teeth."

Wren shrugged. "I guess that's why I couldn't put it out."

"And interesting, the way the bed frames were stacked on top of each other." She pointed into the depths of the cabin's ash, where the metal frames remained in position. Wren managed to restrain any sign of recognition on his face. He'd meant to take them apart again but forgotten.

"They're bunkbeds," he said. "It's how they came."

"Are they? It looks almost like someone was trying to create a fire chimney effect." Rogers paused. "Like a furnace. Ensure that whatever lay on top of those metal frames got plenty of oxygen and caught the full heat of the blaze."

"Or maybe it was just a bunkbed, 'cos kids like them."

"But what about the teeth?" Rogers mused. "And the shell casings. A lot of teeth in eleven men. A lot of shells in eleven AR-15s. If they were ever here, of course." She mused for a long moment, made a show of looking around the woods. "Easiest thing would be to bury them."

Wren said nothing. Throughout the night he'd collected all

the teeth and bone remnants and pounded them to dust with a ten-pound rock hammer, then scattered that dust into the creek. The shell casings had gone much the same way; pounded flat into one giant, unidentifiable brass stack, which he'd then driven ten miles away and buried three feet deep in the middle of the forest.

"Like I say, I'd love to help you with your inquiries, but all that happened last night was this fire."

Rogers nodded. She looked resigned. "That's what I expected. All those eleven men, I guess they got lost in the woods. Between here and their trucks it's a straight line, so it seems they failed at the last stretch. You dodged a bullet."

Wren shrugged. "Woods can be tricky at night."

"I thought that too," Rogers said. "But with your fire blazing? That'd be like a lighthouse."

Wren smiled faintly. "Strange, isn't it? There's no telling. I expect they're out there still."

"I expect they are," Rogers said, taking it slow. "Somewhere in the woods. I've got a feeling we'll never see them again, though."

"That's X followers for you, Sally. Who knows why they do what they do?"

Sally Rogers looked at him. He looked back at her. She'd never liked his extra-judicial killings, but why would she pursue this any further? These 11 men had come to his land armed to kill. He was well within his rights to take them out.

"Who knows," she agreed.

Silence passed between them for a few seconds, interspersed only by members of her team rustling in the tree line.

"So, you've had AI eyes on me?" Wren asked. "A threat matrix, you mentioned."

Rogers took a breath, like she was resetting herself. "We never took our eyes off you, Chris. Frankly, we intercept a lot of hate mail coming your way. Death threats, mostly, from X freaks. Sometimes they pay off. We've headed off plenty before they got this far. These ones slipped through the net. It's a full-time job for five people, keeping this little reverse Weight-Watchers bubble you've built for yourself safe."

Wren smiled wider. It was good to see her, even in this odd circumstance. She was a reminder of a life he was trying to leave behind; but still, she was a friend. Rogers was tough as nails, and loyal, in her way. More than anyone he'd ever met in the Marines, Force Recon or the CIA, he'd want her by his side if his back was to the wall.

"You're welcome to come get with the program any time, Sally. We'll get you moving timbers around site, build a jetty on the creek, really put some meat on those bones."

Rogers snorted. "Yeah. Count me out. And you should count yourself out, too. Where those Ammenites came from, there's dozens more groups all looking to take your head. If one group can hunt you down, the others can too."

"I'll be fine."

"You got lucky," Rogers said firmly. "Your kids weren't here, Chris. That was the first thing we checked. They didn't, I guess. But they could have. Imagine you're out here, miles away from anyone else, and they come in and snatch your kids. What then?"

Wren's easy demeanor hardened. "That's my business."

"You're getting soft. I can't blame you. If anyone's earned some R and R, it's you. But it can't last, Chris. Not like this, anyway."

He stared at her. He'd barely had a chance to think any of this through. He didn't like it, but she wasn't wrong. "So what are you proposing?"

She took a breath. Looked over her shoulder at her team, still scouring the woods. "Are they going to find anything?"

"Nothing to find."

She nodded. "Good. OK. Let's walk. Maybe show me this creek you keep talking about."

Wren grunted. "Follow me."

4

CREEK

The creek was a fifteen-minute walk, and they covered it in silence. The woods normally brought Wren peace, but that wasn't happening today.

It wasn't the deaths. Killing eleven men wasn't a hard thing to do. Destroying all evidence of their existence wasn't so difficult, either. Living with it could be hard, but Wren had killed so many people that the impact was vastly diminished. The justification for these deaths passed a moral threshold he'd set a long time ago, and he didn't second-guess that.

What he was second-guessing was what Rogers had said. If the Ammenites had successfully taken his kids, would he be standing where he was right now?

He didn't think so.

He'd be dead. He would've pulled the trigger himself, if it meant Jake and Quinn had a chance.

Before he knew it, the creek was there. He found himself staring down into its dark waters. Five feet across, up to four feet deep in places, it burbled and trickled a switch-backed path between mossy rocks and gnarled old hickory roots.

There was no sign of the bone ash he'd dumped here the night before.

"It's pretty," Rogers said.

Wren looked at her. He'd almost forgotten she was there.

"I can see why you bought this place," she added.

Wren pointed to the side, where a stack of seasoned lumber lay beneath a lashed-down tarp. "I'm going to build a jetty. A canoe too. There are crystals further along, big clumps of white quartz. You can just pull them right out of the banks." He took a breath. "I haven't showed that to the kids yet. There's a cave at the edge, too, that goes at least a few dozen yards underground, maybe further." He felt himself rambling. "Lots of things to do."

Rogers gave him a moment. "You can still do those things."

He turned to her. "Do you think so?"

"Yes. You just need to get away for a while. Give us some time to clean up Texas. Take the heat off you, put it back on us."

He could see where this was going. What made it worse was that she wasn't wrong. "And in the meantime, you've got a mission for me."

"Specifically for you," Rogers said. "A puzzle that'll earn us a lot of international trust." She paused for a moment. "One that comes from President Ablas herself."

That caught his attention. "The President requested me?"

"Officially, no. But unofficially? She's pissed off she ever had to hear your name again. But it came up, and she's no idiot. It's something you'll want to know about, too." She rustled in her satchel. "Will you look at some images?"

Wren savored the bubbling of the creek. He imagined the calls he'd have to make, if he agreed to this 'mission'. Explaining to Loralei and his kids that he was going off to fight the bad guys again. No lies, this time.

It didn't feel great. The alternative was worse, though.

"Sure."

Rogers handed him a slim black tablet computer. He brought it up.

It was a photo of a corpse, a naked male lying flat on his

back on raw concrete. It was an upper body shot; he looked Asian but with an uncanny pallor, like all the blood had been drained from his body. There were no visible wounds. His arms looked thin, almost wasted, but not otherwise unhealthy. He had dark, short hair, was in his early forties perhaps and wore frameless eyeglasses. Not ugly, not remarkable, just some dead guy lying on raw concrete.

"No blood anywhere here," Wren said. "But he looks like he's been drained like a kosher chicken. This is a secondary crime scene."

"That's our thinking," Rogers said. "DNA evidence bears it out."

"What's with his arms? Looks like severe muscle wastage."

"All that's in his medical records. Myasthenia gravis since he was a child, it's a muscular weakening disease, unrelated to cause of death."

Wren scrolled to another photo. This showed the man's face in close-up. There was some light designer stubble on his chin, scuff marks around his lips where he might have been forced to wear a gag.

He scrolled again. The next shot was a wide angle, putting the corpse in the context of an angular concrete tunnel, lying beside a channel filled with what looked like dark liquid. In-built bulbs beamed a fuzzy white light every ten yards or so.

"Modern sanitation," Wren murmured. "Some kind of sewer?"

Rogers said nothing and he scrolled on. The next shot was of the man's hands. A watch remained on his left wrist, the only thing he was wearing, a Cartier. Worth tens of thousands, if it was real.

"His watch, or posed that way?"

"His, as far as we can tell," Rogers answered.

"The killer didn't take it. So they're making a point. This isn't about money. Something else is going on."

He zoomed into the image, saw more scuff marks where the man's wrists might have been bound with ligatures. He flicked furthers: the ankles had scuff marks and some bruising, eyes were spotted with red flecks. He kept looking for some sign of a wound but found none.

"Where was he bled from?"

"That's where it gets ugly," Rogers said, eyes narrowing. "He was castrated. All his equipment neatly removed. The medical examiner says it happened while he was alive, but it wouldn't have taken long for him to bleed out."

Wren looked up. "Castrated?"

Rogers' expression was grim. "Someone hated this guy a lot. Evidence suggests he was held upright to get most of the blood; there's faint restraint marks around his shoulders."

Wren pictured the scene. At least two killers, then: one holding the victim up, the other bent over with a blade, or possibly one killer with a harness system. It wasn't a pretty picture. "This is a serious pathology, Sally."

"I haven't told you the best part, yet."

"There's a best part?"

"The killer left what looks to be a brand on the inside of his thigh, no bigger than a car cigarette lighter. Last photos in the set."

Wren scrolled on. There were dozens of photographs, the latter ones clearly taken in a white coroner's office, though none offered any obvious clue until he reached the last few. It showed the man's wasted leg, the skin drained white and lit by bright lights. A circular brand mark was raised up in faint pink lines. There seemed to be writing within the circle, but it was too small to make out.

Wren swiped to the next image, a zoomed-in version of the same mark, and saw three words written in the victim's skin, each letter barely a quarter-inch tall and perfectly sharp and clear.

FOR CHRISTOPHER WREN

It came like a sucker punch. He looked at Sally Rogers. "What on Earth is this?"

Now Rogers seemed pale. "The first of five just like it, Chris. Five dead men in Tokyo, Japan. All castrated, and all marked for you."

5

FOR CHRISTOPHER WREN

Wren stared at Rogers for a long moment, mind spinning through everything he knew about Japan.

It wasn't much. He'd passed through airports in Tokyo several times. Once he'd taken three days to roam the city as prep for a black ops mission that never happened, but that had been over a decade ago.

Back then Tokyo had seemed like a Rorschach test to Wren, one of those inkblot tests psychiatrists used to tease out deeper meaning. Everybody saw what they wanted to see in the towering skyscrapers of Tokyo's sprawl. Ancient culture. Cutting edge tech. The old world clashing against the new in sprays of tectonic neon.

But murders?

"Why me?"

Sally Rogers gave a slight shrug. "We don't know. All we know is, this is bad for all of us. You're something of a poster boy for American ineptitude now, and your name on these bodies makes it look like we're somehow exporting our incompetence."

Wren frowned. "I'm a what?"

Rogers made a pained expression. "I'm not surprised you're

unaware. Out here, you got away from it all. Fact is, there's a lot of 'funny' videos out there featuring you as a stand-in for America. Not your fault, of course. Mostly it involves you shooting yourself in the foot in various ways. In one you're the captain of the Titanic, firing a shotgun at the iceberg as the ship sinks. In another you're the Wizard of Oz, tapping frantically on a keyboard while the world economy crashes."

Wren said nothing.

"I can show you some of the memes, if you like. Also late-night comedians across the world reference you frequently, along with tabloid and broadsheet headlines, plus opinion hit pieces. In other instances, you're being painted as an old mule running itself to death on a treadmill trying to reach a carrot, or as a tortured idiot in Abu Ghraib-style robes, attaching cables to your own -"

"I get it," Wren interrupted. "So we're getting bad press. I am. It'll blow over. Who cares?"

"Money cares. Foreign investment follows public opinion, and it's drying up. The country's already been down-ranked from triple-A economic status to A. There's talk of the dollar getting replaced by the Chinese renminbi. Our companies are getting blacklisted, our influence is shrinking as our soft power wanes. Some of our allies are wavering. Every moment those memes circulate and we look like idiots, we're getting measurably weaker while our enemies get stronger.

The creek babbled away by Wren's side.

Things had gotten bad, he supposed. This was the reputational fallout from several years of chaos pouring out of the United States. Always Wren had been at the forefront. It wouldn't matter that he'd been fighting for stability. It just mattered that the instability was there and he was in the thick of it.

"So why involve me at all? You'll just be foregrounding me further. Whether I figure out these killings or not, it'll be my face in the newspapers again. More memes, except now I'll be in

Japan, exporting our chaos, like you say. I'll..." he trailed off as he saw Rogers' face setting. "Ah," he said, finally getting it.

"Yes," Rogers agreed.

"She *wants* it to be about me. President Ablas. Just me acting alone, not the United States. She's looking to separate me from the country, so she can pin it all on my head if it goes wrong."

Rogers shifted position uncomfortably. Wren spun the outcome faster into the future. "Let me guess. I go out there without any pomp or circumstance, right? No military flight, no CIA escort, no help from local assets? Nothing that would make it official."

"The Japanese PSIA will assist you," Rogers offered weakly. "That's their FBI. You'll have your Foundation for support, too. Private, outsourced intelligence."

Wren grimaced. It was genius, in a way. "Yeah. So if I figure this out in a way that's good for the US, Ablas steps in to claim the credit. If I make a bigger mess, she disowns me, says I'm some private citizen acting independently, like a vigilante."

He chewed on that. Rogers said nothing, though she was paling again.

"Maybe revoke my citizenship?" Wren asked. Rogers looked away and his heart sank. "Put all this on me. That'd be a great course correction for the US' image. Hang me out to dry like a sacrificial goat."

Rogers' gaze fixated on the creek.

"I couldn't even come back here, if it goes that far," he went on. "Maybe all this land would be seized." He looked around at the creek, trees, sky. "They'd lock down observation on my family. Arrest me, if I ever turn up. I'd never see my kids again, as long as they stayed on American soil."

Rogers took a deep breath. "All that was unspoken. But, yes. I think that's about what she has planned."

Wren grunted. It was all a big step, but not outlandish. The government had been treating him as expendable for years. "And if I refuse to go? What's happening in Japan's got nothing to do with me. So some Tokyo wacko starts signing his kills with my name, why should I care? My name's common knowledge now, like you say. It's a US public relations problem, maybe, but it isn't mine."

Rogers cleared her throat; it looked like she was trying to spit out a frog. "Well, there's the issue of us helping clear up the Texas X members. If you don't go, I've received very strong hints that there'll be no budget allocated to that effort. You'll be a sitting duck here."

Wren set his jaw. "I can deal with that. We've got strong oversight over the darknet these days. I can flush these X idiots out and deal with them myself."

"That's your decision. But with your kids' names, home address and school in the public arena? It's not a risk I'd take."

Wren gazed at her, then cursed. It was a good point. Yesterday he'd gotten lucky, and he'd never counted on luck.

"So you'll go," Rogers said.

Wren watched the creek. He was starting to get angry. "Ablas and I are going to have words after this is done. For now, she's got me over a barrel. I'll go. The best outcome for her is I screw it up. So I'm not going to screw it up. The Japanese are barely going to know I'm there."

"I'll help in any way I can."

Wren forced a smile. "I know you mean that. And thanks, Sally. But Ablas is using you. I expect it from a politician. Not from you. Don't do this to me again."

She nodded. "Understood."

"OK." He took a breath, surveying the woods a final time. "I guess I'm going to Japan."

6

JAPAN

Wren struggled up from a dark, cold sleep as the plane's wheels hit the runway of Tokyo's Narita International Airport. He rubbed his eyes. A Japanese phrasebook lay on his lap, along with his extensive briefing papers and crumbs from a pack of biscuits he'd eaten sometime in the middle of the night.

He rubbed his eyes and looked out the porthole. The airport was gray; gray buildings, gray runway, gray sky veined with dull dark splotches, threatening rain. A female voice came over the intercom in perky Japanese, Wren presumed welcoming him to the city. The announcement was lengthy and off-puttingly upbeat.

Wren tapped the seat back screen before him. Coming up for seven in the evening already, after a fifteen-hour flight. He did the quick mental math; that was five in the morning back on the Pacific coast. Maybe he'd slept three hours, and he barely felt rested.

The words of his wife, Loralei, echoed through his head. He'd called her from Philadelphia International to explain. They'd had a deal: he quit the life of a special operator, and in return he got to see his kids again.

"It's one time," he'd said. "They're forcing my hand."

"Come back soon," Loralei answered, "or don't come back at all."

Then she hung up.

The voice on the intercom switched over to accented English, pulling him back to the moment. The message was long and ended with the sprightly: "Welcome to Japan!"

Wren's first steps out of the plane, on the connecting bridge to the terminal building, were like walking into a sauna. Hot, wet air slapped his face and filled his lungs, making it feel like he wasn't getting enough oxygen. Even the sky appeared lower, as if it had dropped ten thousand feet since he'd boarded in the US. The effect was oppressive.

"Is it always this hot?" a tourist in back complained.

"This is rainy season," one of the air stewards replied cheerfully. "June, July. Very humid."

Wren strode along, imagining corpses in the sewers exposed to this kind of heat and humidity. He'd spent most of the flight familiarizing himself with the contours of the case; five dead bodies left in a ring around the central 'wards' of Tokyo, in the vast and labyrinthine Tokyo sewers. A judge, a CEO, a surgeon, a government minister and a banker, left to rot in tens of thousands of miles of sewer tunnels.

He pictured that rot setting in fast, driven by the moisture and the heat; mold creeping over the flesh, bringing corruption and decay.

The terminal building was air conditioned like a fridge and snapped him awake. In twenty minutes he passed through customs and into the Arrivals Hall, where men in stiff black suits wearing white gloves and sharp peaked caps stood waiting at a railing, all holding out name cards for clients. Here and there were monks in orange robes, bald heads shining in the bright lights. He scanned the line until he saw his name on a card.

WREN-SAN

The card was in the hands of a lone woman. She stood out

amongst the ranks of uniformed taxi drivers, but she would have stood out anywhere.

She was six feet tall, with thick raven-black hair pulled into a loose ponytail, and she was gorgeous. There was no getting around it. Her eyes were wide ovals, her lips shone, her cheekbones could've cut glass and even the formal fit of her gray pantsuit couldn't hide the swelling hourglass of her body's natural curves.

Wren strode up to her. She'd already picked him out too, it seemed, and ran her gaze up and down in one assessing glare. If anything, she seemed unimpressed.

"Ohayou gozaimasu," Wren said as he drew up to her, trying a Japanese greeting from the phrasebook. "I'm agent Chris Wren."

The woman frowned, her perfectly coiffed brows pulling the smooth skin in tight, then spoke in British-accented English. "Wren-san, I am Makoto Toyama, your partner with the PSIA. You may call me Toyama. There is no need to say '-san' at the end of my name, as that is an honorific given to seniors. I will call you Wren-san, as that is customary. And it is not morning. You just greeted me by saying, 'Good morning.'"

Wren offered a faint smile. So she was a spiky one. "It's morning for me. And please, just call me Chris."

"This way, please," she said, ignoring him, and spun summarily on her heel.

Wren followed, scanning the Arrivals Hall: it was huge, and crammed with tiny booths, each featuring a service person out front perfectly coiffed, holding brochures of some kind. He saw a sign for a 'Limousine Bus', which sounded nice, and several for hot springs tours of the lakes in the shadow of Mt. Fuji. Off to the side there was a DHL booth.

Toyama was already ten yards ahead, her hourglass figure weaving rapidly through the crowd. Wren figured he'd catch up, and broke directly for the DHL booth, where a young man in a bright yellow and red uniform smiled attentively as Wren approached.

"You should have a package for me." Wren said.

It took moments to retrieve it. A small box ordered from the plane, delivered within hours. He had it open by the time Toyama found him and came stalking over.

"Wren-san," she said, "we really must-"

"Call me Chris," he interrupted, scooping the contents from the box. It was a complete T-CAPS earbud kit, Tactical Communication and Protective System, featuring a snug earpiece, microphone and sensors. Not Wren's preferred gear, but on short notice in a foreign country, without access to CIA resources, it would do. He slotted the earbud into his right ear, attached the microphone to his jacket lapel and tucked the sensors into his pocket.

"Let's go," he said, and started away, bringing up his phone.

"What is this device for?" Toyama asked, keeping pace beside him.

Wren clicked through to an app he'd downloaded on the plane and waited twenty seconds until the earpiece chimed in his ear.

"Ready and waiting," came a crisp, clear female voice in Wren's ear.

He looked up at Toyama. "The headset catches whispers from ten feet away, also muffles sound at dangerous levels. It's a great piece of kit. The app I'm using provides outsourced simultaneous translation, someone always on the other end ready to translate. I've used them before."

Toyama frowned, clearly unimpressed. "Interpretation is one of the purposes I am assigned to. This is-"

"I'm sure you're good for more than translation," Wren said, and dropped the box in a trash container as they passed.

Her full lower lip curled a little. "This way," she said, and stormed on.

This time Wren kept pace. At a turnstile for the Narita

Express, the train service into Tokyo, she stopped and handed him a credit card-sized oblong of green plastic.

"This is your travel card. We take longer journeys by train. To take a car in Tokyo is often slower. The underground lines are fast. We're booked onto the express line into Tokyo. You were late debarking from your plane, however, so we may miss-"

While she was talking, Wren scanned his card over the turnstile's pad and pushed through. He'd already read the digital signs overhead. "We can still make it, if we run."

He set off at a light jog. Toyama was another hard charger, he figured, clearly annoyed at what seemed an international babysitting duty. But that was OK. Wren loved hard chargers.

By the time he hit the stairs leading down to their platform, where the sleek white train's doors were chiming to close, she overtook him.

The interior of the train was as sleekly molded as the exterior, and many of the seats were already filled with passengers; the vast majority of them Japanese. The men were trim, dressed in black suits with neckties throttled tight like nooses, sporting short-cropped black hair. The women wore gray suit jackets over skirts, with glossy black ponytails.

Toyama took a seat at the one empty four-top table. Wren sat opposite her. Her eyes were striking; the irises so dark that they merged with her pupils.

"You don't mind riding backward?" Wren asked.

Toyama frowned. "Why would I mind riding backward?"

"Some people do. I'll swap, if you like."

"No," she said flatly. "We'll use this time to acclimate you to law enforcement procedures in Tokyo. It is very different from what you are used to in America. The PSIA, or Public Security Intelligence Agency, is not a militarized service, like your FBI. We don't carry handguns, and we cannot make arrests."

That caught his attention. "You can't even make arrests?"

"Not without a specific warrant."

He mulled it over. "Can I make arrests?"

"Of course not. Now, there are a number of procedures that-"

"I'd rather talk about the case."

She frowned. "The case? Now? On a public train?"

Wren looked around. Nobody was looking at them. One man nearby was already asleep, a neck-cushion firmly ensconced around his collar, jaw slack. "I think we're OK."

"Is that how you conduct yourself in America?" she asked, then muttered something further to herself in low Japanese. Wren barely caught it, but the T-CAPS in his ear did, and relayed it to the interpreter waiting on the other end, who offered a simultaneous translation.

"She said something like: 'Arrogant Americans.'"

Wren laughed.

"What is funny?" Toyama asked.

Wren tapped the earpiece. "It catches whispers, remember?"

Her smooth cheeks reddened slightly.

"Listen," Wren went on, "I realize partnering with me may not be your dream assignment. Being here wasn't my idea either. But we're both here, and the case is serious, so let's make the best of it. What do you say?"

Toyama just stared at him. Those wide-open pupils made for a piercing glare.

"I can have that translated into Japanese, if you like," Wren said, holding up his phone. He tapped a button, and instantly the interpreter on the other end began speaking in Japanese.

At that moment the train pulled away from the station. The acceleration was smooth, rapid and silent, and the station slickly receded. In seconds they emerged from the station into a drab switching yard flanked on all sides by the low gray sky, coursing by at a wickedly fast pace already.

Wren turned back to Toyama.

Now there was a sheet of paper on the table before them, whisked there just as silently as the train's acceleration. It had numerous bullet points and a signature line at the bottom. "I would like to establish standard operating procedures," she said.

"You are renowned for disregarding standard procedure, or 'going rogue', as it can be called. This approach has worked well for you in your home country. It will not work well in Japan."

Wren picked up the paper and scanned it. One of the bullet points was a promise not to handle any offensive weapons. Another was a promise not to involve the members of his Foundation in any way. A third was to avoid saying anything to the media."

"Too late for all three of these," Wren said, tapping each bullet point.

Toyama remained cold and neutral. "What did you do?"

"I already have an offensive weapon. A club in my luggage. It looks like a flashlight, but it's a club. Second, I called my Foundation from the plane. I've got teams already digging into the victims. Subtly, of course."

Toyama looked unamused. "And the third? You already spoke to the media?"

"I posted on my social feed that I'm taking a holiday overseas. I didn't say where, but it's better to have a cover story in place, for the moment someone recognizes me."

Toyama's jaw set hard at that, and tiny patches at the peak of each cheek turned white. It looked kind of cute, Wren supposed.

"You will surrender the club," she said robotically. "You will make no further posts about your 'holiday'. And you will not meet up with any of your 'Foundation' members, without the PSIA's express approval. Essentially, Wren-san, everything you do, say, see or think from this point forward will go through me."

Wren watched her. A harder charger than he'd thought, perhaps, but a little too easy to emotionally manipulate.

"You do realize it's not me signing my name on those dead peoples' bodies, right? That I'm here to help?"

She stabbed the list. Looked like the fourth bullet point to Wren. "No discussion of cases in public."

"I haven't signed it yet."

She pushed the paper closer and laid down a pen firmly.

"You were supposed to sign it before we left the airport, Wren-san. Now, I must insist."

"And if I don't sign this?"

"Then we turn around at Tokyo station and I send you on the next plane back to America. My government and my agency want this matter cleared up as calmly and quietly as possible."

Wren couldn't argue with that. "I feel the exact same way." He signed the paper and handed it back. Toyama produced a slim plastic wallet from her valise and slid the paper in.

"Now," she said, rising from her seat. "I must make several telephone calls. We will speak more when the train arrives."

She stalked away.

Wren watched her go, hips swaying like a metronome. She was right, they did do things differently in Japan. He turned to look out the window, just as the first slashes of rain spattered down across the glass. Moments later the gray skies broke open, and all Wren could see after that was the downpour.

"Welcome to Tokyo," he muttered to himself.

7

WELCOME TO TOYKO

Despite the falling curtain of rain, Wren picked out the thickening of infrastructure as the train pushed into Tokyo. Fields gave way to low apartment blocks of featureless gray concrete, which in turn gave way to taller blocks that crowded in on the train line like cantilevered overhangs on a shadowy Victorian street.

Just as the surging buildings drew within yards of the train, tunnel walls rose up either side that cut off the view. Each wall rose some fifteen feet high on a concave curve then stopped, leaving the sky open.

For noise pollution, Wren knew. He'd traveled from the airport by car when he'd last visited Japan, and the roads had the same thing. Back then it had seemed like an obvious act of consideration; the kind of thing you had to do when forty million people lived on top of each other like this.

But now?

Now it was claustrophobic. Japan seemed very different. Back then on his first visit, the country had been in the throes of spring and everything had seemed beautiful, from the people to the neon-sprayed architecture to the fluttering cherry blossoms in the air.

It had been a joy to walk through parks and along riversides, casing various potential safehouses for an op that never came to fruition. The city had felt like a place of limitless potential, its skyscraper hands straining up to some unseen future in the sky. Now it felt oppressive. The kind of place where men were bled out in the sewers.

There was no sign of Makoto Toyama, so Wren went ahead and checked in on his Foundation darknet. His hackers had come up with the goods on each of the five dead men, but there was nothing yet to tie them together, and nothing to tie them to Wren. The most interesting of the five seemed to be the CEO, Kenji Ando, largely because he'd spent a lot of time in English-speaking environments. Wren figured he could get into the man's head more easily.

After an hour Toyama returned, moments before they were due to arrive, and held out one hand.

"Club, please, Wren-san."

He had it ready and handed it over. A fifteen-inch long 4D flashlight; with the batteries in it weighed a solid few pounds and would brain a man as easily as any police baton.

Toyama tucked it into her valise alongside the paper he'd signed, like a teacher confiscating another piece of contraband. "We'll meet several of my colleagues at Tokyo station. I would appreciate it if you followed procedure to the letter."

"As long as the letter doesn't mean them getting in my way, that's fine."

Toyama eyed him. "You are a man used to getting your own way. That is not how it works in Japan. *deru kugi wa utareru.*"

Wren's translator kicked into gear in his ear. "She said, 'The nail that sticks out gets hammered down.'"

It sounded like an ancient proverb, tested by time. Not tested by him, though. "Easy answer to that, Toyama. Be the hammer, not the nail."

Her lips quirked into a faint smile, like she knew something he didn't.

The train slowed and the curved walls of the tunnel gave way to the open platforms of Tokyo station. Wren stood.

"Douzo," he said, another phrase he'd learned, that meant 'after you.' He accompanied it with a 'ladies first' gesture.

Toyama strode away without a word or a second glance.

The station was cavernous, and people were moving everywhere in a complex series of cross currents, but not like the currents of an American mass transit system. In the US there would be bright colors, and different shapes and sizes, and people shouting and bumping into each other.

Here the people flowed like oil in grooved channels, silent and perfect. It was a crass stereotype to say everyone looked the same, but compared to Grand Central in New York or even Metro Center in Washington, they did. Short, dark-haired, suited, pulling wheeled suitcases behind them in an orderly, meek manner. There was precious little color or noise or conflict, and at 6' 3" Wren towered over everyone.

Toyama led them off the platform, through a turnstile and out onto the open concourse. There were more figures in suits standing around, holding signs. Toyama spotted a group of three men some fifty yards off and made a beeline for them. They were all shorter and slighter than Wren, clean-shaven with short hair, in dark suits.

As they strode up, Wren spoke first. "Good evening. I'm Christopher Wren. Thank you for inviting me here to investigate this case."

One of the three smirked; mid-forties, slicked back black hair, he had the look of a weasel about him. The other two bowed and smoothly handed Wren their name cards. Wren took them carefully with both hands and studied them for a moment, like the guidebook had instructed.

"It is our honor to have you in Japan," the eldest of the men said formally, maybe mid-sixties. "I am Ino Yamaguchi, subsection chief of PSIA. I am overseeing this case."

Wren nodded. "A pleasure to meet you, Yamaguchi-san."

"Was your flight comfortable?"

"It was excellent," Wren said, and held up his phrasebook. "Gave me a chance to brush up on my Japanese."

Yamaguchi's eyes narrowed. "You speak Japanese?"

"I think I've mastered three words so far," Wren allowed. "Toyama-san here has been extremely helpful."

He felt her fuming by his side at the use of the '-san' honorific. The subtext seemed to escape Yamaguchi. "This is excellent. I hope our cooperation will be most fruitful. Now, here are PSIA agents Nakamura and Sato, who will be offering assistance."

Nakamura was in his thirties, with a whisker of a mustache on his upper lip. He bowed. Sato, the weasel, barely tipped his head; instead he muttered something in Japanese to Nakamura.

The T-CAPS caught it, and Wren's translator sprang into action. "He said, 'Maybe the ice queen will screw this ogre.'"

Interesting. Wren looked at Toyama, who gave him a sharp, barely perceptible shake of her head.

Even more interesting.

Yamaguchi seemed oblivious. Maybe he hadn't heard or had chosen not to. Was this the nail getting hammered down?

"I would like to invite you to our offices, Wren-san," Yamaguchi said. "But it is late, and you must be tired. Perhaps you would like to begin your investigation in the morning?"

Sato muttered something else. This time Nakamura smiled.

"He said, 'Investigation of the ice queen's ass.'" Wren's translator offered.

Wren didn't need to look at Toyama this time. It was always better to be the hammer.

"Thank you for your consideration, Yamaguchi-san," he said. "But as I already mentioned to Toyama here, it's morning for me now. I'm ready to work. I'd like to see one of the sewer scenes, if that's possible. And Sato-san." He turned to the weasel-faced man. "To avoid undue embarrassment later, there's something you should know. I have in-ear simultaneous translation, and I can say with confidence that the chances of a romantic enterprise between Toyama and myself are almost as unlikely as the chances of one between her and you."

Nakamura's eyes bugged. Toyama let out a little gasp. Only Sato seemed confused. For his benefit, Wren held up his phone and tapped the button for translation.

His simultaneous translator repeated everything he'd just said in flawless Japanese, loud and clear through the speaker. Sato's eyes widened, then narrowed. Humiliation turning into fury. That was a nice reaction.

"Yes, I think a visit to the latest crime scene will be possible," Yamaguchi said swiftly. Ignoring the things he didn't want to hear and reacting only to business. "Speed is good in this case."

Wren nodded to him, then turned to Toyama. Her cheeks were burning bright red with barely restrained anger.

"Hammers," Wren said with a shrug, then made the ladies' first gesture again. "Douzo."

8

FLOATING WORLD

They took a subway train eight stops to Shinjuku station and didn't speak a word. Wren could feel Toyama building to an explosion, like a thundercloud gathering a charge, but they reached the entrance to the sewers before lightning could strike.

There was a uniformed police officer standing at a metal door set into a tiled wall, at the end of the Marunouchi line westbound platform.

"You've got sewer access here?" Wren asked.

Toyama ignored the question and spoke briefly to the cop, showing him her PSIA badge. The T-CAPS headset caught every word, but it seemed they were too far underground for the signal to reach Wren's translator, so the conversation remained a blank to him.

Didn't matter. In less than a minute the cop opened the door and Toyama gestured Wren forward. "Douzo."

Ahead lay a long, gloomy, cement-walled access passage, illuminated by industrial lamps every twenty feet or so, lined with dozens of pipes, conduits and cables. It was barely three feet wide, with a ceiling that was maybe six feet tall.

"You'll have to bend over," Toyama said frostily. "Looks like the nail will get blunted after all."

Wren almost laughed but held it in. Before stepping through, he took a moment to look to either side along the platform. The rail line stretched away into the wormy dark of tunnels in both directions.

"Is there access to the sewers from the train line itself?"

"Unlikely," Toyama answered readily. Calm and controlled now that they were back to business. "We checked the plans for each of the dump sites. The Tokyo sewers have multiple access points, but mostly that's from above ground via various maintenance ladders, impassable drains, and the basements of adjoining buildings. Access from train lines outside of the stations is not marked anywhere. That doesn't mean it's not possible. The city is vast and complex."

Wren considered that. "You mentioned adjoining buildings. Why would they link to the sewers?"

Toyama gave him a look like he should have known this already, then took a deep breath. "Tokyo is a city built on water, Wren-san. All the land around us is part of the Kanto floodplain, with over a hundred rivers and canals that used to overflow regularly during rainy season. All but one or two of these were encased in concrete decades ago and submerged, but Japan is also a city of earthquakes and floods. Everything shifts, sinks and floats." She took another breath. "There are thousands of miles of flood-prevention tunnels to accommodate this, a whole parallel sewage system in case the existing one fails. There are overflow halls bigger than football stadiums, large enough to capture and bury a small ocean. The amount of overlap in our underground architecture requires advanced three-dimensional modeling. Every new building that goes up must build upon and around existing structures with great care. These foundations are like an interwoven root system, all connected."

Wren was left trying to picture that. It sounded like the tangled root labyrinth of a mangrove forest, stretching over thousands of square miles. "So asking if this route into the sewers is the likely route our killer took is simplistic at best."

"At best," she allowed.

A wave of hot air washed over them both and Wren watched the tunnel's far mouth, waiting for a train to appear. None did, and the rush of air faded like a summer squall.

"Adjoining tunnels," Toyama said. "That could have been any of some fifteen other lines passing by." She gazed at him flatly. "Now, you wanted to see the dump site?"

He nodded, then bowed his head and started forward into the tunnel. The air smelled like iron rust, static electricity and damp. The door clanged shut in back and echoes of their footsteps engulfed them.

"Don't touch the cables to either side," Toyama warned. "Some of them may be live."

They walked for several minutes with echoes spinning madly around them. Soon they reached an intersection where the tunnel separated into four further passages, each identical in appearance.

"This one," Toyama said, taking the lead. Wren made a mental note and followed.

After perhaps five minutes there came the sound of rushing water somewhere, almost as if it was all around them.

"Is that the sewer?" Wren asked.

"It's not the sewer that we're heading to. It could be another sewer, or one of the big drains, or even the course of one of those lost rivers."

"Lost rivers," Wren mused.

They kept walking, and the sound faded after they took a left at another intersection.

"Tokyo used to be called the 'floating world', Wren-san," Toyama said, her voice becoming slightly singsong as they pressed deeper. "That usually refers to the indulgence and wealth of the seventeenth century, where fashion, art and poetry were considered fleeting pleasures. But it also describes the city itself.

All those rivers, canals, streams? Tokyo was once the Venice of the East. Then we capped all our rivers and laid culverts and roads over our streams, almost as if we could escape the past."

She stopped abruptly and turned to face Wren. In the dim light she looked hauntingly beautiful, like the ghost of some lost Edo-era geisha. "If you ever speak about me again the way you did earlier, I will personally see you deported. That's a promise."

Wren regarded her. Emotionally she was under control, but she'd chosen to let her emotions dictate her actions. "Why didn't you say that to Sato?"

Her cheeks blinked white as the anger rose up again. "Sato's been doing that ever since I joined PSIA. He's my *senpai*, my senior, and my job is to be his nail. He is the hammer. If I take it for long enough, I'll rise up. You want to be a hammer, and that's fine. It must feel good to be you. But this is my life and my career. If we're going to work together, you have to respect that."

Now she was furious. Better than the robotic manner she'd treated him to earlier, Wren figured, and not unreasonable.

"I understand your position, Toyama. But Sato wasn't just insulting you, was he? I was insulted too, and insults are about more than just personal offense. If this is our team, I need them to respect me, just as I'll respect them, so there can be trust. Without trust, how can we work together?" He took a breath. She didn't look any happier. "But," he conceded, "you make a good point. This is your life. I'm a tourist here. I will try to hammer less."

That seemed to take some of the edge off her anger. They walked in silence for a few more minutes, before stopping by a metal door embedded in the concrete wall, coated in flaking green paint. Spidery, dark water stains spread from the frame like grasping fingers, as if some noxious corruption on the other side was trying to creep through.

"This is it," Toyama said, then opened the door.

The stench was instant. Wren had been in sewers before. This one had to be the worst, and the stink hit him like a body slam. Human waste, rotten meat, ammonia in the air thick enough to make his eyes water. He squinted and cupped a hand over his mouth.

"Mask?" offered Toyama.

"Thank you."

He fastened the particle filter around his mouth. It helped a little.

Ahead lay a dark band of sewage, running alongside a gray concrete walkway. He recognized some of the features of the walls and ceiling from the crime scene photos. A mottled yellow knob jutted from a pipe at a certain angle. Pocks in the poured concrete matched the photographs. All lit by flickering halogen lights.

"Not a great place to lie in state," he said.

Maybe he caught the ghost of a smile on Toyama's face. "Not at all. Let's take a closer look."

9

LIE IN STATE

Wren stood where the body had been, checking the notes on his phone.

The name of the victim was Kenji Ando. Once a wealthy, up-and-coming CEO of a new tech company that specialized in cell phone parts. Young, highly educated, most of his life ahead of him. The one stand-out part of his record was a rare form of dyslexia known as dyscalculia, a difficulty in acquiring mathematical skills. It seems he'd made it to the top of his company through his sales skills and networking, not his engineering skills.

Either way, it didn't matter. Wren hadn't come to dig into the life of the victim.

He'd come to get into the mind of the killer.

The walkway was three feet wide and some twenty yards long, bounded on either side by metal grates that spanned the tunnel like portcullises. The walls were crammed with more pipes, cables, ducts and wires; some old and rusted, some in shiny new plastic casings. Wren imagined the water, gas, electricity and data of the city above shunting through them constantly.

"What are you thinking?" Toyama asked.

"I'm thinking about logistics," Wren said, then dropped to one knee and mimed rolling a dead body off his shoulder. He did it carefully, guiding the head like he was laying down a baby. Do it without control, and the skull would bang off the concrete. He ran his fingers over the concrete; it was rough. If the killer wasn't careful, the corpse's skin would get scuffed, and forensics hadn't shown that.

"The concrete's rough. It would have taken effort to treat the body this well. Preserved like an exhibit in a museum."

"Our analysts agree," Toyama said. "None of these bodies were dumped for conventional reasons; to hide or dispose of the evidence. Each one was a careful display, something they wanted to be found."

"Maybe to draw our attention to something here." Wren stood and surveyed the walls. "These pipes, any idea what's running through them?"

"We haven't made a study of them, no. Why?"

"Just getting a sense of the scene. What belongs, what doesn't." He took several photos, the flash adding a fresh stutter to the flickering lights. "Those ones look like water. There's electric, new and old. Those ones might be gas. Those new ducts, the red plastic, what are they?"

Toyama peered at the wall like it might open up its secrets. "I could file some information requests. The city planner's office might know. They might not, though. Like I said, it's a warren of different jurisdictions down here."

"Let's try it."

Toyama tapped notes on her phone. "Anything else come to mind?"

"This precise location. Is there anything particular above us?"

Toyama considered. "I don't know. Does that matter?'

"It could. If there's a particular building, it could give us a link."

Toyama wrote down more notes.

"Then, access," Wren said. He paced along the walkway, imagining the killer coming this way. "Many routes in, you said. How far have you got in ruling them out?"

Toyama made a face. "That's a work in progress. Just listing them all takes us into the hundreds, maybe the thousands. As for checking any significant portion of them off? I think we're not going to get very far."

"Hmm." Wren came up to one of the grates limiting the walkway. Beyond it, shadows flickered as the lights sputtered, illuminating some twenty or so feet. "What are these fences for? What's the point of sealing off the sewer, when it's already behind a locked door on the station platform?"

"Safety regulations," Toyama said. "This is a maintenance point. As I understand it, these fenced sections are protected from accidental flood surges. The sewers beyond it, the 'dark sewers', they're called, are not."

"So the 'dark sewers' are dangerous."

"Very. Anything beyond this fence won't have lights, power or ventilation. You could die in a flood surge, get lost in the dark for days, or even suffocate in a methane cloud."

Wren peered into the darkness. "Where do they go?"

"I have no idea. A sewage treatment plant, probably. Some sewers flow directly into Tokyo Bay."

Wren tapped the grate. "Did you look into them as a possible route?"

"No. To my knowledge they're all fenced off like this. No access hatches, welded shut, embedded in concrete. You'd need industrial tools to get through. Why go to so much trouble?"

"Why, indeed. Can you step back a little, Toyama?"

Suspicion flared on her face. "What are you going to do?"

"I'm sure it's within the parameters of your procedures. If you just trust me."

There wasn't a lot of trust on her face. Still, she stepped away from the grate. Wren picked a stance, left leg forward, right back, a few feet from the grate, then he shot his right leg forward in a powerful front kick.

The sole of his foot slammed into the grate and stopped cold. There was barely any reverberation.

"Satisfied?"

Wren took two steps back and launched a second kick from a running start. The impact was bigger and louder, and this time there was a faint rattle.

"Hear that?"

"Hear what? You kicking a sewer fence?"

"The rattling sound. That was metal on metal. For a grate with no moving parts, there should be no rattle."

Toyama raised one eyebrow. "I'm not sure what that proves."

"Not proof. Possibility. Watch."

Wren took hold of the grate with both hands. The gaps between the metal bands were around four inches, allowing plenty of space to grip.

"I don't-" Toyama began, but then Wren put his feet into the lower gaps in the grate and started edging sideways. "Oh no. This is not a good idea, Wren-san."

He kept edging along until he hung directly above the flow of sewage. The stench was even more powerful, as the black flow passed by below. "It's fine. I've actually done something similar before, in a big box full of mud. I almost drowned, that time."

"What?"

"Didn't smell as bad as this, though," Wren muttered, then pulled one foot back to kick the grate again.

The faint rattle was louder.

"You hear that?"

"No."

"Maybe it's the T-CAPS system. It augments quiet sounds. Let me just..."

He edged another step sideways then kicked again, and this

time part of the grate opened up and flapped backward, dropping Wren along with it.

He plunged backward toward the black flow. Toyama called out something. Wren let go of the falling grate and snatched out for something solid. His left hand grabbed empty air. His right hand caught a worn pipe in the wall and just about arrested his fall, though it yanked a good two inches off its housing and cracked, dropping his back within kissing distance of the black sludge.

He came to rest poised near horizontal above the mulch, feet still braced against the grate, barely hanging by one hand from the crumpling pipe.

"Little help," he managed.

Toyama was already on the grate and leaning out. Wren reached up to grab her hand just as the pipe shattered. His full weight yanked her away from the grate. His right shoulder almost grazed the sludge, but then caught.

Toyama cried out. Wren stared in amazement as she held on, at full stretch. She was stronger than she looked. Carefully he pulled himself up, to encircle her against the grate. Briefly their faces were side-by-side, her warm breath on his cheek, the curves of her body pressing hot into his, then he muttered a fast apology and crab-legged back to the walkway.

Toyama followed, wearing a curious expression.

"Thanks," Wren said. "You just saved my life."

Her eyes narrowed. "You're welcome. But if you'd fallen in, I don't think I would have helped you out."

Wren wasn't sure if she was joking. "Noted."

"Just for future reference."

Maybe she was? "Got it."

A moment passed, then they both turned to the grate. The section that had collapsed was around three feet square and seemed to hang on an invisible hinge.

"Everything I heard about these grates was that they're

impassable," Toyama supplied. "So I doubt this access hatch was original."

"You think somebody added it later."

"It seems that way. For access to the dark sewers. Perhaps the same person who killed Kenji Ando."

Wren looked back to the spot where Ando's body had been found, then back to the grate. "This may change everything. That's clearly an access point. Maybe Ando was left here like a parcel at the front door. Some kind of offering, perhaps. But to whom?"

A visible shudder ran through Toyama. Wren wasn't too surprised. He'd dealt with some of the darkest cults there were, but you only had to go back a few hundred years to find people offering human sacrifices all over the world, as a matter of course. Castration certainly bore the hallmarks of a ritual kill. Underground spaces, like tombs, had always been considered sacred.

Facing that dark past head-on could be sickening.

"You think someone's down there?" Toyama asked, staring wide-eyed now into the dark.

Wren gritted his teeth. "Could be. There's only one way to find out. We do happen to have a high-power flashlight with us, after all."

She stared at him blank-faced for a moment, then reached into her valise and brought out the long flashlight.

"Ninety-eight lumens," Wren said. "As useful as a Swiss Army knife."

10

DARK SEWER

Wren clicked on the flashlight and shone it through the bars. The beam was a bright white that illuminated a couple of hundred yards. Just more sewage tunnel. He took to the grate and climbed.

His heart beat hard, but no more hatches collapsed, and in twenty seconds he stood on the other side. Toyama followed.

"This is not within procedure," she said, raising the flashlight on her cell phone.

"You're welcome to go back."

She didn't budge.

Wren started forward, running the flashlight over the floor, walls, ceiling and pipework. They looked the same, but now they receded away at a downward gradient. It grew colder as they descended.

"Nothing," Toyama said.

At a hundred yards, Wren stopped to look more closely, but there was still nothing unusual. Looking back the way they'd come, the flickering lights shone like a signal fire.

They advanced. Two hundred yards went by, then three hundred. With each stretch the lights behind them grew smaller and higher, like the pole star climbing in a dark sky. At four hundred yards out they reached a T-intersection with another tunnel, which ran lower by around ten feet. To continue further they'd have to get on their hands and knees and climb down a ladder. Beside them the flow of sewage simply fell off the edge, becoming a pattering, noxious waterfall.

"It looks like a surge control tunnel," Toyama said, peering down. Her cheeks had a greenish cast. "Lower than this one, so it catches more of any flood. It would have to overfill massively to spread up here."

Wren dropped to his knees, shining the flashlight into the surge tunnel. It ran left to right and looked much the same as the one way they were in, if smaller: a narrow walkway alongside a silty flow; pipes and conduits filling the walls and ceiling; air that felt almost thick enough to keep them out.

"This is as far as I go," Toyama said. There was a gurgle at the back of her throat, like she was holding down a gag. "Nobody could live down here."

Wren squinted into the dark. It didn't add up. He scanned the surge tunnel. Everything was the same: the concrete walkway, the mixture of pipes and cables. Nothing unusual. Nothing out of place.

Then he saw it.

His breath stopped in his throat. He ran the flashlight beam back and caught on something sleek and shiny in the darkness. His heart skipped a beat and his vision tunneled in. Some kind of figure was standing in the middle of the sewage flow, but hardly human. It had oily onyx-black skin, and the face was split by a gargoyle's rictus grin, with gleaming red eyes and a fat, lolling tongue. And it was staring right back at him.

Toyama sucked in a breath beside him. "Is that a-"

Wren flung himself feet-first into the lower tunnel. The fall passed in a second then he hammered down onto the concrete walkway, ankles crying out, pulse pounding and flashlight beam roving like a maddened disco ball.

"Wren-san!" called Toyama in back.

He ran. The tunnel clattered like a heart attack with the pounding of his feet. Walls spiraled, pipes and cables ricocheted in the flashlight's beam. He reached the spot it had been and spun, roving every inch of wall for some kind of passageway or hidden door, but there was nothing to see. In after-images it taunted him, that hideous gargoyle face grinning wildly, its thick tongue waving in the air.

Gone.

He ran some fifty yards on, scanning the walkway and the sewage, expecting at any moment the face to surface from the mire, suck in a gasp of air then submerge again like a-

"Chris!" came Toyama's voice, then a hand came on his shoulder and he spun. She was right there behind him. "We have to go!" she shouted. The T-CAPS amplified her voice to thunder in his head. "Don't you feel the wind?"

Her dark eyes grounded him back in his body. Now he did feel it. A cold wind blasted up the tunnel around them, just like the rush of air they'd felt on the Marunouchi line platform. But this couldn't be a train, not down here. This had to be…

He heard it before he saw it; a distant roaring of water like a lost river finally finding its way, rampaging closer with all the force of a rainy season deluge.

"Run!" he shouted.

They took off at a sprint back to the ladder. At the base the roar became a building roll of thunder. He grabbed Toyama by the hips and hoisted her halfway up the ladder. She grasped hold and climbed over the top, and Wren followed.

Halfway up the freezing surge tide crashed against him like a freight train, engulfing his whole body. His right hand ripped free of the rung and left him clinging only by his left, battered by the sudden torrential flow. He couldn't think, couldn't tell up from down, couldn't see anything. The flashlight was gone, peeling away like a shooting star into the dark, and he couldn't-

A hand found his flailing wrist and pulled. He pulled back

and erupted from the froth of the surge tide with a great gasp, into the dim light cast by Toyama's cell phone.

He pulled himself over the edge and onto the upper walkway, even as the surge climbed up and over the lip.

"It's still rising!" Toyama yelled in his ear, hauling him to his feet. "Come on."

They ran, her cell phone clattering away behind them, charging for the distant bead of flickering light that marked the way home. Fifty yards they made, a hundred, then a rushing wave of icy water smashed into their knees from behind. Toyama was swept sideways, and Wren just caught her before her skull was dashed against the wall.

He yanked her back then stampeded onward, holding her tight and using his mass and momentum as a bulwark against the tide, racing toward the flickering lights ahead as every step came down in water that rose to his thigh, then his waist.

Then the lights went out.

Instant darkness fell across the drumming rip tide. For several lunging steps Wren didn't believe it; maybe he'd hit his head, or something had blocked his vision, or anything but the lights at the end of the tunnel going out.

But they had.

The tunnel rumbled and floodwater thrashed at his waist. Toyama staggered on behind him somewhere, tugged along by his grip. He thrust out his right hand to find the wall, suddenly terrified of stepping into the sewage flow. If he sank in, he may never find his way again.

His fingers stubbed the wall, then his wrist banged off metal, instantly numbing his whole arm. He didn't care and plunged on, both of them gasping over the tumult.

"Almost there," he called back at Toyama. Still counting the yards. Two hundred, now. It couldn't be far. With every yard gained they climbed a little higher, but with every step forward the water beat higher, until Toyama was carried forward on a surge, slamming into Wren's back.

He barely managed to keep his feet under him. Three hundred yards covered, but not enough. She was too light, and he wasn't heavy enough, so he hoisted her over his shoulder and ran on.

"Cellphone in my pocket!" he shouted over the jet-engine assault of the flood; not even sure Toyama was conscious. "Toyama, flashlight!"

Faint white light poured out just in time. Five more yards and he would've run face first into the grate, maybe hard enough to knock himself out. Water was everywhere now, swamping the walkway, the door.

"It shouldn't come this high!" Toyama called in his ear.

Wren jumped and caught the upper bars of the grate, letting the tide push them both through the gap. On the other side the walkway was a whirlpool of rushing, foaming, foul liquid. He scanned the walls until he found the green door, then the most violent surge yet hit and knocked him from his feet.

He tumbled. Toyama was lost. The water carried him upward and in. His face scraped off the ceiling, his elbow struck a pipe and sent his whole arm dead, then he slammed against the far grate.

There was no air, only the wild racing of water all around, pinning him to the metal. Something thudded beside him, trapping his right arm, and for a moment only there was light. Toyama, her head lolling unconscious.

Then the light kicked out and Wren was trapped once more in the dark.

No air.

He remembered tumbling in the Pacific Ocean as an oil rig collapsed around them, trying to rescue the body of one of his most trusted Foundation members, and failing.

Not again.

Defiance pumped adrenaline through his body, and with all his prodigious strength, he pushed back against the pummeling flood water. He scooped Toyama around the waist and thrust back into the flow. She was an anchor dragging him backward, but he was a machine now. Three months of hoisting logs on the farm dawn 'til dusk had made him a human backhoe, and he wasn't going to let a little thing like some rain overflow keep him under.

He yanked on pipes in the black, inching sideways like a climber summiting into an avalanche. Hand over hand he drove on until his hand slammed the edge of the door, sank to the handle and turned.

It opened.

The flood dragged them both through. He hit the far wall as the torrent cascaded in, the door slamming wide open into blaring white light. Wren spun and tumbled five feet in the cross flow, Toyama lost, scrabbling for purchase even as the flood rose again.

Nothing for it. He leaped forward and caught the edge of the flapping door, got his frozen fingers around the jamb and pulled. Getting the door halfway closed was easy, but then he hit the massive force of the surge full on. His feet climbed up the opposite wall until he was wedged across the passage, shoulders against the door and pushing a massive squat that had to cap half a ton. It moved. Toward the end he let out a tremendous bellow, squeezing off the last riotous push until-

The door clanged shut. The flow abated immediately, and Wren dropped to the swirling shallows. In seconds the water dissipated, tumbling away down the corridor until there was only a damp stain to show it had ever been there.

Makoto Toyama was on her knees on the wet cement ten yards away, spluttering hard, black hair loose and bedraggled, staring at Wren with fury in her pitch-black eyes.

"Somebody just tried to kill us!"

Wren strode up, took her cold hand and pulled her to her feet.

"They can't have got far. Can you run?"

She muttered something in Japanese, Wren figured it was a curse, followed by an angry, "Yes!"

"Then let's go."

11

SATO

Wren took the lead, racing back along the way they'd come. Past the roar of the underground river, taking the turns through intersections by memory, mind racing with calculations.

Was this the purpose of the corpses; lure him deep then hit him with a drowning flood of wastewater? Rage endorphins pumped into his system, and he burst through the metal door back onto the Marunouchi platform amped up to fight. The door slammed wide against the tiled wall with a stupendous crash, and Wren found himself staring at a packed platform.

Hundreds of Japanese people thronged the station. There was barely room to move, and white-gloved figures in navy uniforms were physically pushing businesspeople onto the train like they were herding stubborn cattle.

Wren's jaw dropped. For a moment he contemplated charging into the crowd, calling out for everyone to get back, make way, then he saw the first camera phone rising.

He turned his back instantly, just in time for Makoto Toyama to run straight into him. He barely caught her, arms against his chest, then lifted her up and took one big step back into the tunnel.

Her legs kicked until he set her down, reached back around and pulled the door closed again.

In the dim, narrow confines of the passageway they stood, panting.

"What was that?" Toyama demanded.

"I can't be seen," Wren managed between gasps. "Terms of my deal to come out here. No media exposure, no noise, certainly no video of me covered in filth and racing like a madman through the Tokyo underground."

Some of the heat went out of Toyama's eyes. She muttered what had to be another low Japanese curse word.

"Exactly that," Wren confirmed. "We're screwed."

They waited five minutes, exchanging panted confirmations of what they'd seen and what had happened, long enough for the train on the platform to leave and another to pull in, then Toyama went out and made a call from the platform's emergency line.

Within three minutes station security met them at the door. Within twenty more the first members of the PSIA arrived, and thirty later Yamaguchi himself arrived, flanked by Sato and Nakamura. They looked stunned.

By that time, the platform had been sealed off, and Wren and Toyama had been run through a three-stage mobile hazardous materials shower: doused with disinfectant chemicals, scrubbed with soap and water by a team, then rinsed off with cold water. Wearing towels and silver Mylar blankets, Toyama offered her debrief to the other PSIA members while a paramedic administered preventative antibiotics against bacterial infection and a Hepatitis A vaccine shot.

Wren just stood and stayed quiet. His T-CAPS unit and phone were long gone, and he couldn't take part until he got new ones. It wasn't hard to read the official response, though.

"They don't believe us," Toyama said.

"I'm getting that. What about the gargoyle face?"

"It seems they don't believe that, either." Toyama sounded drained. "I'm not sure I even believe it. The flood surge they accept, but we're going to get blamed for it. We shouldn't have been down there. They're already lining up disciplinary protocols for reckless endangerment."

Wren cursed low. "Tell him we need to get back down there."

"Back into the sewer?"

"Yes. We need them to shut down the flood tunnel, whatever it takes. The guy with the gargoyle face, he must've had an escape hatch of some kind, a secret door. Either that or he just committed suicide. Either way, we follow his trail. It's the best lead we've got."

Toyama relayed the request. Yamaguchi answered it seriously and at length, but Sato smirked throughout, muttering away to Nakamura.

"He says no," Toyama translated flatly.

Wren controlled his anger. There was no point making a bigger mess than they were already in. "What do you mean, no?"

"No, they can't make the tunnel safe for access, and no, you and I are not going back down there. Maybe not ever. He says we were both off procedure, and he thinks we might have hallucinated the face. He thinks we could have been high off the sewer swamp gas."

Wren almost laughed but controlled the impulse. It was that or punch someone in the face. "Is he not curious why the flood surge hit just when we were vulnerable? Why the lights went out in perfect synchrony? Is he going to investigate that?"

She relayed the question. Another long answer came. In the middle Sato muttered something that caused Nakamura to smirk. Again, Toyama summarized the long answer briefly.

"He says no."

Wren felt like he was about to explode. "Any reason?"

"He says it's raining. In rainy season, the sewers flood. It's a coincidence. We should never have gone down there at all."

Wren let the anger burn. Fixed his gaze on Sato. Lowered his voice. "And what did the idiot say?"

Toyama grimaced. "I shouldn't say."

"I'm on this team, Toyama," Wren said low, not breaking eye contact with Sato, who seemed to be savoring his anger. "He can't hide like a punk behind the language. Tell me."

She winced, then continued in a quiet voice. "He said he knows what triggered the flood. A million people flushed their toilets at once."

Wren said nothing for a long moment. So this was all the help he was going to get from the PSIA. This was the system she was talking about; more interested in hammering nails than investigating.

Wren took a step closer to Sato. The man was 6', tall for a Japanese but slim. To his credit he didn't step back, staring up at Wren defiantly. It would be so easy to break him in half, Wren figured, but he was protected by the system. Or so he thought.

He was wrong.

"Keep mouthing off and you may take a spin in the sewers yourself," Wren said softly. "Now give me your jacket, your cell phone and your money, then shake my hand and say, 'thank you for your service'."

Sato stared back.

"Toyama," Wren rasped.

"I'm not translating that."

"Translate it or I break his nose and walk. Solve the murders on your own."

A long moment passed. Yamaguchi did nothing. He said nothing. Wren already understood why completely. His authority stretched only so far as it was respected, and Wren wasn't respecting it, so just like every time prior, he chose to ignore what he couldn't control.

Sato began to feel it. The isolation, as Wren's glare cut him off from support.

"Toyama," Wren barked.

At last, she translated.

Sato flushed white as she spoke. His cheeks burned red.

"Douzo," Wren said. "Now."

Sato's fury sprayed hot in his eyes. He began to take off his jacket.

12

DUTY

Wren made a beeline for the surface. Sato's jacket was too tight, but better than the subway boiler suit he wore underneath. At the ticket gates he scanned Sato's phone and emerged into what seemed to be an underground food hall. Everywhere there were booths selling gourmet ingredients: a range of truffle butters, huge slabs of freshly caught tuna, squid squirting around in giant glass tanks, stacks of cheeses. It was quite a contrast from the sewers.

Using Sato's phone, he dialed an emergency number as he walked.

The line rang. He checked the time, coming on for midnight already in Japan, which meant early afternoon in Europe. Hopefully they'd be awake.

The line clicked and a sleepy voice came on. "Christopher?"

Wren's surging pulse calmed a little. It was good to hear her voice. "Hellion, it's me."

"What is happening, Christopher?" she mumbled in her strong Slavic accent. "Why are you calling at," there was a pause for clacking keys, "4 p.m. in afternoon? I was sleeping. Very nice dream."

Wren couldn't stop a hint of good humor breaking through

his anger. Hellion, real name Isabella Matis, was unmoved by most matters of the real world. She was a multi-millionaire hacker at the age of twenty-four, having made her fortune multiple times over; from a misspent youth excelling at competitive video games to a misspent adolescence spent cracking and blackmailing major corporations, governments and banks around the world.

She lived in a rolling convoy of coaches with her best friend and fellow elite hacker, B4cksl4cker. They had a rocky history of extreme rivalry, battling each other across the dark web. B4cksl4cker had a network of slaved Russian botnets and was a genius at programming AI controllers that wielded them like a digital army. Hellion had the strategic skills and incredible speed on the keys to run rings around any other hacker Wren had heard of. Together they went by the name H4cksl4cker, and together they powered the backend of Wren's Foundation.

They slept when and with whomever they wanted to, living whatever kind of life they liked.

"You're going to love this," Wren rumbled. "So I'll save you any beating around the bush. I just got flushed down the toilet, literally tumbling through the Tokyo sewers. There was someone down there, they had a face like a gargoyle, then they disappeared. Seconds later, a flood surge hit. Now I need everything you can find on weird cults worshipping the underground and underground gods in Japan. I also want you to run the deepest pattern analysis of all the tunnels, sewers, train routes, basements, access hatches and passages you can find. We're looking for anything unusual, maybe a hidden place where these freaks worship, some routes they regularly take. I'll send a sketch of the gargoyle face soon, for a recognition algorithm. Also, check any means or mechanism someone might have to trigger a flood surge in the sewers."

He stopped and took a breath.

"Christopher," Hellion said, sounding a little more alert now. "Did you say you were flushed down toilet?"

He steeled himself. "Remember the Anaximanderians in Utah? The mud box? Picture that, in the sewers, hit by a flash flood that was sent our way on purpose. I must've swallowed half a gallon of gray water. Enjoy that, turn it into a ring tone, whatever you like, but help me with this. Someone's trying to kill me out here."

There was another silence, filled with clacking keystrokes. Wren had a sinking feeling that she wasn't searching for the things he'd requested. "Kill you with sewage," Hellion said. "This enemy truly fights dirty."

Wren braced himself. "Not now, Hellion."

"It would have been murder most foul. I think urine over your head, Christopher."

He closed his eyes, praying for patience. "I don't have time for this."

"At least there was not any fire. Then you would have turd degree burns."

He waited. "Are you done?"

"Of course. I would not mock a man who is clearly in deep shi-"

"You're done! OK, Hellion. I may need you as operator for what's coming. Can you handle that?"

"Naturally. I will do my doody."

Wren ran a hand down his face. "See that you do."

He killed the call.

Makoto Toyama was standing in front of him. She'd cleaned up nicely, and still had the red glow in her cheeks from the chemical disinfectant. Wren couldn't be sure, but it looked like she was wearing a borrowed subway worker's jumpsuit. It was distractingly tight in the chest, but Wren focused on her face.

"You shouldn't come with me, Toyama. Someone just tried to kill me."

"Someone tried to kill us both, Wren-san," she countered, steel in her black eyes. "Also, I am your partner for the duration.

This has been made very clear to me. We are not to go outside of our bounds again."

Wren snorted. "So they're making you the hammer."

"The system is the hammer. It is a very big hammer, Wren-san. What you did to Sato will only make things harder for us. He will never regain this lost face."

"He should've thought of that before he started talking smack. Listen, Toyama. Does anyone in your PSIA even want to solve this thing?"

"Of course," she said, getting quieter as she grew angrier, which was an impressive new trick. "But the Japanese system is slow. It reacts to new information very gradually." She paused a moment. "Procedures must be followed. Evidence must be gathered in the correct way, or it will not count."

"Forget evidence. I'll catch the killer."

"We'll catch the killer," she corrected, then flashed him an unexpected smile. "Besides, we have now been flushed down the toilet together. In Japan, this is a true bonding experience."

Wren stared, then let up slightly. Full-on fury only got you so far. "I guess that's a bonding experience anywhere. OK. So we're in this together."

"Good. Now, I don't know about you, Wren-san, but I'm hungry. Let's go get noodles. I know a great ramen place."

She started away. Wren hadn't thought once about eating, but now, as if on cue, his stomach began to rumble.

13

KABUKI-CHO

Toyama led them out through the East gate of Shinjuku station. The rain was still pouring from a black and starless sky, drumming hard on the pavement and lending a soft-focus glow to the towering neon lights of the city.

Wren took a breath. His first proper look at Tokyo.

Across a road glistening with rain shone a giant arch with rippling red bulbs, guarding the entrance to a broad pedestrian esplanade packed full of people, BBQ smoke and a dazzling array of lights.

"That's Kabuki-cho," Toyama shouted over the rain. "Entertainment district."

Wren just stared. After the chaos in the underground, it didn't feel real. Kabuki-cho was a heaving river of color and humanity. Every inch of vertical real estate on the buildings was filled with bright, multicolored signs, from ground level up to at least twenty stories high.

All were written in Japanese characters. None of them were intelligible to Wren, and the effect left him searching for signal in the noise. There was music playing from speakers somewhere, too, some tinny Japanese pop, while a building on the corner churned out an endless roaring racket like a factory production line. Inside people were sitting at what looked like arcade machines, packed in side-by-side.

"It's a lot," Toyama said by his side. Wren turned. She looked different in the subway uniform, with her hair looser and cascading wet around her shoulders, her sharply contoured lipstick and eyeshadow replaced by a softer, more genuine look. "But you've got me as a guide. Come on."

She stepped out onto the crossing and Wren followed. The rain beat on his head and trickled warm down his neck. Strange to think that this same rainwater was fueling the flood surge below.

Soon they were swallowed up in the flow of people pouring through the open mouth of Kabuki-cho. It was nothing like the uniformity of Tokyo Station. Wren was still the tallest person on the street, but the orderly current of businesspeople in suits and boots was replaced by a wild torrent of colors, shapes, and sizes. There were slick-looking young guys spinning laminated menus on their fingers, hawking out cocktails with sexual-sounding names. There were young women dressed in figure-hugging French maid outfits, all black lace and white frills, smiling demurely and handing out pamphlets. There were tourists of all kinds from all countries, some dressed as if for the opera, some in ridiculous cosplay, others ready to hit the clubs. There were even a few monks wandering around, dressed in their orange robes and flapping sandals with shiny bald heads.

A few of these carried umbrellas, but most didn't seem to care about the rain; sucking from vape pens, chatting with friends, leaning against a ten-deep bank of vending machines while swigging beer from tallboy cans.

"This way," Toyama called over the ruckus of voices, twinkly pop music, and the factory thunder of the arcade, steering Wren with a casual touch of her hand on his arm.

They wended their way past smoking outdoor BBQ grills set up under clear plastic awnings tended by wizened old men, by a flock of feather-haired young men in dapper black suits, all looking too cool for school, through a batch of schoolchildren all wearing bright yellow ponchos and out into an open square.

On all sides the buildings popped like Times Square, with gleaming digital billboards displaying the latest range of Hollywood movies. Here Jason Statham stood three stories tall, glaring moodily at Jennifer Lawrence opposite, who was pointing a gun right at him. At ground level there were dozens more plastic-walled booths, all thronged with workers in suits sat on stools nursing chopsticks and sake.

"Here we go," Toyama said, and led Wren to one of the tents with red and white vinyl sidings. He pushed through and in, head stroking the plastic ceiling. There were five picnic benches packed closely together, all but one occupied by men and women in suits, smoking and laughing. They didn't skip a beat when Wren and Toyama entered, dripping wet. An old lady manned a narrow BBQ grill in the corner, surrounded by an assortment of pots on burners. She had steel-gray hair hanging either side of a wide face and was dressed in what looked like a coarse navy robe overlaid with a brown smock.

Toyama went straight to the old lady and spoke in fast Japanese. Wren regretted losing the T-CAPS. He'd need to order another. The woman behind the counter had no such trouble, though, and after laughing and nodding and offering some comment in a smoke-roughened voice, produced a frosted glass bottle, popped out two shot glasses and filled them to the brim.

Toyama took them and turned to Wren.

"Sake," she said. "We toast being alive."

Wren took the glass. He hadn't drunk for months; hadn't felt any urge while out in the woods of Delaware. If ever there was a fitting time, though, surely it was now.

"To being alive."

They clinked then downed the shot. It was like swallowing liquid ice, chased by a fiery aftertaste that burned up Wren's throat and into his nose.

"That's wasabi," Toyama said with a sly smile. "Rice wine brewed with wasabi leaf, my favorite. Come on."

She led them over to the spare picnic table, where the old woman put down the sake bottle, chopsticks, two small white towels and two small plates piled with fine slices of some pink vegetable.

The lady took Toyama's arm, looked at Wren and said something low and fast, which teased out laughter. Toyama replied and the old lady laughed back. Wren raised one eyebrow.

Toyama saw Wren's expression and grinned. It was the first time he'd seen her smile, and it changed her frosty demeanor completely.

"Sit down, Wren-san," she enthused, patting the seat opposite her.

He assessed the bottle, glasses, and the flush already on her cheeks. "Noodles," he said. "Not a drinking binge. We're on the clock here."

The smile spread. "Wren-san. What else do you think we'll do tonight, chase around the city hunting toilet cultists?"

Wren frowned. He had actually been thinking just that. "OK. We eat, have a drink, then we beat the streets until something shakes loose."

"Or we sit and wait for the world to come to us. Wren-san, you have your people out. I have my people out, not only through PSIA channels. Some of my best are right here, in this square, working yakuza contacts. The best thing we can do is wait. And while we wait, we eat. Maybe drink."

"I'm not a big drinker."

She picked up her chopsticks and rooted into the shredded pink vegetables. "Why do I suspect that is a lie?" She lifted a wad of pink to her mouth. "Somebody tried to kill me tonight. That never happened to me before, but I survived. We both did. Then you humiliated Sato, and my career may be over. The world seems brighter. Everything is different. Perhaps drinking is the best idea."

Wren looked into her dark eyes. Maybe it was her first time to face death so directly. For him it was only the second time in the last forty-eight hours. But she had a point. He didn't know the city. Didn't know the players. Even when he got another T-CAPS and simultaneous translator, there wasn't much he could do without her help.

He sat down.

"Can you get me a pencil and paper?"

"Of course."

The old lady supplied them. Wren set to drawing on the wobbly wooden table.

"These are pickled radish," Toyama said as he sketched, pointing to the pink shreds. "They go beautifully with sake. Here." She handed him a fresh shot.

"What happened to procedure?"

Toyama lifted the shot glass, looked Wren straight in the eye, then glugged it back. She even slammed it on the table. "Maybe I'd like to try being the hammer for a change, Wren-san. Now drink."

He heaved a sigh. It seemed there was no use arguing. "Call me Chris," he said, then lifted the second shot, knocked it back and slammed it down on the table too.

Toyama laughed. "Imagine it's Sato's face."

Wren finished his sketch and held it up. "Is that a good likeness?"

She laughed. "Of Sato?"

"No, for the thing in the sewer."

Her good cheer evaporated. She took the paper and held it close. Wren wasn't a great artist, but he liked to doodle, and figured the sketch wasn't a bad likeness; it had the glowing eyes, the oily-black skin and the long, curling tongue.

"Yes," Toyama said firmly. "This is it."

"We definitely both saw it, then," Wren said. "I didn't imagine it."

Toyama shuddered, handed the image back then downed another shot. "We saw it. Him. He is now dead."

"Maybe. Maybe he got away."

Toyama said nothing. Wren took a photo of the sketch and uploaded it for his Foundation to research.

Another shot was already waiting for him. He sipped it and dipped into the pickled radish. It was salty, tangy, and a good complement to the sake. Rain beat on the hut's ceiling, and people passed by in a smeared blur outside, distorted by the plastic wall. The effect was strange but oddly comforting. Here they were in the thick of it, but apart.

He realized Toyama had said something and turned to her. She seemed expectant.

"What?"

"I said, what makes you so sure we're facing a cult? You said it to your team."

"Oh." He thought for a moment, wondering how much to say. The sake was already kicking in, mellowing out his lingering adrenaline and letting some exhaustion through. He raised one hand and started counting off factors on his fingers. "Cults often make sacrifices to their 'gods'. These are usually made at threshold places where two different realities meet. Examples include an altar, a doorway, the entrance to a cave. So the grate between the maintenance space and the dark sewer qualifies."

Toyama shuddered. "Especially if there's someone living down there."

"Especially." Wren took a breath. "Next, there's the castration. That's an offering if ever I saw one. Sacrifices are always killed in a specific, ritualized way." He paused a moment. "Third is the willingness for members to risk themselves to protect the cult. That masked figure we saw below, either he found a passageway that was hidden extremely well, extremely fast, or he dived into the sludge. After that, well. He was washed away."

"We can hope," Toyama muttered. "Those are some good guesses."

"Not evidence, though."

"No."

Wren sipped his sake, thinking about a network of killer cultists spread throughout Tokyo, picking victims and offering them up to some underground god or monster. It sounded crazy, but people did all kinds of crazy things.

Toyama said something again, and he refocused. "Sorry, I'm miles away. What did you say?"

"I said, how do you like my grandmother's place?"

He had no idea what she was talking about, but looked from Toyama to the lady at the grill. She was stirring an iron pot behind the BBQ with one hand, while swiftly turning skewers of meat on the BBQ with the other. She had to be in her late seventies, if not older. But there was a certain resemblance in the wide cheekbones and almond eyes...

"Wait, she's your grandmother?"

"Of course." Toyama seemed pleased. "Why are you so surprised?"

"I don't know. I guess I'm surprised she's working here, in a hut in the red-light district, at her age."

Toyama raised one clipped eyebrow. "What's wrong with her age? She's been here for fifty years, rain or shine. This is her place. Presidents and prime ministers have eaten here."

"Seriously?"

She smiled. "Not seriously. They passed near, though, that's certain." She pointed out through the plastic walls to buildings across the square. "That's a high-brow musical theater. That's the cinema where all the Hollywood stars come for premieres. It's not all red lights and brothels."

Wren surveyed the lights around them, then looked up to the roofline, where one of the buildings was capped with what looked to be a life-size Godzilla head peeking over the seventeenth floor, complete with clawed hand.

"And that?" he asked.

"That one is a brothel," Toyama answered deadpan.

Wren laughed.

"I'm kidding. It's a cinema, too, and a hotel. But there are brothels everywhere. Love hotels, also; that's themed rooms you rent for casual sex, totally anonymous. Anyway, our food's coming."

Toyama's grandmother passed behind them carrying a large plate full of salted green beans. She was just bustling away when she abruptly pointed beside Wren's head and said something fast and loud in his ear.

Toyama perked up immediately and picked up his sketch of the mask.

"She says she recognizes this, Wren-san!"

That perked him up too. He turned to look at the old woman's face. "What is it?"

The old woman nodded, then let loose in more fast Japanese.

"She says it looks like a *yokai*," Toyama translated. "That's a kind of Japanese monster from folklore. She says," Toyama listened, "yes, it's a monster called an *akaname*, a child-like monster. It means 'filth-licker'." She made a face. "Apparently it creeps into bathhouses and toilets to lick away the scum and waste. It has a very long tongue. It's not normally dangerous, though, more of a pest." The old lady went on at breakneck pace. "Now she's asking why you've drawn a picture of it. She says they're not something you see much of these days."

Wren looked at the drawing. A filth-licker. "Tell her it was a dream. A nightmare, actually. And ask her, where would I go to learn more about this?"

Toyama asked. The lady's face went serious, like she was deep in thought, before she answered.

"There's only one place," Toyama translated.

"OK, where?"

The old lady's lips pursed, then she spat out a word in barely intelligible English. "Google!"

That cracked her up. She breezed away, cackling to herself.

Toyama shrugged, put the sketch down. "Don't mind her. She's always like that."

Wren didn't mind. She'd given them something to go on, and he typed it into Sato's phone and sent it to his Foundation.

THE MASK IS A JAPANESE MONSTER CALLED AN AKANAME. IT MEANS FILTH-LICKER. GET ME EVERYTHING YOU HAVE ON IT.

He put the phone down.

The old lady returned to lay two ceramic bowls of steaming noodles and broth on the table. A few seconds later a platter of grated skewered meat arrived beside them. Last to come was a wicker basket laden with a steaming grilled fish, split open like a butterfly.

"Now we fuel up," Toyama said. "Eat a lot and it'll soak up the alcohol, so we can drink more."

Wren shot her a wry glance. "Is that another old Japanese proverb?"

"It's more a way of life."

She knocked her shot down then dug into the food. Wren saw nothing else for it but to join her.

14

HOST

Wren got drunk.

He didn't mean to, but it was easy, like slipping into a comfortable pair of pants. The threat was gone, and here they were in one of the world's greatest cities, without anything more than a sketch of a monster for a lead. So he ate his noodles, and dipped the BBQ chunks of beef and chicken into the spicy, salty red sauce, and shelled the green beans and chugged them back like peanuts at a ball game, and all throughout, he kept downing sake.

"What were you talking about earlier?" Toyama asked, slurring her words. "Something about a mud box, and Anaximan-something?"

Now they were on the move. The rain had stopped, and they were patrolling Kabuki-cho's rain-slick streets like a couple of beat cops, staring down tattooed guys with tight yakuza man buns and swigging flavored beer from tallboy cans.

"Anaximanderians," Wren said. "That was another strange cult."

"Strange how?"

Wren considered. Casting his mind back. "It was a pseudoscience cult, started by an engineer. They took up residence in an abandoned pumping station just off Utah's Great Salt Lake. The leader, he'd worked there until it was decommissioned."

They walked on in silence. Toyama waited.

"He had three trials set up for his people. One of them was a big glass box full of mud, split with a metal grate down the middle. He'd dunk people in one side, lock them in, then tell them to become 'one' with the mud. They were supposed to flow through the grate and bob up on the other side."

He went quiet. Reflecting on that moment from over a year ago. Henry had been there, for that operation. Now Henry was dead.

"Did they?" Toyama asked.

"Cross the grate? The leader did. Of course, he had the system rigged. A hatch opened in the grate, just like the one here, where no one else could see it. But how many of his people kept trying, and kept failing? How many tried so hard that they drowned in the mud, and ended up buried in shallow graves in the Salt Lake desert?"

They walked on. Wren felt the past weighing on him like a boulder. You could come to a foreign country on the other side of the world, but you still couldn't outrun the things you'd done.

"That's dark," Toyama said, too loud. "Why did his followers stay?"

Wren shrugged. Took a slug of his beer. It was kiwi flavored, maybe, or strawberry. The taste was overpoweringly sweet, but he kept drinking it anyway. "Some people are cruel, but charming. Others have a hole in their hearts that they're looking to fill. You're an agent. You know this."

A moment passed.

"You're right. I know it." Her eyes took on a far-off look, like she was drifting on her own tides from the past. "There was one man. A serial killer, it turned out, and the reason I transferred to the PSIA. He used to work around here as a host, around the same time I was a cop on the beat."

They walked through a group of noisy tourists as they spilled out of a karaoke box, still singing lustily.

"What's a host?" Wren asked.

Toyama pointed over at a gang of slick-looking young men in natty silver suits, hanging around outside a club. Behind them on the wall were some twenty large-size headshots of the very same young men, like a cast roster for a film. They were all outlandishly thin, with angular jaws and feathery bleach-blond hair. A certain waifish ideal of good looks, Wren figured.

"Those are hosts. They pull you into the club, then you pay for their time. There are hostesses too. Think of them like mass-market geishas; they sit at your table and entertain you, flatter you, pour your drinks. The top hosts and hostesses charge thousands of dollars an hour."

Wren processed that. He could think of no parallel in the States. "So they're prostitutes?"

"Some of them, if they want. Most make more than enough from tableside entertainment."

Wren grunted. They walked on past the hosts and down a long alley of brightly lit vending machines selling beer, sandwiches, milkshakes and sex toys. The streets were mostly quieter now, just a few odd groups heading to the next club, or lone salarymen wandering drunkenly side to side, their ties disheveled and cheeks ruddy. The lights were all just as bright, though.

"This serial killer was a host," Toyama picked up. "His colleagues thought he was strange, apparently, but that's not so unusual around here. He was good at the job, I heard, convincing women to come into the clubs. Then one day he moved out of the city, a hundred miles west. He set up an online account and started using his hosting skills to attract women to come to his apartment."

She went quiet. Wren let the moment hang.

"The lost kind of women, you know? Women with holes in their hearts. Women who spent time on self-harm and suicide chat boards, hoping someone out there would listen. Maybe the same kind of people who ended up in your mud box cult." She drank a deep slug of her sake. "This man listened. He was a host, charming and persuasive, so it was easy for him to earn their trust. Make them feel special. He said if they came to his apartment, he'd be there with them for their final hours. Help them, if they wanted him to. Just watch their final moments, if they preferred."

They rounded a corner, back on the main road again. The station entrance lay off to the left. The big Kabuki-cho sign glowed bright red. The noisy arcade was still filled with people sitting on stools bolted in front of tall machines, generating an unearthly racket. Wren peered in as they walked by. They seemed to be playing some kind of upright pinball game, filled with flashing lights and ringing bells, but there were no flippers. Silver balls dropped constantly from the top of each machine, bounced off pins randomly and collected in different slots at the base. Some of those balls paid out like a slot machine, piling into a tray waiting by the player's feet, while others were reclaimed by the mechanism. As Wren watched more, it seemed the player's only input was control of a dial that sped or slowed the flow of balls.

"It's a pachinko parlor," Toyama said. "Lots of people here play. It's a kind of gambling. Look at all the balls he has."

She pointed. One young man with his hoodie pulled over his head had five large cartons of silver balls filled up and stacked by his stool.

"He's rich," Wren said.

"He'll cash those for prizes, then he'll go down the street and cash the prizes for cash." She gave a small shrug. "Our gambling laws are obscure, all overseen by the yakuza."

They passed by the pachinko parlor's open doors and the wash of chiming alarms and clattering balls grew deafening. Soon, though, they walked beyond it. Back into Kabuki-cho, through the square where her grandmother's booth had been, now bundled and removed, then on down quieter side streets.

Wren didn't press. He sipped his flavored beer and watched the streets go by.

"I was there when we finally entered his apartment," Toyama said. "It wasn't even a lead we'd tracked down. One of the missing young women had a friend who'd tracked her digital profile back and found her conversation with this host. Encouraging her to talk about her suicidal impulses." Toyama swallowed hard. "When we arrived at his apartment, there were ten PSIA agents with us, maybe fifteen police. We knocked on his door and he just let us in. The place stank like rotting flesh. We asked him what he knew about the missing woman, and he just pointed, said she was in the fridge."

They passed a clutch of what had to be hostesses, young and beautiful women in tight-fitting evening gowns who cat-called them until they passed out of easy range.

"She was in the fridge," Toyama finished. "She was in three cool boxes too, and five plastic cartons, along with seven other dead girls. It seemed he lured them in then he strangled them. He dismembered their bodies and he lived with them in boxes for weeks. He dropped their body parts into his trash regularly, for the sanitation workers to collect."

Wren stopped and put one hand on Toyama's elbow. "So you joined the PSIA."

She looked at him. "That's right. But it's slow, grinding work. You've seen my bosses. They care more about procedure and saving face than stopping crimes."

Wren said nothing for a moment. He didn't want to turn that around on her. Her focus on procedure was clearly a product of the system she was part of.

"You caught him. That's what matters. We'll catch whoever's killing these men, too."

She looked up at him. For a moment he thought he saw her hard shell crack. That's what hammers did, after all. Hit you until you broke. She reached a hand up to her eye and rubbed away a tear before it fell.

"We'll catch them," she agreed. "Exactly. And here, Wren-san, is your hotel." She gestured across a quiet four-lane road.

They'd emerged from a Kabuki-cho side street right in front of a Clarisson Red hotel's forecourt. The tall building looked severe and staid after the tacky, pumped-up gloss of the red-light district.

"You should be booked in for a suite. You're only three blocks from PSIA headquarters, here. I'll meet you in the lobby tomorrow morning, 9 a.m." She pulled her elbow gently away from his hand. "Goodnight, Wren-san."

He wanted to say something more but wasn't sure what. It wasn't his place. With this kind of thing, all you could do was your best. Sometimes talking was not the answer.

Justice helped. But justice, like vengeance, was a powerful drug. You could easily get addicted.

"Oyasumi," Wren called after her. Another phrase from the guidebook, a simple 'goodnight'.

She walked on, weaving slightly, caught up in her own private misery. Wren smiled sadly. Weren't they all?

15

CALL

Some five hours later, Wren woke to a ringing phone. He was momentarily disorientated, not sure where he was. Was this his Delaware cabin? But the cabin had burned down, and the quality of the darkness here felt different.

He rolled over on the mattress and saw the cell phone flashing on the bedside table. He picked it up; the screen blurred and resolved. 6 a.m. on the dot, in Tokyo, Japan. That made it three in the afternoon, Delaware time. He vaguely remembered drinking with Toyama until late, then rambling the streets of Kabuki-cho talking about old cases, until they'd closed things out with a promise to meet at 9 a.m. sharp in the lobby.

The phone was still ringing. Maybe this was her. He answered it.

"Hello?"

There was a pause, followed by a female voice speaking softly. "When did you give up, Christopher?"

Wren blinked, rubbed his eyes and pressed the phone closer to his ear. It wasn't Toyama, but it was a voice he vaguely recognized. "What? When did I give up what?"

"Justice," answered the voice, then the line went dead.

Wren held the phone away, looking at the display. His head

hammered like a steam train; a sake hangover. He tapped through on the incoming number, but it was blocked.

Strange, but not a problem. He tapped in another number and waited for the answer. It took only one ring.

"Christopher, you are early bird," came Hellion's lilting voice. "Are you catching worms?"

"Maybe. Can you check the last number this phone received?"

"Yes, why is this, you receive love call, how is this called, 'booty call', in early hours?"

Wren rubbed his face. "Just check it, please."

"Checking." Keys flew. It was an easy thing for her, hacking into telecom records. "This is Tokyo number. It looks like, yes, public phone. Location is... well. That is interesting."

Wren lumbered to his feet. The dark room spun and his whole body throbbed. "What is?"

"First piece of news, there has been sixth murder, Christopher. Body was found three hours ago. Similar conditions to others, in sewer. This call has been placed from immediately above that location. It's-"

Wren was already moving, stumbling into the bathroom.

"Get me everything on it, and call me a cab. I'm headed there in ten."

He jumped into the shower, dialed the heat to max and blasted the hangover fog back. Ten minutes later he was dressed in navy chinos and a white shirt and heading out. Along the corridor he found a vending machine selling a cloudy-colored energy drink called 'Pocari Sweat' and bought two bottles. He chugged them straight down in the elevator, dropped through the buffet restaurant where he shoved a wedge of grilled salmon and a rice ball in his mouth, then checked at the reception.

"You have something for me, Christopher Wren?"

The attendant handed him a package. He ripped it open. A new cell phone and a fresh T-CAPS system waiting for him, delivered in the night.

Outside, the new day was hot, humid and overcast with more slurry-gray clouds. The rainbow lights of Kabuki-cho had finally given up the ghost, leaving only drab-looking gray buildings behind, like dead fish on the beach after a receding tide. Traffic crawled along the road like sewage underground. The air felt lifeless and compressed, with not a breath of wind

Wren dropped into the waiting cab, gave the direction three times then rigged the T-CAPS system and set up translation on his new phone. The Sato handset he switched off.

"Ready," said his interpreter.

Streets passed by in a blur. The female voice played in his head. Giving up on justice. He called his hackers again and this time got B4cksl4cker.

"Christopher, good morning," said the big man in his rich Armenian bass. He always reminded Wren of a Siberian bear just coming out of hibernation, so cheerful to discover that spring had come.

"What have you got for me?"

"Hellion is checking CCTV above public phone now. As for murder, victim reports are same as before. Castration. Clean body. Dumped in deep sewer."

Wren's head pounded and he rubbed his eyes. That made a sixth offering. "But it's not raining now," he muttered. "No more flood surge."

"Yes, it is not raining in Tokyo. If you are interested, it is very sunny here in-"

"And the rest?" Wren interrupted. "The sewer controls and access, cult members, the *akaname*?"

"We have many things. Tokyo sewers are maze, Christopher. Access routes and surge control systems will take many hours to solve. Like very difficult sudoku. We found several targets of underground cult members, but PSIA already addressed them. More interesting, we have found preeminent expert on mythology, should know something about *akaname*. Most fascinating man, dresses like Victorian gentleman. I will send all these."

"Good, thanks."

The handset vibrated as B4cksl4cker's messages came in, and Wren scanned them swiftly. The cult members were all known quantities; some were ex-members of the infamous Aum Shinrikyo cult, responsible for the Tokyo subway sarin gas attacks in the nineties. Others belonged to Sunlit Dawn; the cult based in Indonesia that Wren had cracked himself most of a decade ago. A quick check with his PSIA records showed they had all been interviewed already.

The expert was fresh intel, though. Dr. Tetsuo Wakayama, once a professor at the illustrious Waseda University, until he started chasing conspiracy theories down unfunded rabbit-holes, and they let him go. His subject was mythology and symbology, and it looked like he'd taken the subject too far. Now he had a little-heard-of podcast, where he roamed Tokyo giving the 'behind-the-scenes truth' on modern corporate symbology, often libelously linking CEOs, judges, government ministers and other high-fliers to dark strains from ancient Japanese myths.

It sounded promising.

The cab parked. The driver said something. Wren paid him with Sato's money and tumbled out.

Harajuku station, just a couple miles south of Shinjuku. The buildings were shorter here, no skyscrapers, and the sidewalks were quieter. Beyond the train line lay a large park. Opposite was a street lined with designer goods' stores.

Wren saw the public phone next to the station's turnstiles and stamped across the street. Maybe twenty minutes after the call. Standing where she must have stood, he spun and picked out three CCTV devices in range.

"Hellion, I see at least three cameras here."

"I am checking them, but there is nothing, Christopher," she answered. "Records are clean; no person on phone in last two hours. It could be VPN bounce, send signal around the world. This woman could be anywhere."

Wren didn't think so. She'd been here. Across the road there was a convenience store and he strode over. As he entered, the two youths on the desk, both sporting bleach-blond hair and red sequined armbands, shouted something at him like, "Irra shy massay!"

"They said welcome," said his interpreter.

"Who is this voice in ear?" B4cksl4cker asked. "Is new friend?"

Wren ignored them both and spoke to the youths on the register, pointing back through the windows. "Did you see a woman over there, at the public phone?"

They smiled at him and held up their hands, chiming in unison. "No English, sorry."

Wren hit the button on the app, and the interpreter translated for him through the speakers.

One of the kids' eyes widened. "Kakkoi!"

"He said 'cool,'" the translator said.

"The public phone," Wren insisted, pointing again across the road. "A woman. Where did she go?"

They stared at him. He hit the button. They grinned and the girl answered, pointing.

"She said there was someone," the translator said, "she looked cool, all in black. She went left."

Wren was already moving.

He ran along the street until it forked over a concrete-channeled river. The park opened up on his right, a stadium lay dead ahead, and two big roads crossed paths on his left. CCTV cameras were everywhere.

"Hellion, there's plenty of cameras here, tell me you have something?"

"Checking. I have nothing so far, Christopher. Either she did not come this way, or these cameras have been digitally tampered with."

Wren cursed. "So she ghosted herself?"

"It seems this way. I will try to retrieve tracks of any ghosting protocol, but I am not hopeful. If this is digital hack, it is extremely professional."

Wren cursed again. He spun but there was nobody to ask; no shop overlooking the intersection, no dog walkers pottering around, no homeless people out panhandling for change. He was about to run into the park and take his chances on spotting her by eye, when a voice called his name from behind.

"Christopher Wren!"

He recognized it. He turned.

Koichi Sato.

16

TROUBLE

Sato wasn't alone.

He stood on the sidewalk barring the way back to the station, along with three other men in dark navy police uniforms. These were taller, thicker, and all seemed to be armed, with bulges under their left arms.

A fair fight, maybe.

Sato was talking in Japanese. One of his new friends was translating into English. Wren ignored them both, strode over and reached into his pocket. Two of the three police officers went for their guns, but all Wren produced was Sato's phone.

"Thanks for the loan," he said, holding it out.

Sato stared at the phone like it was a piece of trash. Wren didn't bother to activate his translator.

"I'll get the suit back to you, dry-cleaned, of course. And cash?" Wren rustled in his other pocket, sending the officers back to their weapons. He came up with a handful of coins and notes, which he held out to Sato. "I went a little too far. I apologize. Why don't we start again?"

Sato was cold with anger. He started barking orders. One of the officers started translating, but Wren's in-ear interpreter was faster.

"He says you're in contravention of procedures," she said. "Apparently you're not allowed within five hundred yards of any current crime scene. They have photographs you can look at."

Wren's eyes widened. "What? I can't come to a crime scene, are you serious?" He hit the button and the interpreter translated.

Sato seemed to ignore this and kept on talking.

"Now he's asking how you even knew about this crime scene. It hasn't been announced and you weren't contacted."

Wren looked in Sato's eyes. There was no sense there of contrition, no hint that they were on the same investigative team. There was only cold and brimming rage. Wren had seen lots of men like him before. Petty bureaucrats that wrapped themselves up in the hierarchy, using whatever power they had to bully those beneath them.

How ridiculous that he thought those rules applied to Wren.

Wren took a step closer, getting back in the slim man's face. "I'm going to that crime scene, Sato, whether you like it or not. Unless you want to accuse me of committing the murders, despite the fact I was eight thousand miles away for the first five, I suggest you let me through."

A slow smile spread across Sato's face. That wasn't good. "Call your government," he said in halting English.

Wren frowned. The officers must have read his surging anger, because they went for their weapons again.

"Be careful, son," Wren said, hitting the button to translate. "Don't do something you can't take back. I've said I'm sorry for taking your phone. Block me here, and there will be an accounting."

Sato didn't budge, just repeated the same line. "Call your government."

Wren's jaw set.

He made the call standing right there. Sato in his face. The three officers like a wall, clearly meant to mark some five-hundred-yard exclusion zone around the crime scene.

After five rings on his private priority line, Sally Rogers answered her phone. Around 7 p.m. back in Washington.

"Chris," was all she said.

"Sally, what's going on? I've got Japanese cops telling me I can't access any of the active crime scenes."

A long beat passed. "There's been a complaint. At the highest levels."

Wren grimaced. "I took some guy's phone. That's it."

"Not his clothes as well? His money? And not some guy, Chris. A PSIA section sub-chief. Shame's a big deal in the Japanese culture; I thought you'd have picked up on that now. You made him lose, so now he's pissed, and that comes back to us. It all counts as noise. We talked about this. While you're out there, you've got to color within the lines."

Wren fumed but swallowed it. Nothing else he could do. So this was what it felt like to be a nail. "If I can't see the crime scenes, how am I supposed to solve the crime?"

There was an uncomfortable lag. "Apparently you took one of their agents into a fenced-off section of sewers, near to the last crime scene? You both almost died?" She let out a pent-up breath. "You've been there one day, Chris, and look at what's happened already. Japan is not like here. I'm sure you're starting to get that. As for the crime scenes, I've heard they're going to share the photographs with you."

Wren could've laughed. "Photographs is a joke. I might as well be back in the States looking at a laptop screen."

"This is what we're working with, Boss. You'll have to play it as it lays."

Wren refocused on Sato. He was clearly loving every minute of the call.

"I'll figure something out," Wren said.

"Chris, don't let that mean you're going to find your own way into the sewers. I think that's what you mean, isn't it? You have to-"

Wren hung up. Then he reached out and took Sato's hand.

The shorter man tried to jerk it back, but it was like trying to pull out of a mantrap. Wren laid Sato's phone on his palm, pressed the bills and coins on top, then folded his fingers firmly closed.

One of the officers had drawn his weapon and was barking orders in Japanese. Idiot.

"He says you should release the sub-section chief," his interpreter said.

Wren didn't. "Enjoy this moment," he said. "While you're playing power games, I'll clean up your damn town."

Then he released, spun on his heel and started away, tapping at his phone.

"Christopher?" came B4cksl4cker's voice. "You wish us to find you independent access to sewer system, yes?"

Wren smiled. "You read my mind."

17

TETSUO WAKAYAMA

Wren took a cab to Waseda, a university district two miles north of Shinjuku. Passing back by Kabuki-cho, with its red-bulb gate lying dormant at 8 a.m., he felt he was starting to get a sense for the city. Tides of businesspeople poured up from each subway station as they went by.

Makoto Toyama was waiting for him outside Waseda University, standing underneath a tall pink sandstone clock tower at the head of an open square, flanked by greenery. A few clusters of students stood dotted around, all with hair dyed in various colors, most dressed bizarrely: some in tartan skirts, some in Day-Glo bright flight jumpsuits, others wearing heavy black and white makeup that made them look like pandas.

Wren paid the cab and strode out toward Toyama.

She looked upset. Dressed in a black pantsuit, this time, wearing a snug jacket that struggled to contain her curves.

"Now you got me kicked off the case," she called as he came up the steps to meet her. "I hope it was worth it."

"Good morning, Toyama. And don't worry, I'll get us back on it."

She snorted. "Really? I heard you almost had a shootout with Sato already."

Wren held up both hands, showing empty palms. "Can't have a shootout with no weapons, right? I'm one hundred percent on procedure so far today."

She eyed him suspiciously. "The day's hardly started."

"Then let's get it rolling. You've got time for a coffee?"

"Coffee? Are we in Waseda to get coffee? I thought you'd want to-"

"I hear this place has great beans." Wren pointed at a coffee shop situated in a glass block at the north side of the open square. "Trust me."

"I trust you less the longer I know you," Toyama muttered, but fell into step beside him. "I see you got your translation gear back."

"I'm living large. Strike me down and I shall rise again twice as strong."

She frowned. "Why so upbeat? Another person died last night and we can't even get into the scene. Shouldn't we be lining up to interview the friends, colleagues and neighbors?"

"I don't line up," Wren said, and pushed through the door into the coffee shop. It was a large and airy space but felt cozy thanks to low-hanging lights and a rustic parquet wooden floor. There was a line five-deep at the counter. "Except for coffee," he corrected. "Coffee's worth lining up for. What are you having?"

She gave him a look. "Are you paying with Sato's money?"

"I gave it all back. He didn't even say thanks. Now, what do you want?"

She sighed. "Flat white, whatever vegan milk they've got."

"Coming right up."

In five minutes, they were sitting and sipping, while Wren kept a close eye on the square.

"OK, so we're clearly waiting for someone. Who is it?"

Wren looked at her. He hadn't told her about the 6 a.m. call and had no intention of doing so. But Wakayama was fair game.

"We're following up a lead about the *akaname*, the filth-licker. I've found an expert, but he's a little cuckoo, maybe. Apparently, he comes to this square every day at half past nine in the morning. He used to be a lecturer at Waseda until they booted him for libel and conspiracies, so now he lectures for free on the steps."

Toyama looked at Wren doubtfully. "There's been a murder this morning. That makes six in total. So we're talking to a crazy man?"

"It's in the unexpected places that you get the answers, Toyama. It's why we went into the dark sewer. It's why I took Sato's jacket. It's why--"

"It's not why you took his jacket. You did that because you're an asshole and you wanted to humiliate him."

Wren raised a pacifying hand. Last night's drinking had really brought them closer together. "Easy girl. I may be an asshole, but he had it coming."

"Girl?"

"I'm five years older than you, at least."

She sighed. "So says the hammer."

He took a glug of his hot black Americano. It really was good. "The hammer of experience. Look, the way I see it, we're both getting used here. Me by the CIA, you by the PSIA, so all tools at my disposal are fair game."

"I'm not getting used."

"Oh no? Remind me, how long have you been with the PSIA?"

She glared at him. "Three years.

Wren smiled. "Three years. You've barely got your foot in the door. But they put you with me on a high-profile murder case with international implications. A little strange, no?"

"It's a great opportunity. I can-"

"You can take the rap if this thing goes south," he said. "You're expendable, Toyama. It's pretty much the terms I'm here on, too. I screw up and they write me off. They can easily write you off to. We're just as much sacrificial offerings as those bodies in the sewers."

Her nose wrinkled. "Procedure point five. No discussing the case in public."

"I'm taking that one as an advisory," Wren said, then stood, lifting his coffee with him. "Now on your feet, Toyama. Seems our man's arrived."

B4cksl4cker hadn't been kidding when he'd described Wakayama as dressing like a Victorian. The man looked like he'd stepped right out of a Jules Verne novel. He wore a fine embroidered cornflower blue waistcoat, a long-tailed wool jacket despite the heat, a ruffled ascot tie around a high white collar, all capped with a tall black top hat.

The young people in the square barely cast him a sideways glance.

"What is this?" Toyama asked as they strode toward him across the square.

"Watch and learn," Wren said, then strode up to Wakayama as he was settling in at the top of the steps.

"Professor Wakayama, my name is Christopher Wren, and this is Makoto Toyama of the PSIA. We'd love to take five minutes of your time to discuss an ongoing investigation."

Wakayama rounded on them. He was slender and tall, perhaps only fifty years old, with alert, fervent eyes set above a finely groomed white beard.

"Christopher Wren?" Wakayama asked in smooth English. "Of the Foundation?"

Wren hadn't expected that. "That's correct. You know me?"

"I know of you." Wakayama peered at him closely, his gaze lingering on the various scars that dappled Wren's face. "Your reputation. We are fellow travelers on the road to truth. But you are a long way from home." He looked at Toyama. "And working with the PSIA?"

"It's an advisory role," she said.

"I see." He refocused on Wren. "Well, how may I be of service?"

"You can look at a picture," Wren said. "Give us your expert opinion." He handed over his phone, showing the image of an *akaname*, taken from a woodblock print dating back some hundred and fifty years. The monster was depicted as an oily black child-devil with red eyes and a long tongue, licking the wall of a bathhouse.

Wakayama looked at it with curiosity. "Ah. This is an *akaname*. It's quite a famous woodblock point, actually, exquisite technique." He looked up. "*Akaname* means 'consumer of filth', or 'eater of sins'. Note the extraordinary tongue. It's one of the lesser *yokai,* which translates as spirits or monsters, more of a pest than a serious threat. But perhaps you already know this?"

"Please, go on."

Wakayama thought for a moment; probably wondering why a man like Wren was asking him these questions, but he went on anyway, smoothly entering lecture mode. "The *akaname* was a mid-seventeenth century invention, I believe, along with a wide range of other lesser *yokai*. These were publicized and spread by woodblock prints in books and papers, and often used by the office of the *shogun* as a kind of moral messaging." Wakayama waved the phone. "This repellent creature, I expect, was used by harried mothers to pressure their children into staying clean, perhaps also by local samurai to ensure the village bathhouse was well-scrubbed. " His eyes narrowed. "But you can find much of this information in a library. You said this was with regard to an ongoing investigation. Why have you come to me?"

Wren exchanged a loaded glance with Toyama. She wouldn't want him to say anything, for procedural reasons.

"What I'm about to tell you can't appear in one of your podcasts or be repeated to anyone in any way."

"Wren-san," cautioned Toyama.

Wakayama only leaned in. "Now you have my attention. And yes, I promise, I will not repeat anything you tell me."

"I saw one," Wren said, tossing the procedures out the window. "At least, a person wearing an *akaname* mask of some kind. It was last night, deep in the sewers beneath Shinjuku station, near an active crime scene."

Wakayama's eyes widened. "Is that so? Well. That is fascinating. A sighting of a *yokai* in the wild."

"Not an actual monster," Wren clarified. "A person in a mask."

"And in the sewers? The perfect place for a filth-licker. Tell me, what was the nature of this crime scene?"

Wren felt Toyama's gaze burning into the side of his head. "I'm not at liberty to discuss that."

"Hmm." Wakayama steepled his fingers. "Fascinating. Well. Perhaps you've exhausted my expertise on the matter, then."

Wren could recognize a gambit when he saw one. Wakayama was a looky-loo who wanted all the gory details. "Again, repeat anything I tell you now, and I'll be knocking on your door within hours, and it won't be with my colleague here, or under the name of the PSIA."

Wakayama nodded eagerly. "You may rely on me."

"Good," Wren said. "It was a ritualistic, highly stylized murder."

18

AKANAME

Wakayama's eyes widened. "I see. That certainly changes things." His lips twitched. "Of a sanitation worker, perhaps?"

Wren took a breath. In for a penny, in for a pound. "Several murders, so far, and always elites. A CEO, a judge, a minister and so on, but no obvious connections between them. They were left naked and scrubbed down, almost entirely unmarked, with all the blood drained from their bodies via castration."

Wakayama remained silent for a long moment. "I've never heard of draining via castration in mythology. Certainly not in connection to the *akaname*. But draining of blood generally, that's a common feature in folklore." He tapped his cheek. "For example, the *akimanto*, or 'Red Cape', could be related. That's a *yokai* that appears to people in bathhouses also, and offers them either a red or a blue cape. If you choose the red cape, you get ripped apart." He thought for a moment. "In some legends the body is literally torn off the spine, then the skin is knotted around the neck bones like a cape, hence the name."

Wren winced. "And if you choose the blue cape?"

"Oh, then you are drained of all blood. Castration would work for that."

Wren looked over at Toyama. She was scribbling notes on a yellow legal pad.

"So we're looking at a fusion of mythologies."

"Possibly," Wakayama allowed. "The only way to escape an *akimanto* is to refuse to choose a cape. It's a simple get-out clause, but that's often the case with *yokai.* They care deeply about shame and respect, just like we Japanese. But still, something is off. Let me think."

Wren waited. Toyama's pen hung poised over her pad. Perhaps a minute passed, long enough for the clocktower overhead to chime for 9:30. The clusters of students began moving as one toward the campus buildings.

"This creature," Wakayama said abruptly, tapping the screen, "as I recall, it's been through several incarnations. One of them was much darker than the rather silly version of it we see today."

Wren leaned in. "Darker how?"

Wakayama handed the phone back, like he didn't want to be close to it anymore. "Well, on one level, the *akaname* just eats dirt and filth. But what are dirt and filth except the offcasts of human life? On a deeper level, it symbolizes a gourmet of the darkest tastes."

Wren felt the hot air closing in around them. "What tastes?"

"Foul ones." Wakayama said clinically. "The darker version of the *akaname* symbolizes sadistic joy in activities like torture, cannibalism, and rape." He took a sharp breath. "Evil, Mr. Wren. Such cruelty has been with us forever, and mythology records that. Once such darker images were all around, representing the casual violence people experienced every day. It's only in recent centuries that the *yokai* have been softened, as we move away from our baser instincts; or at least pretend to. Now those baser instincts must go underground. In this case, it seems quite literally."

Wren knew exactly what Wakayama was talking about. He'd met the real-life monsters who found pleasure in others' pain. He'd hunted them all his life.

"So somebody wearing this mask in the sewers, you think they're invoking this darker version of the myth?"

"I expect so." A heavy silence hung between them. The square was mostly empty, now, and the clock hung still. "Some may even compare this masked creature to your Pinocchios."

Wren blinked.

He hadn't expected that.

He'd destroyed the Pinocchios a year and a half ago. Under the banner of the Blue Fairy symbol, they'd been one of his father's earliest offshoot cults: thousands of men who wore Pinocchio masks and shared sick images of children over the dark Internet. Backed by a mass hacking attack, they'd sought to annihilate anti-pedophile enforcement efforts and enshrine a floating 'Pleasure Island' tanker off the coast off Philadelphia, where all their dark fantasies could be enacted at will.

They'd almost succeeded, until Wren came along and slaughtered them en masse. Ever since, his hackers and his Foundation had come down hard on any sign of their resurgence, largely crushing the secret darknet they thrived upon.

"Because of the mask," Wren said.

"And the appetites," Wakayama said. "The Pinocchios wore masks as they committed their atrocities, didn't they? Until you killed them. That act of vengeance was an appropriate punishment, I think, and you should be lionized for it."

Wren said nothing. Stopping the Pinocchios had involved a wholesale slaughter at Pleasure Island, followed by six months of hunting the worst of them down. It had been one of the darkest periods of his life, traveling the world to execute these sick men one after another, each drenched in the bleakness of their moral black holes. Ultimately, it had landed him in an underground CIA black site as a serial murderer.

"Vengeance shouldn't be lionized," he said softly.

"Oh? Have you had a change of heart about killing them?"

That was a difficult question. "No. I'd do it again. But it's a bad cycle." He took a breath, mind cast back into the past.

"There was a woman who led me to the Pinocchios. She'd suffered the most at their hands; Mona Gebhart, or Clara Baxter, but they all called her the first daughter of the Blue Fairy. Her father had been abusing her for years and livestreaming it on the darknet."

Wakayama's face softened. "That is horrific."

"It was," Wren said flatly. "After she broke free in her teens and turned the tables on her father, she strapped him into his own torture machine and livestreamed it for the Pinocchios to see. That video was running for ten years until I switched the machine off. Her father was an emaciated corpse."

A long silence followed.

"That's where vengeance leads," he finished. "Eye for an eye leaves everyone blind."

Wakayama swallowed hard. "I can only imagine the toll this must have taken on you. For that reason, I would like to end our discussion now. I have lost my career and my reputation already, chasing such cruelty on a small scale through our corrupt system of governance. I have no interest in losing my life to the vengeance of another. Good day."

He started away down the steps.

Wren watched him go, feeling a fresh tendril of rage worming into his heart.

Pinocchios. *Akaname.* Perhaps he should have suspected a connection sooner. But then he hadn't wanted to.

Toyama said something but Wren didn't hear it. Instead his gaze drifted across the square, searching for something that wasn't there. He hadn't thought about the Pinocchios for such a long time. There'd been other matters. The political collapse of his country. The ravings of X. The secession of Texas.

A life with his children on the Delaware farm.

Now every person he saw could be an enemy. An *akaname.* A dark soul hidden inside a normal person.

"Wren-san," Toyama insisted.

He came back to the moment. Toyama was staring at him, concern on her face.

"It's OK," he said softly. "Flashback. It happens sometimes."

She nodded. "I understand. I get them too." A moment passed. "Do you really think we could be dealing with something like the Pinocchios here?"

He couldn't ignore the possibility. Already the scale of the crimes suggested it. If it was true, it changed everything. "Maybe."

Toyama lifted her phone. "Then we need to tell Yamaguchi-san. This is huge. It'll send us in a whole new direction. We-"

Wren laid a hand over her phone. "We don't tell the PSIA. If these *akaname* are anything like the Pinocchios, then there's a high chance the PSIA will have been infiltrated already."

Toyama's eyes flashed open. "The PSIA has not been infiltrated by sewer-dwelling *yokai*! It is an elite institution, comprised of only the best-"

"Elite like Kenji Ando?" Wren asked softly. "Elite like the judge who died, or the government minister? Anyone can have a black heart, Toyama. When I took down the Pinocchios, do you know who they were?"

She gave him a blank look.

"Postmen. Politicians. School teachers. Lottery winners. Nurses, billionaires, street sweepers, brain surgeons. Anyone and everyone. They guard their hearts well, but in the shadows they all put on the mask. If this is real, then they're everywhere. They're walking amongst us right now."

There was silence for a long moment. Toyama looked around. The oppressive gray-white sky felt like the inside of a squeezing fist.

"So, you're saying the victims were somehow involved? Kenji Ando was involved?"

"I'm saying these victims were chosen for a reason. It's our job to find out what that reason is."

19

KENJI ANDO

Wren found a Denny's restaurant up the street from Waseda station, then led them to a corner booth in the window, far from any other denizens at that mismatched hour; too late for breakfast, too early for lunch. The décor was bright and cheery, with lots of yellow, red and pine.

"Can we talk about the case here?" he asked, gesturing around at the empty diner. "It's bending procedure, I know."

Toyama fixed him with a glare. "What's wrong with PSIA headquarters? I can book us a meeting room, requisition evidence, even bring in the interviewing agents."

Wren made a face. "Can I get waffles and bacon in PSIA headquarters?"

"I'm afraid not."

"I rest my case. Plus we might have to deal with Sato again, and once a day's enough for me."

"Good point." Toyama made a show of looking around. "Fine. This will do. So talk."

"I'll order first, if you don't mind." Wren held up a hand to get the waiter's attention. Toyama casually reached over to the plastic tube holding chopsticks, knives, forks and paper napkins, and pushed a recessed button.

A chime rang out. On the far wall their table number came up on a digital display.

"Neat," Wren said.

The waiter came in seconds. Wren ordered a triple helping of bacon, waffles and maple syrup, with strong black coffee.

"You already had coffee," Toyama protested. "Just thirty minutes ago."

"You can never have too much coffee," Wren said, with a wink, and waited for the server to walk away. "So, OK. Tell me everything you know about Kenji Ando."

"Why so keen on Ando? There's five other victims to consider."

Wren shrugged. "I already checked out the others. Your people did, too. There's no pattern, no links between them other than they're all elites. One's as good as another, so I picked Ando. No special reason: let's say his story pulled me in. Small-town boy done good in the big city. I like that. Now I'm getting into his head, and that's like a relationship. Would you cheat on your boyfriend? Or girlfriend, I don't want to be prescriptive."

Toyama sighed. "Boyfriend. And I don't have one. And I wouldn't cheat, even if I did. But we're talking about corpses."

"Closer relationship than with a boyfriend, then. This guy, Ando, needs us more than any living person ever will. We have to avenge his death."

She eyed him sternly. "I can't tell if you're kidding or not. A second ago you were questioning if he was an *akaname* himself."

"I never kid. So, spill it. Ando."

She shook her head, brought up her phone to check her notes, and started talking.

Much of it Wren already knew from the PSIA files he'd reviewed on the plane. Ando was forty-five, the millionaire CEO of an up-and-coming cell phone parts company with factories based in China. He was a lifelong bachelor. No wife, no long-term girlfriend, as far as anyone could tell. He'd been photographed on various red carpets over the last few years, each time with a different minor celebrity on his arm, but none more than once.

Playing the field, it seemed. Or keeping up appearances.

He had few friends, and those he did have, he'd carried with him for decades. There were three top members of his company who'd ridden with him from the beginning, all the way from their hometown together. Like him, they were workaholics, by all accounts.

He took frequent trips overseas, mostly to China, visiting his factories. The records on those trips were thin. PSIA agents had interviewed his close family, which amounted only to his mother. His father had died when he was a baby. His mother was in her sixties and still lived in the same home Kenji had grown up in, in a hot spring town in the shadow of Mt. Fuji.

"And the interviews?" Wren asked, chewing down big mouthfuls of sweet and salty bacon. It tasted pretty much like it did back home. "What did you get on known rivalries, enemies? In particular anything from the three best friends and the mother."

Toyama sipped a green tea while Wren pigged out, scrolling through records on her phone. "I attended the friends' interviews myself. He may have carried them up with him, maybe they were close once, but they weren't anymore; that was my impression. When they were younger, they used to all go for drinks pretty regularly as an office, but that stopped about five years ago." She kept scrolling and sipping. "One woman, Ryusuke Michimura, the CTO, she seems like she was closest to Ando. But even she said she didn't socialize with him anymore, not after the staff parties stopped."

"Stopped," Wren repeated. "Why?"

"Nobody really knew. They figured Ando was so busy. Maybe he'd grown out of it. That was around the time he hit forty. Not everybody wants to party forever."

Wren grunted. "And nobody spotted anything the day he was taken? Any unusual behavior, any oddballs casing the office?"

"No. They all said it was just another day. Few of them spoke much to Ando outside of meetings anyway, by that point. All his staff left that day by 8 p.m., while Ando was still at the office. The security log shows him checking out at 9. It's a short walk from his office to his apartment building. He's got a penthouse right in the middle of Shinjuku, but there's a few stretches on the way without CCTV. Somewhere in there he went missing. Our guess was, whoever took him just dragged him down into the sewers from there, because we tracked every other possible route means of kidnap. No obvious abduction vehicle. No suspects. And that's it. We're up to speed."

Wren chewed his bacon and waffles then took a big pull on his coffee. "And the mother? They interviewed her, right?"

"They did. I wasn't there for that one. They called her in, but uh…" She trailed off. "It looks like she mostly talked about his childhood." She kept scanning notes. "She's in her mid-sixties now. Kenji was her only child, and only surviving family. They tried a few times, but everything was from thirty years ago. Seems he didn't talk to her much, either." She scrolled through screens. "She did talk a lot about, uh, him being a good boy. Apparently, he won some math competitions? She wanted to show them his trophies. In the end, they decided there wasn't much point in pressing further. He hadn't been back home for years, in either case, so they cut her loose."

Wren chewed and thought. "Cut her loose."

"Yes." Toyama put down her phone. "And that's Kenji Ando. Ready to cheat on him with the next victim, now?"

Something niggled at Wren. He brought up his own phone and started looking through the files. He remembered reading something on the plane about…

"Got it," he said.

"Got what?"

"Right here." Wren laid the phone down, already zoomed in

on one of Kenji Ando's school records. "It says he had dyscalculia. That's like dyslexia for numbers."

Toyama surveyed the scanned document. "So?"

"So, don't you think it's odd that his mother's talking about math trophies, when there's no way he was winning any numbers competition with that condition? He'd struggle to sum up a drinks tab."

Toyama was silent for a moment. "That's a good point."

"I guess they didn't raise that in the interview."

Toyama went back to scrolling through her notes. "I don't think they were trying to catch her out. So, no. They had four other victims' relatives and friends to interview."

"Exactly why we don't cheat on our boyfriend," Wren said. "So, tell me, Toyama. Why is Mrs. Ando lying?"

Toyama squinted. "I wouldn't call it lying. Maybe she misremembered?"

"Misremembered trophies her only son didn't win? I don't buy it. She's up to something."

Toyama laughed. "She's an old lady. Long retired. What do you think she's up to?"

Wren pushed his plate away. He'd demolished all three helpings in record time. "Only one way to find out. How far away's Mt. Fuji?"

20

MT. FUJI

The subway ride west passed in silence, both lost in their thoughts. They changed once at Shinjuku, then changed again at Chofu station on the Keio line, heading out into rural Tokyo, the opposite direction from Narita Airport.

Wren leafed again through the interviews with Ando's colleagues as the tall gray towers of Tokyo faded down to a low smear of gray beneath a curdling white sky. There wasn't much fresh. Mostly he was thinking about what the ex-professor, Wakayama, had said.

Darkness everywhere. Hiding in everyone.

It took two hours to reach Lake Hakone, and they arrived just after noon. Wren strode out of the train station and looked out at Mt. Fuji, but its flattened summit was hidden by the low white clouds. Across the gray lake, rooted in drab green forests, the mountain looked like a giant gray hammer head rising featurelessly into white. No color. No trees or greenery on its flanks. Defiant and overbearing.

"Let me do the talking," Toyama said, as they got into a cab to circle around the lake. Wren couldn't take his eyes off the mountain, weaving in and out of tree cover. The roads were narrow and winding, but Fuji was ever-present, shrouded in the dirty cream skies.

Mrs. Ando's house was a twenty-minute drive away, a ramshackle wooden affair built on scrawny metal stilts, projecting out from the road and over a cliff down to the lake. It was shabby and battered, like every other house they'd passed. The heat and humidity had warped and blackened its thin wooden boards with mold. There were several potted plants out front just about clinging to life, one shooting purple-red cherry tomatoes that had already split and were rotting on the vine.

Wren eyed the shaky construction.

"It's fine," Toyama said, as if reading his thoughts. "You're not that heavy."

She knocked on the thin wooden door.

Wren felt like a man invading a tomb, as Mrs. Ando's ghostly footsteps rang through the small house. Each footfall came slow and freighted with grief. The door opened, revealing a shrunken, bowed-over woman dressed in shabby gray knitwear. She looked to be ninety years old, not in her sixties. Grief alone hadn't done that to her, not in a matter of days.

She'd lived hard. Too much sun, too much work, too much pain.

Toyama spoke. Wren's interpreter translated, but listening was hard. Focus came with difficulty. He found his eyes returning again and again to Mt. Fuji, ever-present on the skyline. Looming like an iceberg, the great bulk of its mass hidden under the waves.

She admitted them. They followed her shuffling gait down a narrow, rickety hallway. The walls were made of yellowed paper, torn in places. Dark brown wood bore scuff marks. A step down led to what had to be her living room, floored with six large mats of pressed and bound straw, barely twelve feet by nine. There was a low square coffee table in the middle and two flat cushions either side of it, with two glasses of clear liquid before them. One cushion bore the imprint of Mrs. Ando's weight, the other was plumped and waiting. Beyond it, against the wall, lay a shrine to her son.

In the center was a large photograph of him smiling. To either side were mounded flowers. Far too many flowers, with many of them starting to wilt and brown. There were wooden blocks written with Japanese calligraphy, and unlit candles, and incense sticks burned down to ash. The smell was overpowering: molding hay, the sweet stink of rotting flowers, the musky scent of the incense.

She gestured for them to sit. Neither took the side of the table with the cushion. Wren sat opposite, folding his legs underneath him, barely fitting his back against the wall. Toyama sat kitty-corner, and they waited while she bustled in the tiny adjoining kitchen.

After several moments she returned, and set down an old, syrup-stained bottle of brown liquid.

"It's oolong tea," Toyama said quietly. "It's fine."

Mrs. Ando poured the tea with a shaky hand. Wren and Toyama drank. It was bitter. He found his gaze held by Kenji Ando in the photo. He'd never met the man or seen him in the flesh. Only video of him at various launch events, and photographs of his dead, milk-white body. It was sad, but there was something about his eyes. Like they held a secret.

Something felt off. Uncomfortable.

Toyama began asking questions carefully. Wren's translator interpreted, always a few seconds behind but keeping pace.

"I believe you've spoken to our colleagues already, Mrs. Ando. We're very sorry to disturb your grief again."

"Oh yes. My grief. Yes."

"We'd like to ask you some follow-up questions, if we may?"

"They asked me if my son had enemies." She turned her watery gaze on Wren. "Do you have enemies, sir?"

Wren met her gaze. "I do."

Toyama translated. The old lady nodded. "Everyone does. Enemies. They frame a life."

"We read your earlier answers, Mrs. Ando," Toyama went on. "We wanted to ask about your son's character. Questions they may not have asked you."

She took a weary breath and leaned back in her seat. "He was a good boy. He did his homework. He was very good at math. Would you like to see his trophies? I still keep them."

Wren caught Toyama's eye. "Perhaps later."

"Yes, later." She fell silent.

"He was clearly a very talented student," Toyama continued. "He went on to achieve great things. Can you think of any reason why anyone would want to hurt him?"

A long moment passed. "Hurt him," she repeated. "They asked me that, too. I don't know. He was such a good boy. When I was tired, he used to rub my legs. I worked standing up. I was a nurse. Sometimes he'd massage my feet for hours. Did you know that?"

"Did he ever talk about his life in the city? His friends? His rivalries?"

"Oh, all the time. We spoke on the phone every day. Such a good boy."

Wren leaned back, pulled out the T-CAPS earpiece and brought up his phone. Toyama watched this, but Wren signaled that she continue.

He called through to Hellion.

"Yes, Christopher?"

"Can you check phone records for Kenji Ando's mother? She says he called her every day. But I don't see a phone here. No cell, no landline."

"Checking."

Toyama and Mrs. Ando continued speaking. Soft tones, low voices. Without the T-CAPS Wren could make no sense of it.

Keys clattered on the other end of the phone. As Hellion worked, Wren checked back through Kenji's childhood medical files.

"I show no records of a phone on her address or against her

name," Hellion reported back. "No cell phone, no landline, not for years."

"Thanks," Wren said, and hung up. He slotted the T-CAPS back in. The interpreter was still speaking.

"-so he was always interested in shells. He used to collect them and build such structures. I thought he would be an architect. So creative. He always liked to build."

Wren tapped Toyama's arm. "Can you ask her to show us her phone?"

Toyama gave a slight frown but nodded and translated.

The old lady smiled. It was haunting, like a thing that didn't belong on that prematurely crevassed face. "Of course. Give me one moment."

She rose shakily to her feet.

"Why her phone?" Toyama whispered, as the old lady teetered through to an adjoining room.

"Because those daily calls are not in the PSIA interviews. You'd expect them to follow that up, if they knew. But I just checked; records show she doesn't even have a phone."

Toyama made a face. "Her son's company made cell phone parts. I'm pretty sure she has a phone. It's probably just in his name."

"We'll see."

In a few moments Mrs. Ando returned. She held a disconnected old landline rotary model in one hand. It was a warped cream Bakelite two-part unit, handset and cradle. In the other hand she held the trailing cable. She set the unit down on the table, then carefully plugged the trailing lead into a hole in the coffee table.

"Here," she said.

Toyama looked at Wren. It broke his heart.

"And you called him on that?"

She nodded. "Every day."

Wren studied the unit. It hadn't worked for decades, probably.

"Could you make a call for us now?"

The old lady nodded and picked up the handset. There was no sound, no dialing tone, nothing. Still she held it to her ear.

"This is cruel," Toyama hissed.

"Stay with me," Wren murmured. "Ask her to call her son's number."

"What?"

"Tell her it'll help us identify his phone."

Toyama glared at him for a moment, then turned to Mrs. Ando and asked.

The woman dutifully began dialing the number on the rotary plate. Each number went through slowly and painstakingly, the dial clicking back around after each one. Wren counted fifteen digits in all. Far too many.

She looked up at Toyama through myopic eyes. "It's ringing."

It wasn't ringing. Wren stood. Mrs. Ando didn't seem to notice. Toyama eyed him.

Wren pulled the T-CAPS mic on his collar close to his mouth and whispered as he edged around the tight room. "From now on, only translate what I tell you to say."

He stopped behind Mrs. Ando and looked at Toyama.

"Tell her I'm making an adjustment," he said to Toyama.

Toyama's eyes shone. "I don't like this. I'm not toying with her."

"She won't remember it anyway, Makoto," Wren said. "Please, trust me here."

She stared at him defiantly, then took Mrs. Ando's hand and said something in Japanese.

The old lady muttered a response, and Wren dropped gently to one knee. He plucked the T-CAPS unit off his ear and hung it gently over hers. He took the microphone off his lapel and clipped it to the handset's trailing cable.

Toyama watched, aghast.

Wren worked his way back around the table. He sat down opposite Mrs. Ando. Held up his phone.

"Hello, mother," he said.

It took a second. Across the table, there came the tinny squeak of the T-CAPS unit translating into Mrs. Ando's ear.

Her eyes immediately widened. She clutched the handset with both hands like it was suddenly precious.

"Kenji?" she whispered. "My boy?"

21

MY BOY

Wren barely dared breathe. The old lady clutched the phone so tight he feared the sun-bleached Bakelite might crack.

She spoke in Japanese. Wren gestured to Toyama, whose eyes were blazing. Still she leaned in, pressed her lips close to his ear and translated.

"She says they're telling her he's dead. We're telling her."

Wren nodded, spoke into his phone at a whisper. "I'm not dead, mother. I'm just in some trouble."

The translation jolted the old lady's body like an electric shock. She curled away from the table, body cocooning the handset and speaking quieter still, staring at the blown-up face of her boy amongst the rotting flowers.

Toyama translated. "They're here now. They're listening to us."

"It's OK," Wren said. "They can't hear us."

She answered in a bare whisper, and Toyama translated. "You sound different, Kenji. What's happening?"

"It's the line," Wren said. "That's all. It's good to speak to you, mother."

A tear beaded down the old lady's face.

"We have to stop this," Toyama said, pulling away from Wren. He ignored her.

"It's OK, mother. I'm OK. But I'm scared and alone. I need your help."

Now a tear raced down Toyama's cheek. Still, the T-CAPS continued translating into the old woman's ear, and she continued responding. It didn't matter that Wren couldn't understand her.

"Stop it," Toyama whispered. "This is cruel."

"I'm alone here," Wren went on. "I don't know what to do. They're asking me so many questions. Questions about my enemies. Questions about who would want to hurt me. What should I tell them, mother?"

Mrs. Ando's demeanor changed as her body stiffened. She suddenly focused. The tears dried. She spoke urgently into the dead handset. Wren only looked at Toyama, whose eyes were spreading wide.

"Tell me," Wren mouthed.

Toyama seemed to vibrate, torn between two ideas of what was right, then she leaned in, hot lips now touching Wren's ear. "She says he'll be OK. Nobody can hurt him, but he shouldn't say a thing. Don't tell them anything. He hasn't done anything wrong."

Wren's throat went dry. "Don't tell them what, mother?"

She replied fast and low. "About the girl. About the little girl. You're a good boy, Kenji. I know it. I know it."

Wren's heart skipped a beat. The trapped heat of the room suddenly turned frigid. "What girl, mother? What little girl?"

"The one I hid," Mrs. Ando whispered. "That's over. You're OK, now. You're safe."

"And my enemies?"

This seemed to confuse the old lady. "You mean the police?"

"Not the police. My enemies. The people who'd want to hurt me. The people who wear the masks."

A long silence passed. Then the old lady looked up. She

looked right into Wren's eyes, then into Toyama's, and spoke with a new trembling clarity.

"You're tricking me."

Toyama translated at a whisper.

Then Mrs. Ando dropped the handset. She raked at her ear, pulling away the T-CAPS system and plucking at the microphone.

"Get out!" she shouted abruptly, and Wren didn't need Toyama's translation to understand. She repeated it again and again, getting louder and louder. "Get out! Get out!"

"She's going to hurt herself," Toyama said. "We have to go."

Wren rose. Mrs. Ando was shrieking. Toyama bowed low, said what sounded to be an apology, then led the way. In seconds they were outside, on the hot street, but it didn't feel any better. Mrs. Ando was in the window now, shrieking at them still. Fuji hung over everything, beneath the smothering blanket of a sky.

Wren started walking, trying to put the pieces together.

Toyama strode alongside him. Cars passed them by.

"What just happened?" she asked.

Wren slotted the T-CAPS back, clipped the microphone back in place. "I don't know."

"Then why did you even do that?" Toyama was angry. "What did you think was going to happen?"

Wren took a breath, some fifty yards away already, and stopped. Toyama jostled into him, then stared up into his eyes defiantly. Barely inches apart on the narrow sidewalk.

"Her manner," Wren said, trying to put words to the series of fast deductions he'd made. "I've seen a lot of grieving parents. I've met a lot of people lapsing into dementia, too. When they talk about their children, they give details. Always. If there's anything they remember, it's their children."

Toyama's face screwed up. "So? She gave lots of details."

"They were the wrong details. She was talking about the math thing again, right?"

"She did," Toyama allowed. "But I just don't see how that matters all that much. She got confused. It happens. Maybe she got confused about some little girl. It doesn't mean anything. It's definitely not evidence. She's just old."

Wren shook his head. "You're not listening to me. The last thing that parents lose when dementia strikes is the truth about their children. And when they do lose it, it's gone. They forget their names, their faces, that they ever existed. They don't just invent information." He took a breath, running back over the conversation. "Likewise, the massaging of her legs. You know her son had a muscular condition, yes? I double-checked his medical records. Myasthenia gravis. I don't know what it's called in Japanese. It weakens the muscles, kind of like slow onset polio. It never goes away; it's why his arms and legs were so wasted when you found him. He had it since he was a child. There's no way he could massage her legs for hours. Just not possible.'

Toyama's confusion thickened. "I. So. OK. What does that mean?"

Wren stabbed a finger back at the house. "It means we weren't just dealing with dementia, back there. Dementia's a factor, sure, but it's obscuring something else. She's a liar, Toyama. Not just to us, I expect, or the PSIA or her neighbors, but to herself. Lies she's been telling her whole life. You see how old she looks?"

"She does look old," Toyama allowed.

"Lots of things cause premature aging. Maybe sickness. Cancer will do it, but she's had no sicknesses like that, according to the record. A boy with dyscalculia, the muscle wasting, and raising him alone? Maybe that'll age you. But so much that she looks like she's ninety? That's something else. Incredible, overwhelming stress. It ages the body massively. She's been keeping a secret for decades, I think."

Toyama caught a shallow breath. "The things she said, when

she thought you were Kenji. Don't tell them about the little girls and boys? Where did that come from?"

"I think it's the truth. A truth that's burned her up since he was a child, a truth that led her to inventing this happy fantasy life they lived together, as a cover story. She thought she was helping him, like she must have helped him all his life. Cover up whatever dark things he was doing with little girls. She had to do it, just to get through; tell herself that he was really a good boy."

Toyama nodded. "She did say that a lot."

"That's self-comforting behavior. That kind of repetition. Parents often cover up for killer children. They can't face the reality that their child is evil. So it's not just us she was trying to convince. She's constantly trying to convince herself."

Toyama said nothing. Just stared.

"Now that fantasy life is melding with the dementia. She doesn't know. It might be possible to go back in there, run the whole thing again. We might even push it further, get more details. What little girls? What about the mask?"

Toyama froze. "It was when you mentioned the mask, that was when she saw through us."

Wren just nodded. Waiting for her to make the same leap he already had.

"She must've seen it," she said abruptly. "An *akaname* mask. Or a Pinocchio mask? Maybe a sketch, even, but something." Her eyes lit up. "So, wait. Kenji Ando wasn't an offering? Why would they sacrifice one of their own?"

"Exactly. It's not what we thought," Wren confirmed. "Everything flips."

"If he was an *akaname* himself," Toyama rushed on, her eyes became urgent, "if he was one of them, then why would they kill him? Why leave him on display for us to find?"

"They wouldn't. They wouldn't stamp my name into his skin, either. It wouldn't make sense. The last thing they want is me here, turning over rocks and squashing the bugs that crawl out from underneath."

Toyama's eyes and mouth were wide. "So if it wasn't the *akaname* that killed him, then who was it? And why?"

"Exactly," Wren answered, finally starting to feel like he was getting some purchase on the case. "Who, and why?"

22

WHO AND WHY?

They went back to Mrs. Ando's house. They knocked on the door, and she answered. There was no recognition there. She just didn't speak. Once the door was open, she walked back inside. She sat down in her customary spot at the low table. The Bakelite phone was gone, tucked back away wherever it had come from. The only other difference was the enlarged photograph of her son's face, which had been turned to the wall.

Toyama asked questions. Mrs. Ando didn't even look their way.

"This is bad."

"Perhaps. It looks like dissociative fugue."

Toyama turned to him. "What's that?"

"Kind of like a timeout. Her brain's on lockdown, overwhelmed by events, emotions, the past. It can happen to anyone, usually after trauma. Sexual assault survivors often suffer it. In her case, it's the surging trauma of her son's behavior. The dementia's probably making it worse."

"So is she OK? She'll recover?"

"I expect so. Some medication, some rest, she'll be back to where she was."

"So what do we do? We caused this."

Wren nodded. "Call an ambulance. Just not yet. Thirty minutes won't make any difference."

Toyama's lips pursed.

"That's not an order," Wren said. "I can't give you orders, anyway. I'm going to search the premises. It'd help if you joined me."

Again she seemed to teeter in the balance. Weighing morality against procedure against a desire to know the truth.

"Thirty minutes," she agreed. "I'm setting a timer."

Wren nodded and started back through the house. The boards underfoot creaked and shifted with every step. There were two more rooms downstairs; a miniscule bathroom with a square tub that was barely big enough for Wren to sit down in, and a second reception room.

"What are we looking for?"

"Confirmation," Wren said. "Leads. I'll take upstairs."

He took to the stairs, barely wide enough to accommodate his broad shoulders. The creaking and shifting grew worse. It felt like at any moment the stilts below would give out and the whole structure would surf down into the lake. At the top there was a tiny landing, piled either side with old books. Wren couldn't read any of the titles and looked beyond to two rooms.

One was clearly Mrs. Ando's room. It was a narrow space with more straw-mat floors and built-in cupboards. A futon lay neatly rolled up against one wall, alongside an ancient photograph of a young woman and a young man holding a baby.

Sweethearts. His heart ached. Nobody ever knew what their sweet child was going to become.

The cupboards were filled with clothes and bedding. In the bottom of one he found a box, but inside were perfume-scented love letters. He put it back reverently.

The second room was similarly empty, though it was larger. Kenji's room. A bedroll lay against the wall, underneath a window with a beautiful view of Mt. Fuji. The best room in the house, a place to make the rickety location worthwhile, and she'd kept it for her son.

Her son who never called. Who hadn't even updated her ancient phone. A son who'd left her behind.

The cupboards were crammed with junk. Childhood toys in plastic boxes, clothes for a child, old records, dog-eared books, sketchbooks full of superheroes battling monsters.

Wren leafed through the pages. There was no *akaname*, but there were some disturbing images; blood and wounds sprayed across the yellowed paper. Enough to earn a referral to a child psychologist, in the modern world. Not evidence, but indicative.

At twenty-five minutes, Wren heard sirens drawing near.

Toyama had called the ambulance already.

He stood back to survey the space. He'd checked both cupboards. There was nowhere else to hide anything, except, perhaps…

He worked his fingers around the edges of the straw mats. They were wedged in flush, and he couldn't get his nails in the gap, so he pulled out a key. He'd packed it his luggage without realizing it, must've laid it out on the bedside table last night when drunk and sentimental, then dropped it in his pocket this morning without thinking.

The key to a cabin that no longer existed.

He wedged it between the mats and prized upward. The first lifted, and Wren tipped back. Tiny bugs scuttled away from the light. Stains marked the wooden boards. He lifted the second, and the third, then the sirens drew up and stopped. Any second there'd be paramedics in the house. He couldn't keep on ransacking the house while they were treating Mrs. Ando.

Last chance. He heaved the final straw mat and surveyed the space underneath.

In one corner lay a small plastic Ziploc bag. Wren snatched it up, had time enough to glance over the contents, then the knock came on the door. Looked like a swatch of hair, a locket necklace and a woven grass ring.

Toyama moved to the door downstairs. Wren laid the mats swiftly back in place and was coming down the stairs when the paramedics came in. They shot him a confused glance.

He held out some clothes for the old lady: a warm jacket, a lap blanket, a pair of gloves. The second paramedic through took them with a nod.

Toyama met him on the sidewalk ten minutes later. The glowering sky was threatening rain. Her face was like a mirror, a mask obscuring rage. Wren had half expected this. What he'd done to Mrs. Ando, and pressured her to take part in, was dark. It was far outside anybody's conception of procedure.

"Don't ever ask me to do that again," she said coldly.

"You're angry," Wren said. "I understand. But look."

He handed her the plastic bag. She took it, then focused in when she saw the lock of black hair and the ring. "Where did you find this?"

"In Kenji's old room. Hidden under the mats. And here." He held out the locket. Opened, it contained two tiny ovals cut from a Polaroid photograph. One was a little girl, maybe seven years old. The other was Kenji Ando, at perhaps seventeen.

"My God," Toyama whispered, reaching out. He let her take it. "Is that him?"

"It's him. And I already image-searched the little girl. There were plenty of local news reports at the time. She disappeared twenty-seven years ago, never heard of since."

Toyama's mouth dropped open. The anger with Wren forgotten, beginning to transmute into outrage. "He killed her."

"He was an *akaname*, no doubt," Wren said. "Perhaps a Pinocchio before that. Whoever killed him, well. Maybe they're on our side."

23

STAGE

They didn't talk much on the journey back to Tokyo. Toyama put the small plastic bag on the table between them, the locket lying open. It felt like an indictment. This was the cost of failure.

They reached Shinjuku in mid-afternoon. The slurry sky had opened briefly at some point, cracking piercing sunlight through a gouge in the clouds, but already that wound had sealed over again. Now a low featureless gray ceiling bore down like the lid on a pressure cooker, hot and humid and threatening rain.

At Shinjuku west exit Wren stood in front of a large, open rotary road. Across the way lay several distinctive skyscrapers: a soaring missile shape wrapped with white diagonal stripes like a spiraling web; a gray concrete monstrosity with two towering heads; a large white globe dimpled just like a giant golf ball. He watched cabs pass by; dozens of businesspeople striding between skyscrapers and underground passageways; tourists taking photos and checking maps.

They were all ants. Wren and Toyama were ants. So many millions of people stacked on top of each other, all ants, all getting steadily cooked by the pressure of the steaming skies.

"You OK?" Toyama asked.

He grunted. He often felt this way when he came to big cities. The murder of children just brought it on harder. "Fine. Ando's apartment. It's in that one?"

He pointed at the missile-shaped building.

"The Cocoon," Toyama said. "He had a penthouse suite."

Wren started walking. He tracked the route Ando would have taken from his office to his penthouse. There was visible CCTV along most of the route, with only one unmonitored spot where he might have been taken, where a sewer grate waited.

Wren silently commended the killer. Taking the fight to the enemy by using their own subterranean highways.

Akaname. Pinocchios. There was nothing he hated more.

"What?" Toyama asked, looking down at the grate. "We checked it. No DNA. No evidence."

"That's not definitive."

Toyama cocked her hip. "And what about the flood surge? We went down, and within ten minutes we were almost drowned. If the *akaname* can control that, wouldn't they use it to drown the killer?"

Wren grunted. It was a good question.

The Cocoon's lobby was vast and airy, somehow giving the impression of a bright and pleasant day. Fill lights hidden in the structure, Wren realized. They made for a fake sunny day; temperature controlled to a brisk spring morning.

Toyama flashed her PSIA badge to the guard on reception, offered a few words of explanation, and he took them to the private residents' elevator. It rocketed up.

"It's mostly medical colleges," Toyama explained. "The Cocoon's the second-largest educational building in the world."

"So how did Ando get a penthouse?"

Toyama shrugged.

The dark blue glass of the building's skin tinted the world outside. Tokyo spread before them, eclipsed by the webbing stripes. A gray sprawl that stretched on and on. Up here, you could feel like the king of the ants. The little girl's locket felt like it was burning a hole in his pocket.

"Wren-san," said Toyama. He realized her hand was on his shoulder. He turned.

The elevator opened onto a narrow stretch of hall, at the end of which was a single door. A crack into the building's shell. The guard opened it with a security card and they strode inside.

Wren had seen impressive penthouses before. This wasn't vast, positioned at the tapering top of the Cocoon's missile, but it was incredible. Open plan inside, almost entirely, bar a separate section to the side which he presumed to be the bathroom and utility. Otherwise, it was completely open; to the panorama encircling it, to the sky above. The dark blue glass was replaced by crystal clear views stretching away into the distance. Was that the far-off stub of Mt. Fuji, poking into the clouds? Maybe.

Wren didn't care.

He walked through the space. Surveyed the kitchen with its clean granite worktops and well-stocked chrome wine cooler, the open lounge with its L-shaped gray sofas and sunken TV, dining area with a twenty-seat table cut from a single slab of oak, then came to a stop in the bedroom area, where he just stood.

The bed was round and huge, coated with a black futon trimmed with white ermine. Above the low headboard hung a splattered work of modern art that defied description: perhaps there was a grid system hinting at streets, buildings or sewers; perhaps the thickly textured acrylic paint suggested blood splatters, or frozen waves, or a thousand tiny, sandpaper blades.

"We went through this place in depth already," Toyama said, by his side. "I don't know what we can find."

"And you found nothing," Wren said.

"Nothing. No clues as to why he was selected. He seemed a randomly chosen victim, just like the others. Well, not entirely random. He was an elite, incredibly successful and wealthy, like the rest. He lived here, and his offices are a five-minute walk away, and his body was found in the sewers somewhere beneath us. It was the same for every victim; dumped in the ward they lived in.'

"Not dumped," Wren said. "Displayed. They were a calling card."

Toyama came around in front of Wren, trying to catch his eyes. "A calling card?"

He blinked, refocusing on her face. She was beautiful, intelligent, even incisive, but he couldn't see that now. All he could see was Kenji Ando in this space. Lying on this bed. Dreaming his dark dreams. "A calling card for me."

She frowned. "What does that mean?"

"I don't know yet. But I'm going to find out. Have we got enough pull with Yamaguchi and Sato to start bringing in Ando's co-workers?"

"I don't know. But why would we? We already interviewed them all. None of them knew anything. That day was a normal day. Ando left the office late. They never saw him again."

"I want them here," Wren said. "An interview in situ. With enough PSIA agents or cops to keep them isolated from each other, maybe on a lower floor. So they don't see each other, get any hint of what's coming. Just the top people on his board. Can we do that?"

Toyama's brow creased in curiosity, but she didn't press it. "I'll make some calls."

She stepped away.

Wren stared at the bed. He took three steps and violently pulled back the covers. Beneath lay black silk sheets. Wren felt sick. He went back to the kitchen and opened the wine cooler. He plucked three bottles of red wine, maybe a thousand dollars a bottle, and a corkscrew. Back by the bed, he started pouring the wine directly on the sheets.

"What are you doing?" Toyama called. She ran over, holding the phone to her chest as Wren drained the bottle across the bed. "This is not our property! We can't do this."

"Staging a scene," Wren said, and opened the second bottle.

"Stop it!" Toyama persisted. "Chris."

He turned to her while the wine glugged out. "It doesn't matter, Makoto. Once we share that locket, and it comes out who he was? They'll rip everything here out and trash it. The sheets will be first to go. The mattress. The wine. That painting. The man was a killer of children."

Toyama worked that through her head. Maybe she'd been lost in the revelation and hadn't thought it through. Their discovery of the locket was going to ignite a firestorm, just as soon as they released it. Ando's picture as a teen across from the picture of a missing little girl. A lock of hair. A woven grass ring. DNA analysis of the hair would confirm it. His DNA would seal the deal.

"That evidence will never hold up," she protested. "We don't have chain of custody. We had no search warrant."

Wren shrugged. "So we found it here. Under a floorboard, in the toilet tank, wherever. It's the same thing."

She stared. Working that through, looking for flaws. "OK. Maybe. But. What is this?" She gestured at the bed. "Some empty kind of revenge?"

"It's not revenge," Wren said dully. "It's a scene. Listen. When you interviewed Ando's board members, you did it in PSI offices, yes? In sterile rooms, white walls, nothing but lights and questions."

"Of course! That's procedure."

"This'll heat them up. How many of his colleagues, his friends, ever came here? I'm guessing some. How many of them came here when he had children in his bed?"

Toyama's lip wrinkled. "You think-"

"I think I'm going to rattle them. Shake them up. See how they hold up under pressure. Maybe they never played a role. Maybe they know nothing about the *akaname*. But I'm betting they know something. Some of these people, you know how long they knew Ando." The last of the wine dripped out of the bottle. The sheets were already sodden. The ermine stained. Red liquid dripped onto the marble floor, and the air stank of fruity alcohol.

Toyama stared at the dripping wine. Exactly the kind of impact Wren was hoping to have. Disgust. Even fear. Bringing the sickness into the light. "I suppose," she said trying to shift her gaze between Wren and the ruined bed. "Some were his high school friends. They've known him most of his life."

"Exactly. He brought three of them with him from Hakone. The others he's known for over a decade. You really think they don't know what a creep he was?"

She said nothing.

Wren sprayed the last bottle of wine onto the painting, onto the pillows, onto the headboard and walls.

"OK," Toyama said. Getting a grip on herself. "I get it. But it's very far from procedure."

"Screw procedure. All that matters is the result."

24

MICHIMURA RYUSUKE

The Metropolitan Police came through. Toyama still had some pull with them, it seemed. Over a matter of hours, the top members of Ando's company were brought in for follow-up interviews.

The CFO. The COO. The CTO. The Chair. The Vice Chair. The Secretary. Men and women, all around the same age as Kenji Ando, in their mid-forties. The peak of their careers, perhaps.

They came in coiffed and adept, but that composure broke quickly. The floor was scattered with shards of broken plates and glasses. The bed was ravaged and bloodied with red wine. Wren sat alone at a table in the midst, with the locket open in its plastic bag before him.

Their reactions differed. All were confused. Most were afraid. One even laughed, losing control. One, though, froze.

Michimura Ryusuke. She was Ando's oldest friend from Hakone. They'd gone to school together. They'd climbed up the ranks of start-up companies together. From the moment she walked in, dressed in a prim black skirt, black jacket, striped blue and white shirt, she was nervous. She was short and slim, with her thin hair cropped in a bob, drawing attention to her pallid cheeks.

Her gaze darted here and there, but when she saw the locket on the table, her eyes flared wide. Wren gave her a moment to stew and stare, then pushed the lock of hair alongside it, and the woven grass ring.

She began to tremble. Her eyes fluttered. Her cheeks reddened. All the tell-tale signs he was looking for.

"Tell me," he said.

She looked up at Wren. She looked at Toyama. Her jaw set ever-so slightly, and she answered in smooth Japanese, which Wren's T-CAPS translator quickly converted to English. "Tell you what?"

Wren waited. He watched. He could see her brain spinning hard; trying to figure out what was happening, whether she was at risk, prepping some cover story. But the evidence was there in front of her. The evidence was in her emotional reaction.

"You know what," Wren said, and waited for Toyama to translate. "Ando was your oldest friend. He made you. And here he is, seventeen years old in a locket next to a little girl who went missing twenty-seven years back. In Hakone. And now, as soon as you see this locket," Wren picked up the bag and held it before her eyes, waiting for Toyama to catch up, "you piss yourself." He let the obscenity hang. Toyama hit the word hard, and the T-CAPS confirmed it. There was nothing like a little rough talk to shake a witness up. "I want to know everything. The more, the better. Nothing here's official, and I'm not coming after you, unless you were somehow involved. In which case, you better start running now."

He sat back.

All those words piled up in Michimura Ryusuke's head. The cumulative effect was obvious, coming on top of the wreckage in the apartment, and the locket, and the bizarre death of Ando himself just a few days earlier.

Something inside Ryusuke twisted and the dam broke. Her mouth opened and a torrent of confessions poured out, so fast his T-CAPS interpreter could barely keep up.

"She's always known Ando had an interest in younger girls," she translated. "She knows the girl in the locket. She'd seen Ando with her several times, walking together after school nearly thirty years ago. She teased him about it. He laughed. The girl was like his little sister, he'd said, then asked if she was jealous. It was a joke. It wasn't a big thing."

Ryusuke took a big breath, and the interpreter did too, then they both dived back in.

"Then one day the girl disappeared. Her name was Kaori. It was a big mystery in their small town. Everybody joined the search parties combing the lake, including her and Ando, like everyone else in town. She consoled him, afterward. He sobbed, and they grew closer. For a time she thought the two of them might get together, but it never happened. In any case, she never suspected he'd been involved."

Ryusuke came to a halt. Wren looked in her eyes.

"Bullshit," he said firmly. Toyama translated. He let the curse word hang again. "You did suspect. Or else why are you cracking like this?"

Ryusuke began to sob. Soon enough, the confessions continued. It was all there right beneath the surface. You just needed the right key to open the lock.

"She saw him with young women many times in the years since," the translator raced on. "Teenagers, often. 'My girls', he called them, with a smile. Not girlfriends. Not partners. Certainly not a wife. Just his girls. She went out to clubs with him, work parties where the whole office came along, and she even sang his praises to girls who couldn't even be sixteen. No harm, she thought. Like siblings. It was unusual, but not that bad. He just liked their company. She never saw him kiss them, grope them, do anything untoward. He'd never recovered from the loss of the girl in Hakone, she thought. He was just looking for that little sister again."

Wren said nothing. Just stared and let her keep digging.

"At some point, though, the work parties stopped, and she no longer saw him with his girls," the translator went on. "He started taking trips to China more, for business. Setting up factories. Each time, he came back more exhausted than he'd gone. She assumed it was just hard work, and tried to support him where she could."

Ryusuke's voice hit fever pitch.

"Once she went to his apartment in the middle of a workday. He hadn't come into the office for three days straight, and she was worried he was sick, overworked, maybe half-dead in his bed with no one to look after him. So she came to the Cocoon. The guard knew her and admitted her to the private residents' elevator. She walked right up to his door and knocked."

Tears streamed down Ryusuke's cheeks as she sped on.

"What she saw when he opened the door haunts her still. Kenji Ando was right there in his suit, and behind him was a small figure on the floor, wearing a whole-body leather outfit. It looked the size and shape of a child. It was crawling on the floor. The suit covered the head, and had no eye, mouth or earholes. A leather leash trailed away from a black collar bolted around the neck."

The translator briefly choked up. Ryusuke looked like she was in some kind of a trance. Wren's anger surged but he clamped it down.

"She saw the figure for only a second, because Ando slammed the door and shoved her backward, then tore into her. It was vicious, worse than anything she'd ever experienced. Right there in the hallway, he ripped her apart. She had no right to interrupt his privacy. No right to step away from work in the middle of the day. No right to be here at all, not when she was nothing, when she was a worthless fat pig, not when she was lucky he'd kept her around all these years. Who the hell did she think she was?"

Ryusuke collapsed in gasping tears. Wren had no sympathy to give. He felt like a block of stone, letting the story bounce off him. Toyama moved in, though. She put one hand on the distraught woman's shoulder and whispered something in her ear.

It helped. She pulled herself together and pushed on.

"Ando kept on hammering at her until she was a sobbing mess on the floor. She fled back to the office, but she couldn't work at all for the rest of the day. She couldn't sleep that night. She'd never seen that side of him before and was terrified. She didn't understand what had happened, and she dreaded the next day at work.

"But the next day, it was like everything went back to how it used to be. He was there early and brought coffee for everyone. He was kind to her, friendly, charismatic, generous, acting as if nothing had happened. He even invited everyone to a club that night in Kabuki-cho, just like the old days. Ryusuke went along, half-scared out of her mind, half thinking the fever had finally broken.

"Maybe her friend was back. She blamed the pressures of work. Maybe he was just into kinky sex, and she'd imagined the child-like proportions of the figure in the leather. Maybe it really was none of her business. But midway through that night, Ando seemed to switch off. His eyes pulled far away. Like it was all growing too hard. She caught his eye briefly and felt like there was nothing on the other side. Not the Kenji Ando she'd known. Something else entirely. It terrified her more than him shouting at her in the Cocoon. This time he said nothing. He just left the club, and that was it.

"At work the next day, he was absent again. She didn't go around to his apartment. She didn't ever reach out to him again. He never invited the team to Kabuki-cho again. That was five years ago."

Wren watched as she slowly pulled herself back together. He was having trouble holding in his anger.

"Where did he go, that night?" Toyama translated.

"I don't know," she answered. Wren didn't need the translation to understand that.

"Who did he spend time with? Who was the child in his apartment?"

"I don't know!"

Wren vibrated at the table. Itching to leap up and lay waste to something. Anyone.

"Did you never think to call the police? Tell them about what you'd seen?"

As soon as he said it, he knew it was a step too far. Maybe it was true, but that didn't matter. In her mind, Michimura Ryusuke was a victim too. Maybe she was. But maybe, if she'd done something, if she'd said something, things might have been very different.

But she hadn't.

Toyama read the tea leaves and put a hand on Ryusuke's shoulder. "It's OK," she said. But Ryusuke shrugged it off, and instead she rose to her feet and stabbed a finger at Wren. Now the fear and shame were turning to anger, with almost clockwork predictability. Ando had flipped out at her. Now she was flipping out at him.

"Don't you dare judge me!" she shouted. No need for the T-CAPS for that, either. "I didn't know. I didn't do anything!"

Wren said nothing. Didn't even meet her eye. That was the whole problem. She'd done nothing.

"I didn't know!" she repeated one more time, then spat on the floor and stormed out.

To Wren, it sounded just like Ando's mother. Sitting with her dead Bakelite phone in her hand, insisting what a good boy Kenji was.

Toyama followed her out, making softly worded reassurances. Wren went to the window, barely containing the storm inside. The night view was epic. The low, dark sky glowed with the vibrant pulse of the city. A thousand red lights spread across a thousand skyscrapers hummed on then off in slow unison, beaming out their warning message to low-cruising helicopters.

Stay away from the rocks. The shoals. The sirens below.

Ryusuke had seen that child in the leather suit. She'd just chosen to disbelieve it. She'd wanted to disbelieve it, because believing it would upturn her whole life, her career, everything, and would mean going against Ando.

Ando was at fault, but Ryusuke was an accessory. She was also a victim.

There was nothing to feel but rage. It coursed through him like molten lava, with nowhere to go, because Ando was already dead.

Toyama came to stand at his side. He thought she might criticize him. Tell him he'd gone too far to get so little.

"It's something," she said instead.

He didn't answer. Just gazed out at the slow pulse of the city, battling for self-control. His mind spun with new ways forward, but they all ran up against dead ends. He brought up his phone and checked the feed from his hackers. The most recent update had come in an hour ago. They had no off-book sewer access for him yet. Maybe tomorrow morning.

He put the phone away.

A child in a leather suit. No eye, ear or mouth holes. A leash trailing away. His knuckles tightened. He couldn't stop seeing it.

"Chris," Toyama said. Now her hand came on his arm. He couldn't turn. In the dull reflection of the glass, against the flash of a thousand red lights, he saw her press in. He felt her warmth against his arm.

"It's OK. We'll get there tomorrow. We can't do any more tonight."

He didn't know. He wanted to. Break open every club in Kabuki-cho. Start accosting people in the streets and ripping their invisible masks off. The rage had to go somewhere, but there was nowhere to put it. No Pinocchios to slaughter. No compound to smash into with a cavalcade of self-driving vehicles. Only Tokyo's slow pulse, and all the dark secrets that lay underneath.

"Chris," Toyama said softly. "Noodles. Come on."

She pulled on his hand. He let her guide him out.

25

NOODLES

Toyama walked and Wren followed. It wasn't raining. All he saw were masks on all sides. Faces within faces. They passed through Shinjuku station and emerged on the east side, facing Kabuki-cho's neon red archway.

"Ando came here," Wren said.

"Everyone comes here," Toyama answered.

The old lady's booth was there, like it was waiting for them. The grill sizzled, and smoke plumed up with the smell of grilling meat. The same table was free. Toyama ordered and Wren sat, mind buzzing with a dozen different thoughts. All of them ended in dead ends.

Sake came. There was no toast, but Wren gulped it down. Toyama poured him another glass and he gulped that too.

"This is personal for you," she said.

He didn't say anything. It was a weakness.

"I didn't expect that," she went on. "When we met, I thought-
"

"You thought I had an overblown reputation," Wren said, not even looking at her. "Some guy grandstanding for his own benefit."

He felt her smile. "Something like that. But you're not."

Wren downed another sake. She refilled it.

"You care."

Wren looked up at her. The burn of the sake was coming on already. Hot, sweeping, tingling, better. It helped a little. Maybe a lot would help a lot.

"I'm here for my own reasons."

Toyama snorted. "Bullshit. I don't buy it. The second Ando-san started lying, you shifted. You got angry. I've never seen anything like it. Just, total fury."

Wren looked away. The fury was still there, burning him up.

"I never see that," Toyama went on. "Sato, Nakamura, Yamaguchi, many of my colleagues. It's a job to them. A paycheck. Put the hours in, suck up to the boss, they'll rise up. Personal status. But it's not like that with you. You don't care about any of that."

"Quit trying to analyze me, Toyama."

"I'm done. I get it, now. Why you break the rules. And call me Makoto."

Wren turned to her. There was something different in her eyes now. Where those black pools had been spiky, cold and robotic before, now they seemed like they were opening up.

Her breathing came fast. He saw the flush on her skin, the rapid dappling of her carotid artery, speeding even as he looked at her. He was surprised to find his own body responding the same way.

"I'm not hungry anymore," she said.

Abruptly, neither was Wren. He saw a different hunger in her eyes.

There were plenty of reasons to not pursue that any further, to just go back to his hotel and sleep the whole thing off, but in that moment none of them seemed to matter. Maybe the sake helped, and Wren's body moved without conscious control.

He leaned in, closing the distance between them, but holding back at barely an inch away. Her hot breath glided over his cheeks, the heat of her steaming up his thoughts.

For a moment she seemed surprised, but that quickly faded, then she closed the final inch herself, pressing her lips to his.

Fireworks went off in Wren's chest. She was hot, lusciously soft but firm; overwhelming and pulling him in. Sudden desire burned through him. His skin felt like it was on fire. Every second of the kiss felt like an age, stretching on and sucking him down.

At last, she pulled away. "Forget the noodles," she said huskily.

She stood and took him by the hand. They strode out into the night. Toyama led, and in minutes they stood before a love hotel. There was a vending machine that paid out short- and long-stay keys, with a large display of different themed rooms: one decked out with aliens and a UFO bed, one where the bed was a race car and-

"Do you want-"

"I don't care," Wren interrupted. The fury fueled him. He wanted to grab Toyama right there and it took everything he had to hold back.

She tapped buttons on the vending machine and took the keys, then together they went down a narrow corridor to a tight elevator. Her hips swayed like he hadn't seen before, every step teasing him on.

In the elevator they exploded against each other. Lips on lips, hands roving, elbows banging off the tight walls. They kissed and explored each other, and too soon the chime rang, and the doors opened on the eighth floor, and they staggered down a red-walled corridor to their door.

The room was full of stars and spangles. A US-themed love boudoir. Wren swallowed a laugh, then they were in each other's arms again. Toyama was soft and hot against him, pressing and yearning. She ripped off his shirt and he ripped off hers. Her chest pushed against his, and she let out a gasp.

They tumbled onto the bed, kissing and closing the distance as she tugged at his belt and ripped off her own suit pants, pressing down hard and explosively, until suddenly something shifted.

Wren saw the locket.

In the darkness behind his eyes he saw Kenji Ando's 17-year-old face with the little girl's face opposite. He saw Mrs. Ando sitting broken in her living room, and Michimura Ryusuke's desperate expression as she recounted her story, and he pictured a small, fragile body crawling on the floor in a full leather suit, on the end of a leash, and -

All his passion reverted to fury. His body ached with it. He shouldn't be here, doing this with Toyama. He had no right. He should be out breaking down doors, fighting through the sewers, digging out the truth. He had to get out, to stop whatever this was and get back to what really mattered, when-

"Hey!" Toyama said, short and hot in his face, stopping him cold. She was on top of him now, their bodies enmeshed, looking right into his eyes. "It's OK. You're here with me, Chris."

He didn't understand. He didn't know what she meant. For so long he'd subsisted on rage. He had a wife, or an ex-wife. He had to get out there. He had to-

Toyama grasped his face with her hands, framing his world so he couldn't look away. "You're with me. It's only you and me. We both want this. We both need it."

She held him just long enough. Maybe something inside him stretched out and snapped. She watched it happen. The rage gave way and the pictures in his mind disappeared, and she began to move like before, rhythmically up and down.

His body responded, and the passion came back like a geyser, harder than before. All that mattered was this moment, so hot and delicious. He leaned forward and hoisted her up, and they kept on climbing until finally they hit the peak together, and collapsed in a panting, blazing heap.

26

DERU KUGI

They lay entwined and gasping. Wren felt utterly spent. The rage was gone. The fury, the disgust, the ever-present urge that said he had to be doing something and saving someone was temporarily beaten back.

It was a wonder.

He didn't know when he'd last felt like this. Toyama's hand stroked his scarred, tattooed chest. Her sleek black hair cascaded over both their bodies. His arm curled around her back, encompassing her shoulders, his hand pressed against the hot, heaving side of her chest.

"*Deru kugi wa utareru,*" she whispered in his ear.

He smiled. The T-CAPS was long gone, ripped away and lying on the floor somewhere.

"And what does that mean?"

"Ancient Japanese proverb," she murmured lazily. "The nail that stands out gets hammered down."

He laughed. It felt great. "Deru kugi something something…"

"There you go," she said. "You'll speak Japanese perfectly soon."

"I think I've already mastered '*douzo*'."

"Mastered being annoying with it."

He laughed again.

She caressed his chest. He stroked hers. "This is the first time," he said awkwardly, flush with feelings he hadn't expected, "since I, uh…"

"Shh," Toyama whispered, stroking his chin. "It's OK."

"Since my wife. I didn't think it could be like this again."

"It's been a long time for me too. I'm glad it was with you. Chris."

She tweaked his nipple.

"Ouch," he gasped, then kissed her neck. "Actually, maybe do that again. I think the nail's starting to stand up one more time."

Now she laughed. Started rolling languorously atop him again. "Someone has to be the hammer, yes?"

He laughed. It didn't last long.

This time it was gentler. Longer. The furious passion was gone, leaving only a slow, aching, building joy. Her whole body trembling. As they rose together, she leaned in close and held him until they hit the peak, then they laid in each other's embrace until sleep found them.

In the darkness, Wren was in the desert.

It was night, and he was running. Out there in the black were all his enemies, closing in. They had guns, and knives, and implements of torture. He should've been preparing to fight, readying his own ammunition, but he wasn't. He just watched them all come on, unafraid.

Their blades sliced into his body. Their bullets passed through him. He didn't feel them at all. And when they were done, and all exhausted from their efforts, they disappeared and Wren alone remained.

His wounds healed up. He felt stronger than ever.

A shrill ringing broke through the silence of the desert. In a second it dragged Wren up from sleep, back into the dim, firework-lit room. The walls were red, white and blue. Toyama was stirring by his side. The sweat had dried on their bodies, covers half flung over them, and there came the ringing again.

His phone. He grabbed for it, found it on the floor. 4:23 a.m., said the readout. Nobody should be calling him at that time. Nobody had that number.

"Yeah," he answered.

"Are you having a nice holiday, Christopher?"

It was the woman's voice again, wrenching him up to full wakefulness. She sounded so familiar, but he couldn't quite place her. "You. Who are you?"

"The better question is, who are you?"

"What?"

"You know what you're facing, now. I left you enough clues. But here you are, screwing around. It's time to act."

"Clues? What are you…" he trailed off. "You mean the bodies?"

There was silence on the line.

"Did you kill them? Ando? The *akaname*?"

"Time to decide who you are. International playboy, screwing your way around the world, or the fabled 'Saint Justice'?"

"That's a bullshit comparison," Wren began, but the click had already come, signaling the line was dead.

This time he was ready, and called Hellion at once.

"Very early, Christopher," she said. "You have been called again by noisy morning bitch?"

"Find her for me," Wren said, "I think she's the one killing the *akaname*."

"Juicy," Hellion said, and already her hands were clattering over the keys. Wren was on his feet and padding around the room, gathering his clothes and the T-CAPS system and pulling them on. "I will have cab waiting for you."

"What was that?" Toyama asked. Fully awake too, now getting dressed.

Wren stopped in the midst of buttoning his shirt, looking at her. With her hair disheveled, her makeup smudged, her clothes half-on, she looked more beautiful than ever. He almost wanted to drop everything and jump back into bed.

But that's what the voice on the phone had said. Accusing him of being on holiday. It was ridiculous.

He considered trying to bluff his way out of explaining where he was going, but then why would he do that? Toyama had proven herself several times already. She was smart. He'd trusted her this far.

"I'll tell you in the cab. We've got somewhere to be."

She didn't question it. They got dressed in frenzied silence, and in seconds they were in the elevator riding down. Through a peephole strip of glass in the elevator's wall, the city looked dark, its bright lights shuttered for the coming arrival of dawn.

"I have location," Hellion said in Wren's ear, "is further public phone, am tracking CCTV again."

"Where?"

"It is not far, area called Roppongi. It looks like a whole town of brothels and bars."

Wren looked at Toyama. "Roppongi. "We may be looking at another body."

Her eyes flared. She clearly had lots of questions, but just then the elevator hit ground floor and Wren sped out onto the street. A warm breeze met him under a dark sky. A yellow cab was already waiting at the curb, an old guy at the wheel wearing white gloves. Wren dropped in the back, Toyama followed, and they took off without a word.

Dark streets glided by like the extension of a dream.

"So what's in Roppongi at 4 a.m.?" Toyama asked.

Wren turned to her. Somehow, either in the elevator or while she was getting changed, she'd managed to tidy up her hair and sharpen her makeup. He wouldn't be surprised if she'd brushed her teeth and flossed too.

He wanted to kiss her.

Instead he spilled. "Yesterday, you heard I was at the Harajuku crime scene, right?":

She frowned. "Getting in trouble with Sato-san, right?"

"You ever wonder how I knew there was a crime, there?"

She frowned. "I thought perhaps you had a police scanner. Something like that."

Wren shook his head. "I got a call from a payphone in Harajuku station. A woman's voice, someone who knew me. They asked me, uh." He paused. "A difficult question."

"What question?"

"If I'd given up on justice."

Toyama laughed. "A stupid question. You're addicted, like me."

He smiled. "Maybe. So I go there, hunt for her, but the CCTV footage overlooking the phone has been ghosted."

"Ghosted?"

"She was erased. The footage is there, but she's gone. I run off looking for her, and that's when I bump into my new BFF."

"BFF?"

"Best Friend Forever. Sato."

Toyama's eyes narrowed. "He's not your-"

"Doesn't matter. So just now I got a new call. You heard the conversation, right?"

"Your side of it."

"Right. It's the same woman. She said she's been leaving me enough clues. That's when I asked if she's the one killing the *akaname* like Ando."

Toyama nodded. Thought a moment. "Which means if it is her, she may be on our side, somehow? Illegally, of course."

"Something like that. And we may be headed to another crime scene now. Have you received any notification from PSIA? Has another body been called in?"

Toyama checked her phone. While she scrolled, Wren focused on Hellion.

"Any luck with CCTV?"

"Nothing," she answered. "CCTV is ghosted. Christopher, here is important question. Was agent Toyama in room with when you called me?"

Wren caught a curse. The last thing he needed was his child-like hackers to focus on that. Better to ignore the question entirely. "Any sign we're headed to another crime scene? Are the PSIA there?"

"I cannot see them. If this is crime scene, you may be first there. And yes, she was there, wasn't she? This is very early. Are you having naughty sleepover?"

"None of your business. Keep your mind in the game, Hellion."

"This is more fun game. I wish to know every-"

Wren killed the call, then went back to staring out the window and trying to put the pieces together. Was this woman the reason he'd been called out to Tokyo? Was she somehow killing the *akaname*, then branding his name into their skin just to get his attention?

But why?

It also threw out the sacrificial offering theory completely. He didn't have a theory to replace it. Perhaps-

"Nothing," Toyama said, looking up from her phone. "If there's a body there, we may be the first to find it."

27

ROPPONGI

Roppongi was a mass of tall and glossy buildings with wide streets, overcast by a broad elevated highway running east-west through a five-way built-up crossing. Wren saw clubs, hosts, bars, love hotels; the same kind of seedy dives there were in Kabuki-cho, but interspersed amongst them were designer jewelry stores, offices for high-profile tech companies and the logos of large investment banks.

The cab pulled up.

"It's like a gentrifying Kabuki-cho," Wren muttered, as the cab pulled up at a large intersection, across the street from a fancy crepe shop with the public phone in front.

"What's gentrifying?" Toyama asked.

"Fancy," Wren answered, got out of the cab and strode across the road to the phone.

The shutters were down on the crepe shop. Next door a desultory teen with multiple piercings sat behind the reception desk of a brightly lit pink lobby, its walls festooned with big-eyed manga pictures. Wren stopped at the phone and spun around.

Of course, there was no sign of the woman. Multiple CCTV

cameras hung from the underside of the rumbling highway overhead, but Hellion had already said they were all ghosted.

"What's this?" Wren asked, striding toward the pink lobby.

"Manga kissa," Toyama answered. "Like an Internet café, also full of manga comics."

Wren pulled the door open. "Do the honors, please."

Toyama led the way up to the desk. The teen looked bored. He had bleached blond hair and a nose ring, fat loops in his ears, cheek piercings, lip piercings and eyebrows that were more metal than hair. Toyama held up her PSIA badge and started asking questions. The T-CAPS translator echoed the answers seconds later for Wren's benefit.

"He asked what kind of badge that was."

Wren groaned. Toyama answered and asked the question again. The teen couldn't have looked more bored if he tried, but forced out an answer.

"He says he doesn't know. Maybe he saw her. Probably she crossed the street."

That was enough nonsense for Wren. He leaned over the counter and grabbed the kid by his nose piercing then pulled him gently forward like he was leading a cull.

The kid's eyes flared wide with panic, hands instantly windmilling helplessly.

"Where?" Wren asked, pointing out the glass.

The kid babbled in Japanese.

Toyama put a hand on Wren's arm as the T-CAPS answered. "He doesn't know, he says. But he says she came out of the subway opposite, if that helps."

"Chris," Toyama said. She was trying to sound severe but struggling to contain her amusement.

"*Arigatou*," Wren said, then let go. "You've been most helpful."

They left the manga kissa and surveyed the intersection. As far as Wren could pick out, there were three entrances leading down to the subway below, each one on a different point of the five-way intersection.

"Which one?"

"They all go to the same place," Toyama answered. "Come on."

They went for the middle one. In seconds they were clattering down tiled steps, emerging into the underground ticketing area. Wren rifled his pockets for his transit card, but it was gone. He settled for vaulting over the ticket stiles, only to find Toyama talking to a gray-faced ticket vendor in a booth. The vendor looked at Wren in surprise, then at Toyama's badge in surprise, then nodded. He opened the booth, stepped out, and held his ID card to the magnetic stripe to open the wide turnstile.

"You could've jumped," Wren said.

"Look before you leap, Chris," Toyama said with a smile. "Would jumping get us a key into the sewers?"

He couldn't argue with that. "Lead on."

The guy did, starting down a rolling escalator at a respectable pace.

Wren placed a call to Hellion as they descended.

"Yes, Christopher."

"In case there's a body here, we'll want all possible access routes for how she got it into the subway. How's your map of the sewers coming along?"

"Yes, we are checking this now. Map is mostly complete, thank you for asking. As before, I am seeing thousands of routes. This is not helpful, so we are attempting to limit. However, you will be glad to hear we have access to first location, *akaname* sighting, through backchannels."

"That is good. Cue it up and see what you can do here."

"It is time sensitive access. But yes. Now, enjoy second trip into sewers with your new girlfriend. Very romantic date. Very pretty lady. I did not know this was your type."

Wren muted her.

They were hurrying along a narrow platform, fringed on

either side by subway lines. Few commuters were out at this time. On a bench at the center laid a suited office worker, his tie around his head like Rambo, his shoes splayed beneath him, sleeping with his briefcase as a pillow.

"That's normal," Toyama said, as they passed.

Wren smiled. "He's not the victim, then."

"Not clean enough."

He laughed low.

The attendant led them to the end of the platform, where it butted into the wall between the two tunnels. A long rush of hot air preceded a train whipping by on their right. Inset into the wall was a metal door.

The guy spoke and Wren's T-CAPS translated. "He says this is it. He has the key."

He rustled with a huge key fob.

"Are you sure you want to come down here?" Wren asked.

"Are you?" countered Toyama.

He nodded. The attendant got the key in the door and turned it. The door opened inward, revealing a familiar-looking tunnel stretching away into darkness, flanked with pipes, lights tinkling to life as some unseen movement detector registered their arrival.

In the distance, barely visible at the outermost limits of the awakened light, a dark figure was running.

28

INTO THE DARK

Wren broke into an instant sprint.

The tunnel walls flew by as his feet pounded the damp concrete flooring, lights flickering to life ahead as he ran. The tide of illumination snapped at the heels of the receding figure, just barely keeping him in sight. Toyama's voice rang out in back, but he couldn't hear it over the sudden rushing of blood in his ears.

An *akaname*!

The figure ran all-out, and Wren gave everything he had to keep pace, elbows and knees pumping for thirty seconds, a minute.

Then the figure disappeared.

In ten seconds Wren saw the reason; the tunnel split left and right. Lights were dappling to life on the left, while on the right lay in darkness. He had only seconds left to choose. Get it wrong and the lead was gone. Delay, and the moment was lost.

He chose right and plunged into the thick dark.

Lights burst up around him, barely keeping pace as he charged full tilt at the shadows. The wild racket of his own footfalls and racing heart eliminated any chance of picking out the *akaname*, but he had a feeling. On opening the door to the sewer, the *akaname* had been in darkness. There was no patch of light already lit. Only as the lights rippled out ahead had it been exposed.

They were creatures of the dark, after all.

Then he saw it. Heels racing at the feathery edge of the flickering lights.

"Stop!" he shouted.

Then it was gone.

Wren reached the point where it had vanished and spun. He saw pipes, cables, and just before all the lights went dead, ladder rungs leading up.

Instant darkness, all-consuming.

There was no time to bring up his phone and bring up the flashlight. He remembered where the rungs were, three steps ahead and off to the left, and went for them. The second he laid his fingers around the knurled metal, he felt the vibrations trembling down from above.

The *akaname* was escaping.

Wren launched himself upward. Powerful arms pulled, powerful legs pushed, and he skipped multiple rungs at a time, catching the next handhold and foothold by feel. Jump, catch, pull, push, jump, catch.

The darkness became a cacophony of footfalls, grunts, caught breaths. His back brushed a wall in the dark, his shoulder rang dizzily off some metal outcropping, but he kept on leapfrogging upward. The *akaname* was right there. He could feel it. Fifty feet already gone and climbing higher. How far up was street level? Maybe a hundred, max two hundred feet? They'd come down thirty or so steps to the ticketing area, ridden an escalator another hundred's worth, so that meant-

Light cracked ahead as a trapdoor of some sort opened. Wren heard a familiar roaring sound, echoing crazily down the chute, saw the *akaname* clambering out, and redoubled his bursts of upward speed.

Jump, catch, jump, catch. Just as the trapdoor was

hammering down, Wren ducked his head in and burst through it like a rocket launch. His back crashed into the metal hatch and sent it peeling away with a wild clang. Wren's momentum stalled and he cast his arms either side to catch the floor, before he fell back down.

It was a storeroom of some kind, filled with small blue crates, mop buckets and the roaring sound of a factory. The *akaname* was right there, staring down at him, dressed all in black. Its mask was a repellent, bulky monstrosity; the goggling red eyes, the horns, the long crawling tongue that slunk out and over the shoulder, back to some kind of backpack.

Instantly Wren understood.

It wasn't so much a mask as a helmet. Infrared cameras in the eyes. Some kind of re-breather apparatus in the long tongue leading to an oxygen cylinder in the backpack. Its whole body encased in a shiny black wetsuit. That's how the previous *akaname* had survived the flooded sewer under Shinjuku. It really had plunged into the sewage flow.

The *akaname* didn't wait for Wren's analysis; instead it aimed a wild kick at his face which he barely managed to dodge, then ripped open a door and raced out. The clanging, ratcheting chaos noise abruptly grew overwhelming. Wren pulled himself the whole way out of the chute and gave chase.

He spun out into the thick of a vast, smoke-filled, lights blaring pachinko parlor.

The upright pinball machines were everywhere, and everywhere sat punters taking their chances at the random game, cigarettes in their mouths and puffing out smoke. Churning metal balls cascaded all around in their hundreds, clanging off the pins, setting off alarms and sudden reward flows crashing into the waiting blue crates, bright lights flaring.

Wren was momentarily overwhelmed after the dark and relative quiet of the sewer. He spun, seeking out the black-encased figure of the *akaname*, seeking the signal in the noise of so much noise and motion.

Then he saw him. Ten yards off and accelerating. The helmet was gone, tossed already, but that shiny black suit was unmistakable.

Wren burst into motion. Three hundred pounds shifting to full-on ram mode, hammering a path between the seated players, spinning them on their chairs, sending crates of balls spraying out across the plain white floor. He made good distance, but the *akaname* was faster. Slim and slick like an eel, it whipped in and out of spaces Wren had to crash through.

It was getting away. Now Wren saw the exit doors ahead, clear glass leading out to the lights of the street beyond. The *akaname* was almost there, and Wren was only halfway. There was no way he was going to make it.

He dropped low on one stride and dunked both hands deep into a blue crate filled with stainless steel balls. He came up with two fistfuls and flung the first from his right hand like buckshot from a shotgun.

The spray spread, taking out collateral damage all the way to the doors, tinkling off the ceiling panels and breaking several lights, smacking firmly into the cheeks of focused players, racing ahead to put starburst cracks into the glass of the exit doors, but still catching the *akaname* with a solid thump of ten or so balls dead in the back.

Maybe half-a-pound of steel all-told, accelerated to ninety miles per hour in half a second flat, making for about ten Newtons of impact force into the *akaname*'s back. Enough to feel it, hardly enough to knock him off his stride, but perhaps enough to-

The *akaname* spun his head in mid-run, right into a second spray of balls from Wren's left hand, which spattered his face and pulled out a scream.

He ran sideways. He banged into a pachinko machine hard, which began vomiting a flood of balls. The crate overflowed in seconds, and balls spilled out across the floor.

Wren was almost there. The *akaname* was reeling, probing at

his face. A ball must've hit his eye, because Wren glimpsed blood pouring between his black-gloved hands. Five more steps, and-

Something massive hit Wren from the side, driving him off course and hard into one of the machines, which itself began to vomit more steel balls. His shoulder crunched through the display glass, and he brought his free elbow down on the back of the hulking, suited Japanese guy who'd just shoulder tackled him.

The guy grunted but didn't let go. He even tried to get his feet under him and lift Wren. Wren got one foot on the floor then sent it back up like a rocket, his knee finding the guy's jaw for his trouble. The big man grunted and swayed, trying to toss Wren away like a rag doll.

Wren flew maybe two feet before he hit an empty stool, bounced and went down in the gap between the clamoring machines and the stools. His head rang and his shoulder throbbed, but he sprang quickly to his feet as players on all sides fled from their machines.

Wren only had eyes for the guy, filling the aisle between the machines. He had to be the biggest Japanese man Wren had ever seen, dressed in a bulging black suit over a white shirt with a neat black tie. Security, had to be, but with face tattoos stretching down his neck. 6' 6" at least, an easy match for Wren's three hundred pounds, now shaking off the blow to his jaw.

Wren could hardly see anything beyond him and the flood of scrabbling players. Not the doors, the *akaname*, nothing.

Easiest way out was through.

He charged three steps. The guy came to meet him, right arm pulling back for an almighty punch, left hand stretching out to grapple Wren's collar. Wren ignored convention and threw himself into a huge double-foot drop kick.

He sailed through the air. The big guy's expression changed as Wren's weight aligned like an arrow on a single vector. His leading hand did nothing to throw the arrow off target. His big fist swatted air as Wren's boots crunched in; one on the guy's chest, one flat across his nose.

He flew back. More than ten Newtons force, without a doubt. Wren dropped and caught himself flat on the deck. Stainless steel balls dug into his palms and he slipped. He tried to get up and failed three times, slipping wildly each time. The only good news was the security guard was having the same problem.

Wren finally found his feet and turned, now totally disorientated in the clamor and clang. More security guards were coming in from behind, all dressed in black and white like penguins. The constant crash of the machines was getting to him. Balls coated the floor, making it near impassable.

Wren opted for a steppingstone, and leaped onto the big guy's back as he floundered on all fours. He thumped flat to his chest, and Wren jumped to a recently vacated stool, then from stool to stool until he reached the exit. Guards chased him but struggled and slipped on the balls. The cracked glass doors swung open, revealing a street, the overpass above, and no sign of the *akaname*.

None at all.

No shine of his black skin. No lolling tongue. No burning red eyes.

What he did see, though, were Japanese patrol cars racing by. Not to him, it seemed. He padded out over the sidewalk and picked out the intersection he'd started from. The crepe shop was there, the pink lobby of the manga kissa beside it.

Cops were thronging it. Maybe PSIA agents too.

He cursed low. Made a quick calculation. They'd already banned him from crime scenes. If he turned up now, with the pachinko place in chaos, at the scene before the PSIA even arrived, maybe they'd deport him on the spot.

He couldn't allow that. Not now.

The pachinko parlor bristled with security guards, coming to the door now. Wren wanted to beat a path through them, dig out that mask and start questioning, but could see no easy way through. At best he'd leave half a dozen innocent guys battered in his wake.

One heck of a mess.

Instead he turned and started off in the other direction at a fast jog, bringing up his phone to talk to Toyama.

29

JONATHAN'S

"Chris," she answered, sounding flustered. "You're OK, thank God. What happened, where are you?"

"I almost had him," Wren answered. "Little creep's mask has scuba gear attached. But listen, where are you right now, did you call the cops?"

"What? No, I'm on the platform again, I came after you but lost you after the turn. Where are you?"

His mind spun hard. "OK. Cops are all over street level. I think you need to get out of there, take a train or whatever you can. We're going to look bad. They're going to try and pin this on us, Makoto."

There was silence from her end.

"They're there," Wren concluded.

"Yamaguchi-san," Toyama answered. "Sato-san. They haven't seen me yet. They will in about thirty seconds."

Wren cursed. Debated going back as he kept striding forward, sirens blaring all around now. Maybe then he could draw their attention to the pachinko place, even sweep up the mask, but then maybe not. In their glee at catching him out, they'd probably let the whole thing slide.

"Can you get in the tunnel unobserved?"

"I guess, uh. Yes."

"Then do it. Take the right branch, after maybe six hundred yards there's a ladder leading up. You'll come out in a pachinko parlor and we'll meet after that. Now go."

"Going," she responded. He heard her slapping footfalls, then the clang of the door opening, then the signal died.

He dialed fast through to Hellion.

"Yes, Christopher. Date went poorly?"

"Can you ghost me and Toyama from all CCTV footage?"

He heard the sound of knuckles cracking. "This is good challenge. If noisy morning bitch can do it, I can do it."

"Then do it fast, PSIA are going to isolate it in seconds."

Keys were already flying down the T-CAPS system. "No problem, Christopher."

"Also any CCTV a pachinko parlor three hundred yards south may have. I wrecked the place. An *akaname* popped out of it just ahead of me, the guy in a black wetsuit. If you can track him, that'd be huge."

"Yes, we will do this. Goodbye, Christopher."

She hung up.

He took a right, working his way deeper into backstreets and away from the intersection and the overpass. It didn't matter where, as long as it was away.

Twitches of unspent adrenaline spiked through his body like popping candy. He kept walking, thinking, looking out at the sky. A dark shrine passed on his left, many low stone graves surrounded by long wooden stakes, each written with the names of the deceased. In a gap in the skyline to the right, he glimpsed the gleaming red iron bulk of Tokyo Tower. It looked like a neon version of the Eiffel Tower.

He had to think. He had to act, but all he could do now was get himself out of the scene.

He'd almost had his hands on an *akaname*. The slippery bastard was wearing a full scuba suit. Spelunking in the sewers. For what?

He brought out his phone and tapped out a message for the Foundation to read.

AKANAME UNDER TOKYO ARE WEARING FULL SCUBA GEAR WITH INFRARED VISION IN THEIR MASKS. WHY?

He had no answers. Every step further he thought about Toyama, and whether she was going to make it out safely. He thought about Hellion and the CCTV, and whether she could cover their tracks. Even the best hackers in the world couldn't do anything about the testimony of the subway attendant, or the pachinko parlor guards, but testimony wasn't CCTV.

Incriminating, but not a knockout blow. Less of a mess, and wren was in the mess reduction business. At least, he had been. Maybe, going forward...

His phone rang. He almost fumbled answering it, he was so hopped up.

"Yeah?"

"It's me," came Toyama's voice. "I'm out. Heading away from the pachinko parlor. It looks like a bomb dropped on it. What did you do?"

"Exited. OK, head south. I'll find us a place to get breakfast."

She laughed. "Breakfast? Chris, do you realize we just fled an active crime scene? Maybe I just lost my career. They'll have CCTV of us, let alone witness testimony, and-"

"I'm taking care of CCTV, so that shouldn't be-"

"Taking care of CCTV? What does that mean? Your Foundation? That's expressly against-"

"The killer of these *akaname* is doing it, the *akaname* are doing it themselves, so I think we're OK. It's what it takes."

There was silence for a long moment, broken only by her rough breathing. "OK. Screw it. I'm off the main road. It's done. Where are you?"

Wren looked up. He must've covered five blocks already. That'd be enough. He saw a 24-hour family restaurant with an English name.

"Jonathan's," he said. "Five blocks south-east. I'll see you inside."

Wren settled in, at a back corner table where he could watch the street outside. In five minutes Hellion called him. "Done, Christopher. I am also tracking wetsuit man you chased, but he disappears from footage also, once passing under bridge. Everyone has ghosting ability!"

Wren grunted. Somehow he'd expected that. "Thank you, Hellion. Keep me posted."

Fifteen minutes later, Toyama appeared on the street outside. She entered, came over to Wren, sat down and let loose what had to be a long and florid curse in Japanese. His T-CAPS interpreter made short work of it. It was certainly florid.

"You OK?" Wren asked.

"Maybe I just wrecked my career."

"You and me both," Wren allowed, then reached over and pressed the call button on the plastic tube in the center of the table.

"I'm glad you've mastered that, though," Toyama observed.

"I'm a fast learner."

The waiter came. Wren ordered a half-pound burger and fries, a corn soup, a black coffee and a plate of waffles and bacon. Toyama ordered miso soup, grilled mackerel and rice, and an oolong tea. They sat for a moment in silence afterward. Coming on for 6 a.m., by the wall clock. Outside it was getting light. Taking stock of the mess they were in.

"So that was a big mess," Wren started.

Toyama blew out a long, slow breath. "Correct."

"I was so close to grabbing the little filth-licker. I pinged him with two handfuls of pachinko balls. Then a big security guy got in the way. Tattoos all over him."

Toyama grunted, laid a hand out across the table. Wren took it and squeezed briefly. That was nice. "I saw. Yakuza."

"Yakuza," Wren repeated.

"Yes. They're everywhere, these days." She took a fortifying breath. "We turn a blind eye to almost everything they do, Chris. They're into politics, into legitimate businesses, into charity. They run half the prisons, all the construction, all the gambling, all the prostitution, half the hospitality. It's a fragile balance for us; there's unspoken rules that say we're supposed to ignore a certain amount of criminality, as long as it's peaceful and ordered."

Wren sipped his coffee. "That's following procedure, huh?"

She winced.

"Sorry. That's a low blow. And I get it. We've got the same thing back home. Corporate interests rewrite the laws constantly, to excuse the fact they were breaking them. It's crazy, but it's ingrained."

"Same," Toyama said, heaved a sigh and sipped on her oolong tea. "So, where are we up to?"

Wren considered. "First up, we know more now than we did a day ago. Ando, we strongly suspect, was an *akaname*. He was into kids, and we suspect the *akaname* are the same. It's in the name, after all. Second up, whoever's killing these assholes, they're on our side. Writing my name on their bodies, it's crazy, but perhaps she was trying to pull me in so I can do something about them."

Toyama put down her soup. "Why you?"

"I don't know. Because I've brought down other big groups, before, like the Blue Fairy. So, point three, let's assume these *akaname* are big and powerful. They've got guys flooding the sewers like lice, moving through the dark and swimming in sewage, wearing tricked out *yokai* masks with infrared and scuba rebreathers."

"For what?"

"No clue. Something sick, is my guess. I read in the briefing books, there's huge sewers underneath Tokyo. Maybe they've got some portions of that set aside, and they're using them as a secret brothel for underage prostitution. That's a euphemism, of course. You can't prostitute a child. It's rape, every time."

Toyama grunted into her oolong tea. Wren's burger arrived, and he tucked in with gusto. He hadn't eaten anything since around lunchtime the day before.

"There are huge sewers, you're right," Toyama mused. "There's something called the G-CANS, which is a massive flood prevention system. Vast, stadium-sized halls underground, to catch extreme overflow during rainy season."

Wren considered. "You know, when I was facing the Pinocchios, they tried to operate in plain sight as well. They retrofitted a shipping tanker with a whole spa-temple-abuse facility. They sailed it around the world, picking up children from war zones, and wanted to moor it off the coast of the US for rich pricks to get their sick jollies."

Toyama nodded slowly. "I read about that. You destroyed them, right?"

"Yeah. So if we find something like that here, a whole sewer filled with sickos, I'm destroying them all over again."

"Cockroaches."

"Vermin."

They were silent for a moment. Wren wolfed down the burger and started in on the fries. Toyama neatly filleted the pink salmon flesh off the bone.

"Point four," she said. "It's highly likely the yakuza are involved."

Wren tilted his head.

"Like I said, they're into everything. You already figured there might be *akaname* in the PSIA, the police, in government. To get that far, they're either in the yakuza as well, or they *are* the yakuza."

"OK. The security guys in that pachinko place, they all had face tattoos. The way I read it, that's taboo in Japan."

"Exactly. Tattoos mean gangsters, which means yakuza. That parlor was definitely yakuza-run, like every single gambling place in this country. And the *akaname* chose to come up a ladder directly into one. That can't be a coincidence."

"Agreed. They also helped him escape. I'd love to question those knuckleheads."

Toyama smiled. "I've seen you questioning. Do we need to bloody up another penthouse suite?"

Wren smiled. "I'll settle for bloodying up them."

They sat and ate for a few minutes. Wren blitzed through his pancakes and bacon, pushing the little button twice to request more maple syrup. He slurped down his corn soup and took regular hits of his coffee.

"First though," he said, "I want to-"

Toyama's phone rang. Wren fell silent. She brought it up and looked at the screen, then winced.

"It's Yamaguchi-san. I think I've got to take it."

Wren just nodded. "Can't argue with that. He's going to press you, though, Makoto. Just remember, no matter what they say, they've got no CCTV of us in there. Just one daydreaming subway attendant. We can ride this out."

She nodded and stood. "I'll take it outside."

Wren sat, surveying his empty plates and drained coffee cup. He still felt a little hungry, so he hit the button and ordered a 10oz steak, medium rare, with peppercorn sauce and fries, plus a refill on the coffee. That ought to do it.

30

SWORD

It was 8:30 a.m. when Makoto Toyama strode back into the Jonathan's looking furious.

He stood up to meet her. "It's bad?"

"It's bad," she confirmed. The tendons in her neck strained white. "Let's pay up and walk. I can't sit for this."

Wren nodded, went to the register and paid. They gave him a handful of cute white mints. Toyama was already out the door and stalking away. Wren caught up easily and held out the mints. She stared at them for a second, then grabbed several and chewed them aggressively.

Wren waited as her florid cheeks worked the mints hard, crunching and crushing. The air was already heating up, the same pressure cooker feel Wren was getting used to, bearing down from the low white sky.

After thirty seconds Toyama took a right turn down an alleyway, where she stopped by some dumpsters to glare at Wren.

"What did your hackers do?"

Wren's eyes narrowed. "Nothing. I don't think so, anyway. Why, what happened?"

"Apparently, the PSIA database was hacked last night. A neat job, I heard, but not invisible. And not just PSIA, either. Government organizations and corporations across Japan got hit in the same wave. Nobody knows the extent of this, yet, or how much data was lost, but it all looks to be information related to our case."

Wren felt a little nauseated. Hellion and B4cksl4cker didn't usually leave a trail of any kind. "You think it was my team?"

"It doesn't matter what I think!" Toyama railed, suddenly letting loose. "It matters what Yamaguchi thinks. It matters what his superiors think. It's bad enough you, and me too, keep turning up at crime scenes before they're even announced. That's breaking procedures of all kinds, especially since you were barred. On top of that, Sato doesn't buy the missing CCTV angle. It may cover us from legal exposure, but it won't keep me in a job." She sucked in a breath. Wren let her have her head of steam.

"So, Yamaguchi knows we were here. Sato's whispering bullshit in his ear and loving it, though he hardly needs any encouragement." She sucked another breath. "Chris, he didn't outright say it, but I get the feeling they suspect we're involved. For that reason, we both just got grounded, due to report into PSIA, where we'll be assigned desk work for the duration." She held up a hand. "And before you say it, there'll be no special exceptions for you. You're here on a police-cooperation visa. Ignore what they say, they'll whip you out of Tokyo faster than you can say '*douzo*'."

She took a breath, then followed up with a torrent of fast, angry Japanese.

Wren's translator kicked in, delivering an interpretation with incongruous good cheer. "She says Yamaguchi is a pencil-pushing desk jockey, a half-ass idiot only good for riding his master's lap, and that Sato is a sadistic scum sucker of the lowest degree. She used several sexual swear words, also."

Wren said nothing. He was going to have serious words with his hackers. They weren't usually so sloppy. Right now was not the moment, though. All he could do now was take responsibility.

"I'm sorry, Toyama. I'll talk to my team. I'll apologize to anyone I need to. But here's the truth. I'm not riding a desk for this investigation. If I can just solve the case, all this goes away."

Toyama stared at him, then shook her head. "That's not how it works here, Chris. We are not in a Lethal Weapon movie. This is Japan. Rebels who break the rules but get the job done are not rewarded. Solving the murders will not help either of us, if we do it in the wrong way. Results matter less than proper procedure!"

Wren said nothing. There was nothing to say. It seemed like she was angry at him, maybe, but he knew she was mostly angry at her boss, the system, the whole thing. If it helped to shout at Wren a little, he could handle it. Better for her to get it out of her system.

"We are lucky they have not sent an arrest warrant for us both," she went on. "You remain an American intelligence agent. Our closest ally. This is your only card. Possibly the only thing protecting us both."

Wren considered. That was one way of thinking of it. He spun forward and back. There was no good answer. Any way you looked at it, he'd jeopardized her position with his recklessness. That felt bad.

It didn't mean he was going to stop.

"You say it's my only card. It's a pretty good card, though."

She blinked. "What?"

"It's a good card. Listen, Makoto. They want us on a tight leash, following procedure into irrelevance, and I get that. I even understand it, to some degree. But your bosses are not my bosses. My bosses do care about results, as long as it's done quietly." He paused a moment, waiting for her to catch up. "Tell me, have the media got hold of these hacks yet, or any of this BS?"

"Of course not! These are top-secret databases, and all these murders have embargos. The media cannot and will not..."

She trailed off.

"They won't publicize it," Wren finished for her. "Correct? It's humiliating for everyone, plus anybody who publishes will fall foul of the same procedures that are coming for us. The same system that knocked Wakayama out of his professorship. Right? And nobody wants that mess. So we're good so far." He took a breath, making up his mind. "Now, Yamaguchi and Sato may be angry at me, but so what? That's nothing new. Half the problems I ever solved were done in spite of my bosses. If we solve these murders, I'm thinking everyone will hush it up nicely, because it's a win. My side's happy. Your side, while not happy, will take the win rather than upset the political apple cart." He paused for a breath. "But that's on me. I should've realized, this is too much for you to risk. Your career, your good name, maybe even your freedom." He looked into her black eyes. "You were right about the system here; I get that now. I was wrong. It's a hammer, and if you want to progress up the ranks, you have to let it hit you. But I don't. So." He took a heavy breath. He didn't want this. "Tell them I'm acting alone. I'm the rogue nail. Not you."

She stared at him. "No. I'm part of this."

"So stay part of it. But the right way. From a desk."

Her black eyes blazed. "Are you trying to fall on your sword for me, over this? You've got no right. You can't do it alone."

"Better than both of us falling on our swords."

He touched her elbow gently, then spun on his heel and strode away. It had been great while it lasted, but it never could have lasted any further.

"Where are you going?" she called after him.

"I've got leads."

"What leads?"

He didn't answer. Better that she didn't know.

31

GOLDEN GAI

Wren turned left then right, and found himself walking alongside a huge cemetery. Stone grave columns spread on through the trees as far as he could see, each fenced by tall wooden stakes marked with the names of the departed.

People wandered on pathways through the cemetery. Some held flowers, others carried jugs of sake. Somewhere a monk was singing low, strange syllables, and the scent of incense hung on the heavy air. It seemed peaceful.

Wren didn't feel peaceful. He called Hellion, and she answered in seconds.

"Yes, Christopher. You are free man, still."

"I'm on a wing and a prayer, Hellion. The PSIA just flipped on me, but not because of the crime scene thing. Apparently, they've got records of you and B4cksl4cker hacking all the government databases last night, looking for intel on the sewers, the murder victims. They're putting that on me, trying to lock me behind a desk."

He kept any anger out of his voice.

"Impossible, Christopher," Hellion responded. "This is mistake."

Wren squeezed his hands to tight fists. "That you couldn't have left some sign? They said it was a neat job. Maybe they had better security than-"

"No, impossible. We did not hack their databases last night."

Wren frowned. "So, wait, what-"

"We hacked them first day you arrived. Two days ago. Very smooth, in and out, and believe this, they did not notice. Since then was processing. Now, second hack last night? Let me check."

"Check what?"

"Back door. B4cksl4cker? Wake up!"

"He's asleep?"

"He is always asleep, Christopher. Very lazy man, yes? Also beautiful woman in his trailer last night, much like yourself, and the noises I hear-"

"I don't need the details. What backdoor?"

"Yes! Backdoor. Always place backdoor, Christopher, with tracking code. B4cksl4cker!"

"Yes, what, why are you shouting?" B4cksl4cker grumbled onto the line.

"Christopher Wren wishes to know why you were not on duty last night, enjoying too many pleasures, and-"

"No," Wren countered flatly. "The backdoor. Who hacked the PSIA last night?"

"Ah, hack?" B4cksl4cker said, like that explained everything. "Let us check this. It will take time."

Wren grunted. "OK. Also keep an eye out for the woman who's been calling me. She could be the key to all this. And now, tell me all that hacking and processing was for something. Have you got me a way into the sewers?"

Keys clamored down the line. "Checking algorithm progress. Very complex. But yes, we have it!" Wren breathed a sigh of relief. "It is fun. Sending details to your phone now."

Wren didn't bother to question their idea of fun. "And the

control for the flood overflow system. Did you find out how they triggered the surge?"

"Yes. This is gate system, installed in many places throughout sewers."

Wren's heart did a double pulse. "And the operator? Who ordered that surge?"

"Impossible to say. It is half automatic system, half remotely controlled by Tokyo Sanitation Department. Trigger could be either, or easy to hack the signal required."

Wren blinked. "It's not hardwired?"

"It is. But many nodes on this network are open. I can open and close these hatches, Christopher. Do you wish me to?"

Wren blinked. "I don't know. Maybe. Standby."

"Standing by. Sending details."

His phone chirped as a series of files came in. Wren reached the corner of the cemetery then hailed a cab, digging into the files as he breezed back north.

The documents were thorough. They gave a location, a time, and the method of access. After that, there were 3D maps of the overlapping underground network that were as complicated as industrial wiring diagrams. Wren zoomed and shifted the angles, getting to grips with the route. It looked like entry via an older building's basement, then a variety of sewers, dark sewers, maintenance access hatches, and even a stretch running along an active subway track.

The schedule for the trains was included, along with a note.

THIS TRAIN SCHEDULE LIKELY CORRECT

Wren snorted. That was something reassuring to hang your life on. He pushed the phone back in his pocket as the cab pulled to a halt.

Back in Shinjuku.

Wren paid and stepped out of the cab. The air was just getting hotter as the day drew on, growing wet and claustrophobic. He looked around, getting his bearings. He was near Kabuki-cho again, but this was a quieter, different kind of neighborhood. Where Kabuki-cho was all tall buildings craning upward, with noisy pachinko parlors and sparkly J-pop music and tourists flooding by like riders on an escalator, everything new and tacky, this place was old.

Beat-up. Worn. Low wooden buildings surrounded him, assaulted by time, humidity and weeds.

A tall, weathered tourist map was mounted at the head of a tiny blacktop clearing, like the entrance to a theme park. 'Golden Gai', read the legend at the top. It showed five or six long, ancient-looking alleyways in parallel, each lined with minuscule bars and restaurants, depicted in a cartoony style. Some looked no bigger than a telephone booth. Wren strode forward, past a police box where two young cops were eating ramen noodles and reading a newspaper, and peered down the nearest alley.

It was barely a yard wide. No chance of getting a vehicle down there. On both sides it was flanked by the same kind of ancient, wooden traditional buildings he'd seen out in Hakone, in the shadow of Mt. Fuji.

Here the shadow came from the encroaching skyscrapers. They hung on all sides, great beasts of glass and steel hanging like marauders from the future. This place felt like an architectural cemetery. Peaceful by day. Walls coated in creeping black mold and yellowed handbills for bands popular in decades past.

Wren walked along the stone-flagged alley. Through the narrow windows he glimpsed tight U-shaped bars, each boasting a few seats max. Some seemed to have themes, reminding him of the love hotel they'd stayed in the previous night. One had medical detritus everywhere: the cups looked like beakers, the snacks dishes were operating trays, and blow-up dolls decked out like nurses and doctors hung from the low rafters.

There was a bar crammed with books, where the customers would have to affect a permanent lean to sit at the bar, to make room for the shelving behind them. There was a bar themed like a subway museum, its walls decorated with engineering switchboards, old topographic maps and subway name banners. Many bars had potted plants in front and bicycles. One had a washing line hung across the narrow alley, upon which hung three tatty string wifebeaters.

Most of the bars were empty and gray in the wan morning light, though a few still boasted inhabitants, sitting at the bar like ghosts of a forgotten era, drinking or eating, staring into the distance. It was a beautiful kind of place, in its way. Creepy, maybe. It made Wren think of Toyama's description of the 'floating world': a decadent place of narrow alleys and fragrant canals. Quite a contrast to everything he'd seen of Tokyo so far; like an intimate art installation built out of the city's lost detritus.

Wren checked his map and took a turn down another long alley. Here there was knotweed growing everywhere, threatening to muffle all the buildings in a creeping sea of green. He stopped halfway down in front of a karaoke bar. Peering through the windows, he figured it had room for maybe six people at a time. The door was wooden and locked with a deadbolt. The window was single-glazed and rattled in the frame. It wouldn't take much to force either.

Wren looked both ways, but there was nobody nearby. No police on patrol. Nobody in the overshadowing buildings watching down, at least as far as he could see. He opted for the door, and pushed down on the handle then simply leaned his weight against it.

The thin door flexed. The frame creaked. Wren pushed a little harder, until the bolt on the other side sheared out of its rotten housing and the door jerked open. Metal clattered on stone flags on the other side then fell silent. Nobody seemed to notice. Nothing untoward in this silent grave of a district. Wren folded himself smoothly in and pushed the door closed behind him.

Then a hand got in the way.

Wren's heart skipped a beat. He almost slammed the door shut with a massive front kick, trapping the limb in place. Maybe lopping it off at the wrist. But he held back at the last moment, largely because of what the hand held in its palm.

A long black flashlight. High-powered beam. Exactly the same model he'd lost in the sewers last time. A face followed it.

"Makoto," Wren breathed out.

"I thought you could use one of these," she said, with half a smile, waving the flashlight. "Or were you just going to use your cellphone flashlight?"

Wren set his jaw. "Why would I need a flashlight?"

Toyama smirked. "What trip into the sewers would be complete without one? Unless you're not here, in an ancient bar slated for demolition, not looking for a route into the sewers. Perhaps you really are in need of some morning karaoke?"

"You overheard me. You've been following me,"

Toyama came fully in and let the door close behind her. "You're surprisingly easy to follow, for a secret agent."

"I'm not a secret agent."

"Probably not a very good singer, either. However, I must say-"

"You shouldn't be following me," Wren interrupted. "We already agreed that you-"

"No," Toyama said firmly, stepping up to poke him sternly in the chest. "You agreed. I didn't agree to anything."

He opened his mouth, closed it, opened it again. "It's better for you that way. For your career."

"Ha!" she said, then fired off a curse in Japanese. His T-CAPS interpreter translated it as 'Arrogant, ignorant American.' "You decided for me, and thought I would go along, because, why? Japanese women are demure? We're all damsels in distress?"

"It's not that. I'm nobody's hero. I just wanted to-"

"Rescue the fair maiden? I understand. It's sweet, but I can decide for myself."

Wren held up his hands. He was clearly on the losing end of this argument. "OK. You got me."

"Yes, I do, Wren-san," Toyama said, and poked him in the chest again. "Now just stand there looking pretty." Then she leaned in and gave him a hard kiss full on the lips. It was wholly unexpected, and fired up an engine in the pit of Wren's belly.

He couldn't do anything but kiss her in return.

When Toyama pulled back, her black eyes were dancing with amusement. "So, are you going to tell me how breaking into a karaoke box helps us get down to the sewers? Or did you really just feel like a Billy Joel interlude?"

Wren felt bamboozled. Not just by the kiss. When had anyone ever called him 'pretty'? Still, he managed a smile. "I do like Billy Joel, actually. But maybe later." He cleared his throat, getting a hold of himself. "Right now, I'm looking for a World War Two bomb shelter somewhere underneath this building, that'll take us directly into the dark sewers."

Toyama nodded thoughtfully. "A bomb shelter, is it? Well, we can't stand around all day looking pretty, then. Let's get to it, or do I have to start hammering nails?"

"Yes, ma'am."

32

BOMB SHELTER

There wasn't much floor to check. The bar was around four yards square, half of which contained five customer stools, half of which was the tiny kitchen area in back. The air smelled of soy sauce, musty wood and the yeasty waft of spilled beer.

"Here," Toyama said within thirty seconds. "The floor's hollow. Help me with this."

She was behind the bar, trying to get her feet out of the way of the worn-down straw mats. Wren leaned through the entry opening and helped. Together they got the single panel up and tipped to the side. Beneath it lay a metal hatch flush to the concrete, no handle or pull ring in evidence.

"We'll need a pry bar," Toyama said.

Wren kneeled down, produced his trusty cabin key and slotted it into the slim gap between metal and concrete. It was enough to pry the lid up half an inch, which allowed Wren to get his fingers in and pull it all the way open. It creaked on a rusty hinge, revealing a narrow concrete-walled chute leading down, fitted with an ancient metal ladder.

They both stood staring down into the dark. Cold wafted up over their faces.

"If you say '*douzo*' I'll throw you down there," Toyama said.

Wren smiled. "I wouldn't dream of it."

He sat down on the floor, legs dangling into the gap. His feet found the rungs and he tested them. Maybe eighty years old, but they seemed dry and sturdy enough.

"Wish me luck," he said, and started down.

Her face receded as he descended into the cold, clammy underground. Fifteen rungs passed until he reached the bottom. He shone his cell phone light, illuminating a space some four yards across, perhaps fifty yards long, stretching into shadow. It looked like an Anderson-style shelter; a half-pipe-shaped space submerged in poured concrete. The curved corrugated iron roof arched from side to side, around seven feet tall at the apex, shallowing out to nothing at the edges. In every spot it was completely brown and flaking with rust.

Wren scanned the light around. There were several crates stacked nearby that could be sake or beer; supplies for the bar. Water dripped somewhere. The corrugated roofing was cracked in places, revealing raw earth.

"This place is huge," came Toyama's voice, abruptly by his side. Wren almost jumped. She really could move silently, even on clanging metal rungs. "It must have served the whole neighborhood. You could fit hundreds of people down here. I thought there were none of these left."

She flicked the high-powered flashlight on, and it illuminated the far end of the shelter. In the stark light, the place looked less intimidating than forgotten. There were a few threadbare gray blankets rumpled by the far wall, an ancient bicycle, several more wooden crates. There were large Japanese kanji written on the wall in a faded red stencil pattern, and a shiny new metal door with a bright lock plate.

"It says 'EMERGENCY OVERFLOW'," Toyama said.

Wren strode over. This access point was on the map, but not the metal door.

"Your key going to work on that?" Toyama asked.

Wren surveyed the door. It would've served him to bring down some power tools. A portable ram, maybe. As it was, he'd have to make do with what he had. He ran his fingers across the door and tried the handle. It was locked solid. He looked wider; at the frame the door had been set into. It looked like a new cement pour embedded in the old cement that had fixed the Anderson half-pipe in place.

Construction of his own cabin in Delaware had given him a deeper appreciation for the value of a solid door with a strong lock. More important than a strong door, though, was the strength of the frame it sealed.

Wren picked up the bicycle. It was frail, the solid rubber wheels hanging limp off the spokes, the connections rusting themselves brittle. The metal of the frame was sturdy enough, though. "Maybe this is the key," he said. "Stand back."

"I can go get us a pry bar," Toyama offered, while stepping back.

Wren swung the bike experimentally, bringing it like his maul in a sideways chop into the corrugated metal beside the door. It hit with a muted clang. The back wheel sheared off its bolts and crumpled. The rear wheel mount dug a crimp through the old, corroded iron.

Wren hit it a few more times, opening the crimp up more, until the wheel rattled off completely, leaving just the impact-bright silver point of the rear axle mounts. He set the bike down then took a closer look at the slashed corrugated wall. He slipped his right hand cautiously through one of the gaps in the sheet iron and pulled cautiously.

It ripped away with a roar like a sheet of Velcro, and half of the wall pulled away with it in an avalanche of crumbled, rotten old concrete.

Toyama shouted something in Japanese and danced back. Wren stepped smoothly to the side, then peered at the remains of the wall. It had come away in a clean line from where the fresh concrete had been poured around the new door frame, to a depth of some six inches. He didn't think it would be much further to go.

"How did you know that was going to happen?" Toyama asked.

"It's old," Wren said, then swung the bike again. Muscles he'd honed over months of chopping trees and clearing the farm burst into action, knotting and firing with explosive force. He hammered the wall five times, ten times in fast succession. In the forest, it might take fifty strokes with the maul to bring down a mid-size sassafras. Each swing sent the bike's rear axle into powdery concrete, throwing off dust and sending fresh rubble dropping down.

"Is that safe?" Toyama shouted. Wren just kept on hammering the bike into the wall, until on lucky stroke twenty-three a hole burst through into darkness.

Wren dropped the bike, pushed his hand then his arm through the hole, reached over to the door and turned the lock. It clicked. He stepped back and gestured to the door with a grin.

"Douzo."

Toyama fired him an evil glare but went to the door and tried the knob. It turned. The door opened. "We're lucky the shelter doesn't collapse on our heads," she said.

"It still might. Best hurry."

She redoubled the evil glare then went through, perhaps with a little more urgency. Wren followed with a smile. Beyond lay a tunnel curving away into darkness. There were only a handful of cables and pipes slung along the walls, and no built-in electric lights.

"This is crazy," Toyama said. "What even is this?"

"This, according to the map, is a service tunnel."

"Service for what?"

"It doesn't say. But it runs for about three hundred yards."

Toyama gulped audibly. "Well, all right then." She started forward.

The tunnel ran in a gentle curve. Wren noted the onset of

electrical lights after a hundred or so yards. All dead, but wired in. After three hundred yards they came to an intersection.

"How far is it to the crime scene?"

Wren studied the map on his phone. "Quite far." He took the right branch off the intersection, into a damp tunnel leading deeper down. "This section is apparently old government escape tunnels. There should be all kinds of bunkers up ahead."

"Government bunkers?"

"A telegraph exchange, military barracks, habitation, a private mail line that goes all the way back to Tokyo station."

"Huh. And this is the data your hackers took last night?"

"Oh, right. About that. That wasn't them."

Toyama's hand came on his shoulder. "It wasn't them? Who was it, then?"

Wren turned and shrugged. "I don't know. I believe them, though. They're investigating. Hopefully we get answers soon.

They walked on. Time passed as they descended in wary silence. The first room they came to was a dusty, empty block of space, barely five yards around and two tall. The walls were peppered with sprays of ancient, rusted wires cased in black rubber, alongside screw-points. On the floor were scuff marks in the concrete where heavy machinery had been moved out. The air was stale but there was some movement.

"Telephone exchanges," Toyama said, pointing at the wall. "Looks like they disposed of it all."

Wren just grunted. Something about being underground made him quieter. He consulted the map and took the northeast door leading out. This tunnel was paved in stone, and they clacked along it for twenty minutes, taking steps up and down at times. Several times they heard the rumble of nearby motion; trains passing or hidden rivers rushing. At one point they passed a thick ventilation grille in the wall through which a hot wind blew. Beyond lay darkness only, until a rumbling drew near and the tunnel flooded with the light of an oncoming train.

It was surreal, peering from a grate in the wall through to

commuters whipping by, in the sanitized tube of the train carriage. They had no idea of the secret world all around them.

"I think that was the Oedo line," Toyama said afterward. "We've got to be very deep, now."

Wren nodded and kept on. At one point they crossed into more modern maintenance tunnels. Familiar plastic-cased pipes and cables ran either side, and light flickered to life as they approached. After another twenty minutes, that led to a sewer, but not the sewer they were looking for. They put on masks and walked on. There was a grating blocking off the dark sewer, just like before, and Wren climbed out to locate and open the hatch.

It was there.

"It could be a superhighway down here," Toyama said. "Ultimate shortcuts. I'd guess we've got to be under Shinjuku station."

Wren checked the time on his phone. They were halfway done with their circuitous journey, and it was already 11 a.m. He pressed on into the dark, lit by the flash of Toyama's flashlight.

Dark tunnels flowed by, broken by the trudge of their feet. After a long stretch in the dark sewer, they climbed back into a maintenance section, crossed through to a dry tunnel, then opened a door into what looked like an empty subway station.

Toyama said something low in Japanese.

"What is it?" Wren asked, his T-CAPS translator out of operation given the depth.

"I've heard of this place," Toyama said, hustling along to locate the station name, emblazoned in tile on the walls. Wren followed, noting the gleaming condition of the rails in the train's bay, as well as the posters behind billboard glass. The style of the models looked like something from the 70s: old hair, old clothes, not a cellphone in sight. There were disposal trays for cigarette butts attached to the walls in places.

"It's the Shinjuku ghost station," Toyama said, standing in front of an empty white space where the name should have been.

"Rumored, but never confirmed. They don't want urban explorers coming down here, trying to take photos."

Wren snorted. "Why would anyone want to take photos of this? It's just old and dirty."

Toyama tutted. "It's history, Chris. I'm definitely coming back here, after all this.'

Wren just shrugged and pointed. "It's this way."

They exited the platform and went up a flight of dark stairs to an ancient mechanical turnstile. The machinery still worked, which seemed to excite Toyama. Then they went back down the other side, entering the tunnel running in the other direction, and dropped down onto the tracks.

"This next section, we're going to be on live tracks for a while."

"Bring it on."

They walked on. The sound of passing trains grew louder, until up ahead the tunnel conjoined into another. A train rushed by like a huge, storming bull. They approached the edge and waited for it to pass.

"Now," Wren said, and ran out into the draft of the train.

They ran pell-mell into darkness for around three minutes, until the sound of another train came racing up behind them.

"Chris!" Toyama shouted.

He scanned the walls as they ran. The lights of the train in back spilled off the walls. There would be no time for the driver to brake. He was looking for a very specific alcove, within which there was a ladder leading down, which would take them into the part of the network they really needed to access.

"Chris!" Toyama yelled, as the train screamed around a long corner behind them.

Then he saw it. A dark shadow. "Here!" he cried and dived for the alcove. Toyama followed him, and they shuddered in each other's embrace as the train's carriages slammed by one after another.

Toyama cursed in Japanese. Wren let her go when it was done.

"Karaoke would've been better," she muttered.

"Here we are," he said, opening a loose side door that led into stairs leading down.

"Tell me we're nearly there."

"It's all dark sewers from here." Wren tried to sound upbeat. "As far as I can tell."

"Our good luck," Toyama said, and started down the steps.

33

CRIME SCENE

It was around noon when they arrived in the storm surge sewer.

The tunnel looked like any other. There was nothing much to see but darkness and the flow of filth. No *akaname*. Nothing.

"This is it?" Toyama asked.

Wren climbed the ladder to peer back at the flickering lights of the maintenance hatch, beyond the grate.

"This is it."

Together, they surveyed the walkway. It wasn't as filthy as Wren had feared. The deluge had been mostly rainwater run-off, after all, giving the sewers a good scrub. He ran his eyes over the walls.

"Did you ever get your information request back on what all these pipes are for?"

"No," Toyama said. "Your hackers couldn't get that?"

"No. I doubt any of it's online."

He walked over to the spot he'd seen the *akaname*. He closed his eyes and pictured its flapping tongue, its red eyes and its slimy black skin. Now he knew those were the air hose, the infrared camera eyes and the full body wetsuit of its scuba outfit.

A cold breeze blew up the tunnel. Maybe the signal for another flood surge, but he didn't think so. The forecast hadn't said rain.

He stood for a time, looking and thinking. He imagined the *akaname* rearing up from the flow, disturbed at its work, to be caught in the flood light of Wren's flashlight beam. Then in a second it was gone.

He scanned the tunnel nearby, looking for a ladder leading up or down, but there were none. If the *akaname* had escaped the flood surge alive, it had to be through some kind of escape hatch beneath the surface.

"He must've dived right here," Toyama said, looking down at the murk.

Wren dropped to a squat by her side, roaming his cell phone light along the surface of the water. The walls above the flow were rimed with black mold. Without a scuba suit of his own, there was no way to see what lay beneath the surface. Even then, he'd struggle to see anything through the murk. What he really needed was to drain all of this filth away.

Then the thought came to him.

He stood up and turned to Toyama. "You mentioned huge overflow halls, big enough to fit a sports stadium in. Are those near here?"

"I suppose so," she allowed. "The G-CANS system. They're everywhere."

"And it stands to reason they're deeper than the standard sewers."

She frowned. "What are you thinking, Chris?"

"I want to drain this sludge. All of it. My hackers can override the sewer gates, just like the *akaname* did. If they can close the flow leading down here and open up the surge control channels to the G-CANS, this tunnel should drain."

Toyama frowned. "I don't know if that's possible. It's certainly not how the system's designed."

"It wasn't designed to flash-surge us, either, but they used it that way. The result was rapid. Maybe this could be, too."

Toyama pondered that. "OK. But even if they can, what's the point? When we found the bodies, we already dredged the sewage flow. Anything left behind, DNA, murder weapon, whatever, it was already long swept away."

"I'm not looking for that kind of evidence."

"So what kind of evidence are you looking for?"

"I'll know it when I see it."

Toyama laughed. Wren felt the exact opposite; like he was finally getting the bit between his teeth. Of course, this was what it all added up to. He played it forward and back and came to the only possible conclusion.

"I can give you the number for my hackers. Hellion and B4cksl4cker. If you go out through the Marunouchi line and send them a message, maybe they can close the inflow and open up outflows to the G-CANS."

"That's a big maybe."

"I know. But it feels right. I think we're on the edge of something."

Toyama looked thoughtful. "Something that will definitely get us both fired, or worse. Tampering with the drainage system for a city, Chris. If your hackers get it wrong, they might cause a flood surge of their own. We don't know where sanitation workers are in the system. They could die. You might die. I don't want that on my conscience."

"So we'll tell them to be careful. They're good at systems, Makoto."

She shook her head. "I don't like it. It's reckless. What if I send this message, and you never surface again? I'm not going to feel good about that. I may go to jail for manslaughter. Plus, you'll be dead."

Wren looked her in the eye. It was a good reason for caution, but he was done with caution. It was put up or shut up time.

"I understand that. I think we're at a linchpin moment,

though. We need to know what the *akaname* are doing down here. It's something bad, Makoto. Something big, too, I think. Maybe bigger than Tokyo, bigger even than Japan. And this is the only way I can think of to find out." He took a breath. "If you have another idea, I want to hear it."

She stared at him, saying nothing.

"I need you. I'd do it myself, but the second I surface up there, they'll never let me back down again."

Toyama jutted her chin out. "So go. You send the message. I'll stay."

"Not a chance," he said sharply. "Unacceptable."

She shook her head. "You've got a death wish. No, Chris. I'm not doing that. I can't."

They stood in silence for a long moment. The waterfall of waste nearby pattered on.

"That man," Wren began. "The host who was tricking women to his apartment, so they could commit suicide with him there? Then he strangled them. If you could go back, what would you risk to stop him one kill earlier?"

Toyama's eyes hardened. "Low blow, Chris."

"I know. I'm sorry. But it's where we are. I think it's what the woman making these dawn calls has been trying to tell me. You and me, we're not like Yamaguchi or Sato. This work's not a job for us. It's a calling. I'm addicted, I can admit it, if recovering. You're addicted, too, I think. That can be a force for good. The world needs crazies like us."

She shook her head. "It's too much risk. We'll find another way."

Wren pushed it to the edge. "Imagine if you could've stopped that host before he ever left Kabuki-cho. Put him in the ground before he cut them up and put them in boxes. Even without evidence. Outside of procedure. Wouldn't you have done it?"

She stared. Wren could feel her vibrating with the decision.

"I know what I'm asking. But you came this far. I think it's worth the risk."

Her eyes blazed in the light. She stamped the few steps toward him. Her hands were balled into fists. Wren wasn't sure if she was going to punch him, curse him or kiss him.

"Give me the number," she said instead.

He did.

"Tell me the message."

He did.

She handed him the flashlight. "I'll never forgive you if you die."

"As it should be," Wren said.

She spun and walked away, leaving Wren alone in the darkness.

34

DRAINAGE

Wren turned the flashlight off to conserve the battery. The dark swelled and shrank around him. Every sound became the surge of an *akaname* army rising through the sewage.

He waited. There came the distant clang as Toyama opened the hatch in the grate, followed by the slam of the metal door leading out. Then there was nothing but the pattering of the waste waterfall.

Minutes passed. Wren thought about the case. He thought about his kids back in Delaware, waiting to take their hayride around the farm. He squeezed the key to the cabin in his pocket.

Toyama should be back on the Marunouchi line platform by now. Maybe PSIA agents were taking her into custody. Asking her questions. Already preparing a team to come in and arrest Wren too.

He imagined a team of them running back through the tunnels. Past the lost river. Up to the grate, steeling themselves to enter the dark sewer beyond.

Then he heard it.

All his senses leaped to attention. It wasn't exactly a new sound so much as a change in the same sound.

The pattering of the waste waterfall was slowing.

Wren flashed the light back on and instantly saw the difference. The level of the sewage flow had dropped a good few inches. He bent closer to study it, but nothing had been revealed yet. The level was dropping steadily though.

Then came the clang from the main tunnel.

Loud footfalls followed. People running and shouting.

Wren cursed under his breath. He just needed a few minutes more, but already spill light from fresh flashlights was dancing across the surge tunnels walls. It sounded like a whole squad was storming the sewer.

Two hundred yards. A hundred yards. The sewage level kept dropping. Then they were there, four faces hovering above four flashlight beams that poured through the opening to the tunnel above. Orders barked out in Japanese and echoed around the confined space.

Wren felt like an *akaname*, clinging to the ladder with his flashlight off. Watching as the four beams of light played over the walls, the walkway, the ceiling, and finally down to-

Wren reached up and grabbed the nearest man by the scruff of his collar and pulled. There was a terrified shriek as he was sucked down into the dark. Wren swept him down and around, dropping him to his back hard enough to incapacitate but not hard enough to seriously hurt. He reached up to grab another while they were still screaming and freaking out, when a sudden burst of light and an incredible blast of sound rang out.

Wren dropped away from the ladder, holding his hands to his ears as the echoes peeled through his head.

A gunshot. It must have discharged right by his head. He staggered away a few steps further, looking up at the opening where three faces remained. One of them he knew. The one who was also holding a gun. A weasel face over a familiar jacket.

Sato.

His flashlight beam homed in on Wren, and Wren froze.

Echoes of the gunshot pinged around the tunnel like balls in

a pachinko machine, mirrored by riotous thoughts in Wren's head. PSIA members weren't supposed to have guns. It was certainly far from procedure for them to fire.

Sato fired again. This time the bullet scored the raw concrete a few inches from Wren's feet to ricochet away down the tunnel. The sound was incredible and painful, shooting Wren's pulse up through the roof.

He didn't show it. Sato did though, with a creeping, sick grin.

"Do … not … move," he said in hesitant English. Wren barely heard him over the tinnitus of the first shot.

"I'm pretty sure firing your weapon like that is outside procedure," he said.

Sato finished his descent, never taking the gun off Wren. He stood above his fallen team member, while the two in the upper tunnel pinned Wren down with their flashlight beams.

"On … your … knees," he said.

There was no mistaking the furious joy in Sato's eyes. Finally getting the upper hand.

"How long have you been standing guard on that train platform?" Wren countered, as Sato approached. The man even moved like a weasel, shoulders bobbing sinuously, hooded dark eyes drinking Wren in, the gun barrel trained on his chest.

"You … are … arrest," he said.

Wren shook his head. "I didn't get that, son. Try again."

Sato scowled and fired once more. This time the bullet scored a gouge in the walkway between Wren's feet. He didn't flinch, but it was a close-run thing.

"Now that was definitely not procedure."

"Smart … mouth … American," Sato hissed, getting more incensed by the moment. He produced a set of handcuffs. "Put … on."

He tossed the cuffs at Wren. They hit his chest and landed on the floor.

"I don't think they'll match my eyes. If I can't coordinate, Sato, I eliminate."

Sato's eyes flared wide. Maybe he caught some of that, and it pissed him off enough to fire again, again hitting the concrete between Wren's legs.

"I'm starting to think you're doing that on purpose."

Sato's cheeks flushed red. His hand shook with adrenaline as he leveled the gun on Wren's face. "Put ... on ... now"

Wren studied him. The man was pathetic. Perhaps an *akaname*, but more likely just a petty, empty little bully trying to enforce his puny authority. His kind were ten-a-penny.

"No."

Sato took a step closer. Raked back the hammer on the gun. "Now."

Wren had no problem staring down the barrel of a gun.

"I said no. Now get lost, while the real police get some investigating done."

Then he turned his back on Sato. He dropped to one knee to look down at the flow of sludge. That was all the man was worth. Wren also knew it would infuriate him like nothing else.

The level of the flow had dropped precipitously in the last minute or so. He could almost see-

Sato charged.

Wren felt it coming more than he saw it. The gun swinging back like a club, Sato's arm sweeping it down.

Wren was ready, and reached up to catch Sato at the wrist and bicep, his hips pushing back as he rose to his feet. The man basically did it to himself, Wren just redirected his force into a textbook over-the-shoulder judo throw.

Sato flew through the air. Wren stripped the gun from his right hand as he passed. His legs hit the far wall first, then his side, then he was falling. Wren stepped sideways to avoid the splash back.

Sato landed. Turgid brown sludge, thickened now that the sewer was draining, split either side like soft custard to admit him in. Foul waves rocked against the walls. A blast of stink puffed up. Sato's screaming face submerged.

Wren disassembled the gun mechanically, a Smith and Wesson M&P; polymer framed, built for military and police use, semi-automatic, chambered for seventeen cartridges. He tossed the magazine into the sludge on one side, ejected the chambered round and tossed it in the other direction, then placed the frame and the barrel carefully side-by-side on the concrete by his feet.

In the tunnel above, the two remaining faces stared down in disbelief. The third guy was just climbing dizzily to his feet. In the muck of the sewer below Sato was thrashing desperately. Wren looked down at his frantic, palsied eyes.

"You thought it was pretty funny when I got flushed. How funny is it now?"

Sato spluttered and slapped his hands on the walkway, trying to clamber up, but everything on him was slick and slimy and he couldn't get a grip. Wren turned to his colleagues. "Aren't you going to help him?"

They stared back for a moment too long. That told Wren everything he needed to know. Then they came down skittishly, taking tiny steps up to the edge. One gagged as he stood over Sato. Sato screamed furious orders, spitting filth. Wren just waited, watching the waterline as it sank below Sato's waist, dropping down his thigh. At last Sato just flung his hands up, and his team members gave their hands back and pulled him up.

The stench was rank. Sato slopped onto the concrete like a landed fish, flopping and foul. He found his feet, eyes red with rage and muck, and took a step toward his gun parts.

So did Wren. "No. You're lucky. Now get lost."

Sato's face burned with naked hatred. But he turned. He stalked to the ladder and started up.

Wren watched until he was gone, then turned back to the sewer. By his calculation, the timer had just started again. Sato wasn't going to forget that extravagant humiliation in a hurry. The second he got back up into cell phone range, he was going to call every bit of firepower he could down on Wren's head.

So let him.

Soon all four of them were gone. Slipping and sliding, cursing each other, slapping along the tunnel above back to the grate.

Wren redoubled his attention on the sewer 'canal'. Now it was largely empty. No chance Wren was dropping in there, but he didn't need to. Sato had drawn his attention right to the only feature in the smooth, poured-concrete U-shape, the only item he could use to get any grip.

A red molded plastic box was mounted low on the wall, previously completely submerged several feet beneath the flow of waste. From it ran three meaty orange cables, each an inch around and bracketed to the concrete. The same kind of cables they sank into the oceans to connect continents. Wide enough to contain a hundred bundled optical fiber cables, capable of carrying countless petabytes of data per second. The three cables each ran away along the walls of the sewage canal in both directions, for as far as Wren's flashlight could illuminate.

His breath stopped.

One of the cables was missing. There was an open port in the side of the box, and multiple empty brackets stretching away along the one remaining wall. He stared for a long moment. Tracking the cables to the box, then away from the box. He'd never seen anything quite like it.

He dropped down into the filth. It didn't seem to matter anymore. He got his hands on the existing cables and started wrenching them away from the box. His hands slipped on the slick metal, but he kept working until he got it. A locking dial had to be turned, then a waterproof ring lifted, a gasket pried out, then the cable could screw free.

He did that for all three. It took hot, sweating minutes. His eyes stung but he had no intention of rubbing them. Just as the last came undone, revealing the glassy fibers within, more clangs came from above.

Wren cursed low. Barely time enough.

This time the stamping of feet was thunderous. A dozen

people, maybe. Perhaps all armed: an urgent SWAT response team charging through the grate, down the dark sewer and into the surge tunnel.

There they would find only an empty, silent canal, with Sato's P&M lying disassembled on the walkway. If they looked close enough, they'd see three thick orange cables hanging limply from the wall, and an empty space where something large and boxy had been mounted.

No longer.

35

OTAKU

The trek back beneath Tokyo passed at an easy run. The box was bulky but not heavy, and Wren carried it like a suitcase. He had no fear of the PSIA agents following him. To them, the sewers were dark and full of terror.

To Wren, they were becoming a home away from home.

In one of the tunnels he found a clump of old rags and used them to scour the worst of the muck off his hands, feet and the box. It still stank, but there was nothing he could do about that.

The train tunnel slowed him somewhat. He stood in the alcove watching trains go by for a long time, timing their passage and studying the timetable Hellion had provided. This time he was running on the tracks directly at the oncoming train, not away from it, and that shaved the window considerably.

It didn't seem possible, until after forty-five minutes he found his opportunity; a big enough gap in the hourly schedule. He had to wait another hour for the next window to come, then he dropped onto the track and sprinted for all he was worth, right into the coming cushion of air pushed ahead by the oncoming train.

He made the dive into cover with a second to spare; panting

for all he was worth, sweating hard, the train shuttling by just a foot away. Three hundred pounds of muscle was great for the hundred meters, but for the eight hundred? Not so much.

He continued back through the ghost station and the World War two telephone exchange, toward Golden Gai. It was coming up for 4 p.m. when he finally re-entered the Anderson shelter beneath the karaoke bar. The rotten concrete wall had collapsed further in his absence. Perhaps the whole area was going to subside into a crater soon, triggered by the next rainfall deluge.

He climbed up the ladder. The hatch cover above was shut and he pushed against it, but it didn't budge. He pushed again, then it opened on its own. For a teetering second, he feared bullets were going to greet him, but instead it was Makoto Toyama's beautiful face, lit by golden afternoon light.

"You took your time," she said. "Finally decided you wanted some Billy Joel?"

Wren laughed. "And you're a sight for sore eyes. I'll sing anything you ask."

She laughed too and backed up to give him room. He pushed the box through first, then followed. By that time, Toyama was halfway across the tiny bar, hand cupped across her face.

"My God, did you take a bath down there?"

He grinned. "You should see the other guy."

Her smile battled with a stern frown. The smile won out, but the frown kept trying valiantly. "I did. Sato. What did you do?"

"I gave him a swirlie."

"I don't know what that is."

"Basically, he wanted to know what it was like to be flushed down the toilet. Jealous, I guess. So I showed him."

Her hand crept back to pinch her nose. "It smells like you went for a second pass yourself, too. Were you wrestling in it?"

Wren spread his arms wide and stepped toward her. "Not going to give me a hug?"

Her eyes flared and she escaped through the door, leaving

Wren chuckling. While she was gone, he closed the hatch, then turned to the tiny sink and started scrubbing his hands. The stink rising off them was indeed eye-watering. He brought soap into the mix, scrubbing hard and getting under his fingernails. Then he turned to the box.

Toyama was hovering in the doorway now, like a nervous bird. "That's not any better, Chris."

He lifted one of his feet. The sludge had caked five inches up his slacks. A lot of it had dried and crumbled away in his long trek, but the stain was still there. "I need new shoes. And pants."

"I think we can stretch to a whole new outfit. And what's that?"

Wren looked down at the box. It could use a scrub down too, but the sink wasn't big enough. In the cold light of day, it looked unassuming. An orange box with a couple of junction ports built in. Like an oversized modem, maybe.

"This is the *akaname* secret. The guy we saw there must've been wiring this in below the level of the sewage, connecting it to a thick fiber-optic cable. My guess is a secret data line, carrying, well. Who knows?"

"A secret data line?"

"I tracked it for a while. They had four cables rigged to feed into it, two out and two in. The two cables I followed stretched for at least five hundred yards. At that point I had to take a different route, but the cables continued on."

Toyama's jaw set. "They disguised it beneath the sewage. That's why he was wearing the *akaname* mask. OK. So, we need to crack this box open and take a look."

"Agreed." Wren started taking photos of the box. "I'll get my hackers on it. They can identify it and advise next steps. We just need somewhere to hole up."

"Not your hotel," Toyama said. "They'll be watching it. Not my apartment, either. Definitely not PSIA headquarters. Somewhere anonymous."

Wren thought for a second, then gave a half smile. "I know just the place."

Toyama's eyes widened. "Not the love hotel."

Wren grinned. "Yes, the love hotel. It's totally anonymous. And the décor?" He finished taking photos and tapped out a quick message to his hackers.

FOUND THIS BOX UNDER THE SEWAGE FLOW, CONNECTED TO INCH-THICK FIBER-OPTIC DATA CABLES. WHAT IS IT, AND WHAT GEAR DO WE NEED TO HACK IT?

He attached the photos, then hit send and looked up at Toyama. She looked disgusted; maybe that was the smell still, or she was lost in contemplation of the love hotel's decorations.

"Why are you not under arrest, actually?" Wren asked. "Sato must've been furious."

She grimaced. "He was. I've never seen him that angry. But he had nothing on me, as I wasn't actually barred from the crime scenes. That was just you."

"Ah. Good point."

"They still tried, Sato especially, since I was obviously down there with you. But I played my own card."

"What card?"

She held up her phone. "I took some video of him on the platform, coated in all that filth. It's my private phone, and we were on a public thoroughfare, so he couldn't do anything about it."

That took Wren a second. "You blackmailed him?"

Toyama's cheeks colored slightly. "Not exactly. Just a little."

He laughed. "You've come a long way, Makoto."

"Like I said, I'm done being a nail. Now, let's go crack this box."

Outside, a hot afternoon sun shone down from a cloudless blue sky. Wren basked in the sunlight on his cheeks. It was the first time since his arrival that the sky hadn't been a looming white wall broken by rain. In this light, even the broken-down buildings of Golden Gai looked gorgeous: the strangling knotweed was greener, the faded wooden boards of the tiny bars more characterful.

Toyama scouted around until she found a hose and rinsed down Wren's legs and feet, then stole one of the wifebeaters off the nearby line and wiped down the box. The smell diminished. They headed out of Golden Gai, and on the main street through Kabuki-cho she dropped into a Uniqlo clothing shop and came out with a new pair of jeans, boots, socks and a T-shirt.

The love hotel was right where they'd left it, down a side street and wholly anonymous; the last place her PSIA colleagues would search for either of them. The vending machine selling keys blinked with its selection of themed rooms. This time Wren noticed the sign that read 'REST - 4 HOURS. STAY - 8 HOURS.'

"Not the US room," Wren said. "I can't face all those fireworks again. Somewhere with a desk where we can work on this box."

Toyama perused the rooms. "There's not a lot of desks in these rooms. This one has a massage table? But, uh, no. Wait, maybe this one." She made her selection and hit the button for 'STAY'.

Wren stripped in the elevator, bundling his clothes and boots into the Uniqlo bag, then headed into the room as Toyama held the door open. It was Bali themed, with walls decked in bamboo and woven grasses, tiki torches in sconces and the smell of lemongrass in the air.

Maybe that's why Toyama had picked it.

He hit the shower and amped the flow up to scalding. For maybe twenty minutes he scrubbed the sewers off him, unloading all the little complementary bottles of shampoo and body wash. When he stepped out into a fog of steam, he felt warm and cozy. Toyama had set his new clothes down just inside the door, and he pulled on the blue jeans and socks. The T-shirt had a picture of a manga character called Astro Boy on it; a half robot, half human boy with plasticky black Lego-man hair. The label said it was double-L size, but it looked like an M-size max. Still, he squeezed into it and it just about stretched over his broad frame.

Toyama laughed when he came out, then clapped her hand to her mouth. "Sorry."

"Japan double-L is tight."

"Better than sewer clothing, though, right? You look like you ate an *otaku*. Maybe a handful of them."

"What's an *otaku*?"

"A nerd. But it's OK. Nerds are cool now. Here, look at this."

She was sitting on a stool by a fake wooden dresser, with the orange box laid out on top. She'd already cracked open the case. Inside there were a lot of electrical bits and pieces, circuit boards and wires.

"Looks difficult. Can you make anything of that?"

"No. But I sent pictures to your hackers. Maybe they'll have something."

She handed Wren his phone and he made the call, tapping it over to speakerphone.

"Christopher," came Hellion's voice, filling the small, tacky room. "You have been rolling in sewers again, yes? I have many jokes still about-"

"Email them to me," Wren interrupted. "Tell us about the box."

"Yes, email." She sounded disappointed. "We have studied this box thoroughly. It looks like signal booster, very high technology version. It catches incoming light signal on optic fiber, increases power, and sends it on. Four ports, and you saw four cables, yes? Two in, two out, so this equals two boosters for two data streams."

"OK," Wren said, taking a seat on a rattan stool beside Toyama. "So what do we do?"

"Well, best thing is go back to sewers for third time, plug

box in again, and we will catch all traffic passing through. Can you do this?"

Wren laughed.

"I think we can rule that out," Toyama said. "The sewer's crawling with PSIA now."

A moment passed. "I am speaking with beautiful maiden, Agent Makoto Toyama, yes?"

Wren went to hit the speakerphone button, suspecting what was coming, but Toyama snatched the phone first. "Yes, it is. Hello, Hellion."

"Yes, it is I, Hellion! I must say thank you, Agent Toyama-san. Our Christopher has-"

"Hellion," Wren cautioned, reaching again for the phone, but Toyama held it away.

"Yes, our Christopher has not had night-time athletics for very long time, and it has made him grumpy like Russian black bear. Years, this has been now! Very long time. Many animals live and die in this time."

Toyama's mouth dropped into a wide, scandalized 'O'. Wren grappled for the phone, but she popped up and scurried to the other side of the bed.

"Always grunting, always urgent, very much built-up manliness," Hellion continued, oblivious. "Now you have helped him find relief, and this is most welcome relief for us, and all in Foundation. We are very grateful. If possible, can you provide these athletics for him again at least one time, most charitable act, it will be enormous favor to us both, and-"

Wren finally grasped the phone and hit the speakerphone. Hellion's voice disappeared to a tinny squawk. He looked at Toyama, whose cheeks were crinkling toward a laughing fit.

"I like her," she said.

"Please ignore everything she said," Wren urged, feeling the flush come onto his cheeks. "She's terrible."

"She's adorable."

The phone was still squawking. He put it to his ear. "Hellion, you're off speakerphone. Can you behave, please?"

"This is best behavior, Christopher. I am concerned very much for your mental health. Agent Toyama-san is wonderful calming influence, and-"

Wren hung up and re-dialed for B4cksl4cker. The big Armenian's deep voice answered in seconds.

"Christopher, apologies. You wish to speak about booster box, yes? "

"Yes," Wren said, and hit speakerphone again.

Toyama looked disappointed.

"Re-plugging to catch full data flow is best option," B4cksl4cker said. "But there is chance of data still lodged in box buffer circuits. This will require connection of certain cables. After connection, we will hack and decrypt contents most carefully, without wiping data. Will require time."

Wren's brow furrowed in concentration. "What cables, and how long?"

"Commercially available. Easy to buy. I will send shopping list and directions for use. Time depends on quality of cryptography. Hopefully within twelve hours."

Wren totted that up. By the morning. "Thank you, that'll be great."

B4cksl4cker ended the call. Wren's phone buzzed as his directions came through. The occasional spurt of laughter blurted from between Toyama's pressed lips.

"I'll get those," she said, and swiped the phone from his hands. "I'm not a wanted felon."

As soon as the door was closed behind her, she laughed raucously. The sound diminished slightly as she passed down the hall and got in the elevator. Wren smiled and sat down on the edge of the bed.

That was nice, he guessed.

The room was quiet except for the ticking of the AC. There was a small window, but it only looked out on a view of another building's vents. He cracked it open and a warm breeze blew in, lulling him softly. It had been a long day, after all, and he'd trekked through the sewers for around seven hours.

He found the TV remote and switched it on. An episode of FRIENDS was playing, dubbed into Japanese. Joey and Chandler were up to their old tricks, wearing each other's clothes. He watched for a few minutes, eyelids gradually drooping, until he sagged back and fell asleep.

36

BOX

Wren woke to the sumptuous smell of piping-hot pizza. He blinked. The room was dark but for the desk, where Toyama was illuminated by two lamps. There were three large pizza boxes on the table before her, the top one with its lid open, the contents steaming gently.

His stomach growled, and he realized immediately how famished he was, but there was something more important first.

"Where's the booster box?"

Toyama turned abruptly. There was a part-surprised, part-guilty look on her face, as she quickly chewed and swallowed her mouthful. Like a kid caught with her hand in the cookie jar. "I was about to wake you up. There's plenty of pizza left."

Wren sat up. The TV was still on, but muted. "And the box?"

Toyama waved a hand. "I bagged it up and trashed it. It's not sanitary, Chris, not next to pizza. I wiped down all the surfaces first with bleach."

"You trashed it?"

"It's OK, Hellion said she lifted everything she could. They're cracking the data now. The box is just junk."

Wren's heart settled back down. Once more, the aroma of hot

cheese and spicy pepperoni overwhelmed his senses. "And did they find anything?"

"Not yet. They got the data, but it's encrypted, as expected. They're prepping for a nightlong hack. You want some pizza?"

Now he smiled. He hadn't eaten anything since breakfast. "Of course I want some pizza."

He hustled up off the bed and sat beside her. She smiled, then started to demolish another slice of Hawaiian. "I was so hungry," she said through a half-full mouth. "I couldn't wait."

"I hear you." Wren scooped up his first slice and took a big bite.

It was indescribably delicious. The hot cheese had a golden, caramelized crust. The dough was crunchy at the edges and soft in the middle. The pineapple chunks popped in bursts of sweetness, while the tender salt of the ham just about carried him away on a cloud of succulence.

He let out a low, warm sigh of contentment.

Toyama hit the mute button on the TV, and it chirped to life. Now it was an episode of Frasier. Wren smiled as the Japanese voice actor attempted Niles' feigned outrage.

"And I got sake," Toyama said, reaching down to pull up a frosted black bottle. "No glasses, so we can drink it neat. If you're in the mood."

Wren didn't speak, mouth too full of his second slice, but he reached a hand out.

"Ladies first," Toyama said, and took a long pull, then handed it to Wren.

He glugged it down. It was cold, then hot, then fiery, then the wasabi hit bounced inside his nose and made his eyes water. Then it warmed his belly, and a fresh tide of relaxation swelled over him.

"Good?" she asked.

He realized he was sighing happily again.

"Yeth," he managed, stuffing his third slice into his mouth.

They sat like that for some time, eating and drinking, half-watching Frasier. Soon the first pizza box was finished and they moved onto the second. Pepperoni. The slices of spicy Italian meat were delicate and mouth-watering. Wren kept on eating like he had a hole in his middle. Toyama kept up impressively. They both took breaks to drink, like they were *akaname* divers coming up for air.

Soon the second pizza was done and they moved onto the third: the pièce de résistance, a Meat Feast, fully loaded with spicy nduja sausage, pulled barbecue beef, crispy chicken skin and smoked ham. Although he was starting to get full, Wren began salivating anew.

They tucked in wordlessly. The pace slowing, but not the enjoyment. Frasier ended and another show began. Wren found himself smiling and laughing, even though the show was Japanese and he had no real idea what was going on. The T-CAPS system lay on the bamboo side table; Toyama must've taken it out of his ear.

He checked his phone. Only 9 p.m. He'd been asleep for a few hours. There were a few messages from Hellion, but nothing relevant, just emojis of eggplants, peaches and champagne corks popping.

By the time the pizza was all done, Wren felt completely sated and not a little bit drunk. It felt good. He noticed, in a bleary way, that the TV had been muted again, and Toyama was looking at him.

"I think I'm fired," she said.

Her eyes were red. She was holding her phone.

Wren touched her arm. "I'm sorry."

She laughed. "Maybe it's good. I'll join your Foundation and become a vigilante."

That seemed remarkably funny, and Wren laughed too. "That's great. You'll be very welcome. We could use someone with your language skills."

"Just my language skills?"

He laughed.

She punched his shoulder. "I'll give you a swirlie."

"Already had one."

"You look like it. You're filthy."

He looked at her. She looked back at him. It felt perfectly natural. Like the whole day, the sewers, the pizza, the sake, all of this was meant to be. They stood up at the same time, went for each other at the same time, locked into an embrace then kissed hot and tumbled onto the Bali-themed bed.

37

GET OUT OF THERE

Wren woke to the shrill ringing of a phone. He blinked hard, rolled, and saw the handset flashing and vibrating on the nightstand beside him. He brought it up and checked the time.

4:23 a.m.

"What?" Toyama mumbled beside him.

"Dunno," he said, and answered.

"You need to get out of there," a voice said sharply in his ear. It was female and sounded just the same as last time.

"You."

"They're coming. I just saw it. You've got minutes only. They're in the building. Get out, or your quest to keep your family safe ends here, Christopher Wren."

He stared for a second. Processing that she knew his name, knew his 'quest'. Trying to figure out where he knew her voice from. Starting to spin up an active response.

"Who's coming?"

"Who do you think? Now get up! You and the girl. I'm showing roof access from the top floor. Get up there and we'll figure something out."

Wren blinked. "We? Just who are you?"

"Not important. They're in the elevator and on the stairs right now. There're dozens of them, and they have guns. Go!"

Toyama was already on her feet, pulling on pants and a top. Wren leaped up too, thinking fast. No time to get dressed, not if they were in the elevator already. "Wait here," he said. "Call armed police and don't come out."

Then he went straight to the door, flung it open and scanned the corridor. It was narrow, red-carpeted and red-walled with a shiny gold ceiling. The elevator was at the end, and it was coming. Eighth floor. The ticker showed them at five already.

He sprinted over, bare feet pounding the grainy carpet. Seconds only, and no time to spare. He plucked a fire extinguisher off the wall as he passed; a big red model filled with carbon dioxide dust. The elevator was at the seventh floor. Wren sucked in a deep breath, then pulled the pin and discharged the extinguisher's jet right at the closed doors.

White powder flumed out in a powerful stream, quickly filling the narrow corridor with a thick, obscuring cloud.

The elevator pinged. Wren pressed himself to the wall, extinguisher held in both hands and still discharging. The doors opened, and immediately shouts called out as the powder washed in, followed by the deafening crack of gunfire.

Bullets sprayed and ricocheted in the contained space, pinging off the lift and the shaft and burning down the corridor. The first figure lurched out into the corridor, coughing hard with his hands to his eyes. Wren brought the extinguisher round in a massive hammer blow.

He could have chosen the face, likely to rip the guy's head off his shoulders like a T-ball out of the cup, but he opted for the sternum. Center mass. Like sending a battering ram into the lock plate of a door, the guy took the full force of the blow in the chest and was scooped up and sent hurtling backwards, smashing into his crowding fellows like a bowling ball into the pins.

They went down in a flailing gaggle, crying out with what

little air they had. More guns fired wild, more ricochets ripped down the corridor and Wren hugged the wall long enough for a gasping, desperate break to come in the chaos, as their weapons maxed out on ammunition.

Then he stepped in. He could barely see, but it didn't matter. In the tiny elevator, everyone was a target for him. He felt his way, stamping with bare heels on calves and feet, driving elbows down and out into exposed flesh, pounding the bodies around him like the whirling blade inside a food processor.

In the close quarters, they went berserk in response. Maybe four guys, all of them thick and meaty. All the better for Wren to properly tenderize them. They thrashed out and hit each other. Wren drove his knees into their hard bellies, crunched his forehead down into their noses, swung his elbows like a scythe felling wheat until the job was done.

In twenty seconds the elevator fell still and silent but for muffled groans.

The smoke was starting to clear.

Wren dropped to one knee amongst the tumbled bodies and fished for their weapons. He came up with two: Smith and Wesson M&P pistols; polymer framed, built for military and police use, semi-automatic, chambered for seventeen cartridges. There were magazines scattered on the floor, and he reloaded just as a door at the far end of the corridor opened to the stairwell and more men poured in.

The corridor was narrow, forcing them into a straight line. From within his cloud of white smoke, still on the same held breath, Wren sighted both M&Ps and fired.

The guns bucked in his hands, and he steeled his grip to stay on target. The first guy went down, and the second went down, and the third was already falling from a through-and-through, then the fourth dropped as he tried to spin away and back out. The fifth dropped to his knees and returned three wild shots into the smoke until Wren clipped him between the eyes.

The door to the stairs swung closed.

The silence after the thunder was deafening. Wren waited, but nobody else poured through. He didn't think that was it. The woman on the phone had said there were dozens. This was nine only. Still, he cast around for more magazines amongst the big guys on the floor.

They had pomaded hair and face tattoos everywhere, like the security guys in the pachinko parlor. Yakuza. He came up with two magazines then was up and running, staring at the door to the stairwell while reloading.

He reached the door to their room and banged twice. "It's me, Chris."

It opened. Toyama stood there with her phone to her ear. He held out the second M&P to her.

"Come on," he said. "We have to go."

She took the gun in one hand. Over her shoulder was a bulging satchel. "Armed police are coming. Four minutes out."

"Let's get to the roof." Wren started for the elevator at a run. Toyama followed.

"What on earth happened here?" she shouted after him, looking left and right as they stamped into the remains of the white cloud.

"They made a mistake," Wren said, and started hoisting bodies out of the elevator like he was shoveling earth. Unconscious figures crumpled in the corridor behind them.

"Some mistake," Toyama muttered, and punched the button to close the doors.

"Tell me you've got clothes in that bag," Wren asked as the elevator chimed.

She smiled, holding her nerve admirably despite the conditions. "I've got clothes in this bag."

The doors started to close. At the same moment the far door to the stairs opened again and more bodies poured through, this time firing from behind the makeshift shield of a metal tabletop.

Wren shoved Toyama against the wall and a few bullets zipped between them to tear holes through the elevator wall, then the doors closed and the ascent began. Wren grabbed the satchel and started pulling on his clothes.

38

ROOFTOP

The elevator hit the twenty-first floor and Wren strode out first. He had his boots and pants on, his shirt partly buttoned, and the Smith and Wesson M&P held out.

The corridor was sea-blue; dark navy flooring, cornflower blue walls and a translucent glass ceiling with rippling pale lights running within it, like they were looking up from underwater at the sun on the waves.

"Armed police are three minutes out," Toyama reported, her phone hard at her ear.

"Not fast enough," Wren said, starting along the corridor at a run. In a few seconds he reached the door to the stairwell, pressed against the wall then cracked the door open and peered through.

The stairs were a switchback design of metal beams and gantry grilles attached to the exterior of the building. Above the railing shone the pulsing red lights of Tokyo. Wren stepped out onto the gantry and leaned over the railing to look down, then leaned back fast as gunshots pealed out from below.

"Three floors down," he said. "We go up."

The stairs leading up lay behind a padlocked gate. Wren put

one foot on the gate, one on the railing and both hands on the vertical I-beam. He judged the distance, pulled back, then flung himself out over the railing. For a second he was exposed, swinging sideways above the precipitous drop, then he came in fast over the railing on the other side of the gate.

Bullets chased him, clanging musically off the surrounding beams.

"I'll cover you," he urged Toyama. "Fast as you can."

She swallowed hard, then gripped the I-beam.

Wren leaned out over the railing and fired at the stairwell three stories down; five fast shots that chipped sparks from the metal structure. Enough to buy Toyama time to swing herself out then back in, far more gracefully than Wren.

She hit the stairs and Wren caught her, just as answering gunfire smacked off the underside of the stairs. Thundering footfalls vibrated up through the structure's beams.

Wren started up at a sprint.

Two switchback turns later, they spilled out onto the roof. An open expanse of gray concrete stretched the full footprint of the building before them, surrounded on all sides by the gushing lights of Kabuki-cho. He surveyed the building's four edges swiftly.

On the west side another building rose taller, maybe a hotel: there were figures silhouetted at the windows, gazing out over the beauty of the city. Useless. The other three sides all dropped away. He tried to remember what lay around them.

"Check the south side for a drop down," he said, pointing, then broke for the north-east corner. The roof thundered under his feet.

At the corner he stopped and peered down both sides. To the north the nearest building was across a wide street and five stories down. Too big a jump; even if they could clear the gap, the fall would kill them.

The east side looked more promising, with an adjoining building around five stories down. Too far, but it had some kind of large, rounded structure cantilevered out over the edge, reinforced with scaffolding in back, like an artificial green hill. It was still a big jump, maybe two full stories, but if they cleared the gap, and if the odd structure had some spring in its surface, they should be able to control their landing and drop down safely onto the rooftop without spinning off to the ground far below.

He turned to Toyama, who was running back over to him. "Only a drop to the street at the south."

"What's that?" Wren called, pointing at the structure.

She reached him and peered over the edge. The hill had a row of strange small cone-like shapes running back from its peak. Beyond it lay a large-scale picture of Jason Statham, and Wren finally realized where they were.

Above the cinema square where Toyama's grandmother's noodles hut was. Which meant-

"It's Godzilla," Toyama said abruptly. She pointed at the hill. "There's his head, those are his spines, and there," she pointed to a smaller, adjoining structure that clamped over the edge of the building. "That's his claw. Why?"

Wren laughed. Saved by Godzilla. "We're going to have to jump on his head. I'll go first. Do you think you can do it?"

Toyama's eyed widened. "Jump on his head? What if we roll off?"

"Maybe the booths below will catch you," Wren offered. Barely even a joke. He was already pacing out his run-up. Any second now the yakuza would appear up the stairs and open fire, at least a dozen or more of them, if the voice on the phone could be believed. Maybe they could take out a few, but this wasn't the tight confines of a love hotel corridor, and he no longer had the element of surprise.

Shouts came from behind, then the first hail of covering gunfire, and Wren looked at Toyama.

She was already in the air.

His jaw dropped. He stared out as she flew through the dark. Five yards covered already and dropping fast. Her hands windmilled, she looked like she was about to overbalance and hit headfirst, then somehow she turned it into a somersault.

Wren's jaw dropped as she spun tight, opened up, and landed on the back of Godzilla's head with a massive bang. The structure shifted slightly, rocking inches forward before catching and pulling back, then Toyama turned and waved.

"Come on!"

The first shot zinged by over his shoulder. There was no time for a run-up. He stepped up to the edge and kicked off with all his strength.

He didn't get nearly the clearance Toyama managed. The air ripped around him too fast, he flew and he fell, then he hit the lower flanks of Godzilla's head low and hard. One foot shot straight through whatever material made up his skin, while the other skidded down on the steep slope of his neck.

Wren's legs pulled in very different directions as his momentum dragged them hard apart. Maybe something creaked in his groin, he cried out in pain, then Toyama was there, pulling him up and out. He got his hands on one of Godzilla's spines and managed to clamber up to his feet.

His groin felt raw but OK. His leg that had torn through the surface was on fire, his slacks already dampening with blood, but there was no time to worry about that.

"This way!" Toyama shouted and led the way over Godzilla's bulbous head. Down to their left lay the main Kabuki-cho square, all the booths gone at this late hour, sparsely populated with a few milling revelers. Wren heard the whine of incoming sirens, but they were too far away still.

A few bullets struck Godzilla's head, ripping out tufts that sprayed like fiberglass. Toyama grabbed Wren's hand and they jumped, dropping to slide down the far side of the great monster's head. They hit the roof just as the potshots from behind became a fusillade of incoming fire.

They hunkered tight against the scaffolding while bullets shredded Godzilla's skin and clashed around the framework inside. Toyama took a breath then rolled smoothly out to the side, took aim, and fired three times. Wren pushed out just in time to see her clip a flying yakuza right out of the air. His balance went as the shot spun him, and he hit Godzilla's head on the wrong side with a horrible crunch, then bounced once and away.

The crash of his final landing came an agonizing wait later, as he met the flags of the square below at breakneck pace.

Wren took a breath, beading tight on the group of yakuza on the rooftop, now staring down at them. Looked like ten guys at least. None of them attempted the leap, though, and none of them fired.

"I think we're OK," Toyama panted.

Both of them were sucking for air. The ten faces over the edge of the roof top abruptly pulled away. The sirens were getting louder.

"Your leg," Toyama said.

"It's fine," Wren said, but made no move to stop her as she ducked into her satchel, miraculously still hanging over her shoulder. She came out with what looked like her bra.

"Here," she said, and pulled up Wren's pants to start wrapping his wounds.

He almost laughed. Good thing Toyama had an ample chest. The bra cups fit nicely around the swell of his calf.

"Where did you learn to jump like that?" he asked.

"Gymnastics," she answered, focused on wrapping his injuries. They looked like surface scratches, messy but nothing too serious. "I was set for the Olympics at fifteen, but I pulled my shoulder. There's no going back from that."

He pictured her spinning mid-air again. "Incredible. A somersault onto Godzilla's head."

She finished up wrapping the bra and pulled out her panties.

"Seriously, it's OK," Wren protested.

"Something wrong with my underwear?" she asked pointedly. "Not good enough for a field dressing?"

"No it's just-"

"What people are going to say? I thought you were the hammer, Chris, didn't care about what others say."

He could only smile, then wince as she pulled the panties tight. "I think we proved without doubt who the hammer is, here."

She laughed. "And don't you forget it. That jump was terrible, by the way." She ripped a strip of fabric off her shirt, wound it around his leg and knotted it. "Like someone threw a bag of trash off the roof."

"I've got heavy bones," Wren countered.

"I've never seen a worse landing," she muttered as she worked. "Who does the splits like that? We'll get you on the pommel horse practicing dismounts."

She kept on muttering while she worked. Wren watched the roofline. It seemed they were going to be OK.

39

ARMED POLICE

Armed police flooded the rooftop, rifles up. There was no denying it. This was a mess.

"Don't tell them about the *akaname*," Wren said, in the moments before everything changed. "Not about Ando, not about the phone call, not about the booster box. OK?"

Toyama just nodded, then the police were on them, a tide of figures in black. Toyama barked out fast explanations, pointing up at the roofline. Wren picked out the word 'yakuza', then strong arms were lifting him up.

They were separated. Wren was escorted away first, supported beneath both arms. He could walk OK but wasn't about to resist and make things worse. The elevator carried him down through a block of karaoke rooms and comic book shops. At ground level in the square, a scrum of beat cops was already fencing off the dead yakuza.

A van was waiting in the middle of the square, and they put Wren in the back seat. No cuffs, which was good. He thought about making a break for it, but the mess was made now, and best faced down. Three guys got in, surrounding him, then the van pulled away. Through tinted windows he watched the empty, bright streets of Kabuki-cho flash by, until they arrived in just a few minutes. He didn't recognize the building as they pulled into its underground parking lot, but he knew where it had to be.

PSIA headquarters.

The door slid open and they ran him in. Another elevator, maybe five floors up, then he was into a small field hospital. A gurney was laid out for him, a doctor and nurse waiting. They cut his slacks off, cautiously probed the underwear wrapping his leg, then set to work.

Anesthetic was injected. Stitches were made. Within twenty minutes he was transported again, given clean blue pants, then dumped in a room. It looked like a detainment cell: low bed, sink, toilet. This impression was confirmed as a bolt in the door clanked home.

Wren sat on the bed and let loose one soft, low curse.

Minutes passed, stretching out to ten, fifteen, thirty. His mind ran a mile a minute, but there was nowhere to go, only looping around the same set of facts.

The *akaname* had the yakuza on the payroll, or the *akaname* were the yakuza; either way they were getting scared. Scared enough to attempt an assassination on two law enforcement officers. It meant Wren and Toyama were getting close to something. Ando was the key. Push the key into the right slot then twist, and everything would fall into place.

He felt he was just one step away from bringing the whole thing down.

If he wasn't deported instantly. If Toyama wasn't reassigned. This was the exact kind of mess Rogers had warned him about making. Not his fault, but when was it ever?

He smirked at that thought. Often, actually.

He considered going up to the door and banging the house down. Demanding a lawyer, the American consul or ambassador, but that would just be more noise. Sometimes you just had to face the music, and no better way to do that than by bowing your head and acting like a nail.

The water in the sink tasted fine. He drank half a gallon, then laid out on the bed. Kicked off his shoes. Put the pillow over his face to block out the light, and promptly fell asleep.

There were no dreams. No assassination attempts. He woke to hands on his shoulders. More armed police in full riot gear, including helmets and visors. They got him up but gave him time to slip his boots back on. Four men with their tasers and batons in their hands, like they thought he was about to flip out.

"What time is it?" Wren asked, rubbing the blear from his eyes. "I gotta use the head."

They spoke to him in Japanese.

"Privacy," Wren said. "How about a little?"

They didn't show any signs of understanding. Neither did they move to compel him.

"Fine." Wren went to the toilet and did his business. After that he washed his face and his hands, then checked his leg. Blood clots had dried and caked around the stitches, seven in total. They were all neat and well-placed. There were three lacerations, but only one looked deep; the others were held together with butterfly bandages. Finally, he made a drawn-out pretense of brushing his teeth with his finger.

It didn't achieve much, but it was all a test, really.

The guards continued waiting, making no effort to compel him. So he hadn't fallen that far.

He buttoned his shirt. Checked his reflection in their shiny faceplates. "Ready for prom," he announced.

The lead police guy barked something in Japanese.

"Sure thing," Wren allowed. "Take me to your leader."

They led him out. Still no cuffs. That was good. Another elevator, another ride, then another room. To the left was a mirrored one-way window. To the right was a video camera trained on an interrogation desk with four seats. Two men were waiting for him, already seated on the other side.

Yamaguchi. Sato.

They didn't bother to stand. Wren held in a quip about Sato cleaning up well. Time to do his best nail impression.

"Please, would you sit down, Wren-san?" Yamaguchi said.

Wren sat. No smart-mouthing. No backchat. Just soft-handed compliance.

Sato muttered something in Japanese. Maybe not even loud enough for Yamaguchi to hear. The guy had a real problem with volume.

Wren took a deep, calming breath. This was going to be harder than he'd thought.

40

DEBRIEF

An aide switched on the camera.

Yamaguchi looked pained. Sato looked like he was settling in for an enjoyable show. There were papers on the table; looked like official reports mixed in with photographs of dead yakuza.

Yamaguchi started proceedings by bowing his head low to the table.

"Wren-san. I would like to apologize for what has happened here. This is clearly a matter of internal Japanese security. Our 'yakuza'. Gang members are out of control. I would like to thank you for your involvement, and apologize again for what happened."

Wren blinked. Yamaguchi bobbed up to make eye contact. Sato smirked. This wasn't the chewing out Wren had anticipated at all.

Yamaguchi went on. "For this reason, it has been decided by the Diet, our government, that this affair is best concluded internally." Yamaguchi bobbed back into a bow. "You will be escorted immediately and safely to a waiting plane and returned to America. Again, Japan apologizes unreservedly for putting you in this danger."

It didn't feel right. Wren felt the situation slipping out of control. This wasn't a disciplinary hearing. This was a brush-off.

"I'm making progress on the murder case. These attacks just prove it. You don't need to send me anywhere."

"Wren-san, you are a credit to your agency." Yamaguchi spoke while remaining bowed low. But it didn't feel respectful. It felt like a brush-off. "Your conduct has been exemplary. We will pass on our thanks to your government. This is an internal matter, however."

There it was. Now Wren got it. The magic word: internal. This wasn't a brush-off; it was a pay-off. Yamaguchi had to know why Wren had been sent out here alone; to manage the image of the US and take the fall as a patsy if he failed. Now he was offering to undo all that; to take the shame on himself, and on Japan, rather than risk Wren digging any deeper and, what?

Find some *akaname* in the PSIA ranks?

Wren felt the crossroads fork before him.

If he just shut his mouth and played by their rules, he'd get to go home free and clear. Keep his citizenship. Keep his farm and his family. Take no blame and carry no consequences.

And he thought about it.

For a long few seconds, looking at the top of Yamaguchi's head and the gloating eyes of Sato, he seriously considered it. When he'd come out three days ago, that was all he'd wanted. This case had nothing to do with him, after all.

Except.

He thought of the voice on the phone. So familiar. Taunting him, then warning him. Maybe the very person who'd killed Ando and the rest. Without that voice, he'd be dead. Toyama would be dead.

If he left, the *akaname* would continue. Men like Ando would keep doing what they were doing. He saw the image of a child dressed all in leather again, a leash around its neck, crawling on the floor with no eye holes, no ear holes, no mouth hole.

With Wren on a plane headed home.

"No," he said.

Yamaguchi bobbed up. "Wren-san?"

He hadn't planned for this. Hadn't expected events to take this turn, and his mind raced hard. Sato looked torn. Like he wasn't sure if this was good or bad. Neither was Wren.

"I'm not ready to go back yet," Wren clarified, still casting around for some way to make it stick.

"Wren-san, this is an attitude that does you great credit," Yamaguchi gushed. "We appreciate your dedication. But truly, this is the time for Japan to insist. We must resolve this matter internally."

Internally. That same word again. A pay-off. A brush-under-the-rug. The *akaname* everywhere, working whatever dark deeds they lurked in the sewers for, licking up filth with impunity. Maybe Yamaguchi was one of them. Maybe members of the Diet were. The six dead men so far were all elites. Maybe Wren was getting too close.

But Wren had cards still. He'd said as much to Toyama. At least one card. Playing it was a gamble, though. It meant putting everything at risk, everything he'd fought for in Delaware.

But to give up and get on that flight? That was worse. He'd never look himself in the eye again.

And that thought gave him the way through: shame.

"I disagree, Yamaguchi-san," he said, then folded into a deep bow himself. He'd never bowed that low in his life, forehead to the cold metal table. He heard Sato's gasp and savored it. "It is I who must apologize. This is my fault. This is the fault of the CIA and the American government. I was sent out here unprepared and under-resourced. It is our shame, not yours. This should never have happened."

A smothering silence descended, like a low white sky crushing down. Wren kept his head to the table, feeling the weight of shame build. The political complications stretched out from that room, making ripple effects on both America and

Japan's images. For this failure to emerge from Japan would shred the last fig leaf America had, and that would go badly for them all.

President Ablas would try to pin the blame on Wren, but he didn't have to make that easy for her. He didn't have to be her patsy. Instead he could come out loud and fast, blaming her.

Make the biggest mess yet.

He could feel the room shifting.

"Wren-san," Yamaguchi tried, again, "this is-"

"I must insist. This is my country's shame. This is our failure to bear." He snuck a sideways glance at the camera, at the one-way glass. "You were right to detain me here without access to my ambassador. You are right to send me back in disgrace. My behavior has been disgraceful. I have failed to resolve the crimes. Despite the incredibly able assistance of PSIA officer Makoto Toyama, I have squandered opportunities. This is due to my training and lack of support. On behalf of the United States, I apologize without reservation."

He didn't look up. He didn't need to.

The camera was recording it all. They'd made all this formal, witnessed and recorded, in hopes of locking Wren down right now. Doubtless there were observers beyond the one-way glass, perhaps even the US ambassador. It's what Wren would do.

Now he was flipping all that on their heads.

"Wren-san," wheedled Yamaguchi, as he started to grasp the situation he was in.

Wren looked up. He stood up. Sato glared at him in disgust.

"I will go at once," Wren said. Doubling down on the pressure and forcing Yamaguchi to choose. "I can't bear the shame. My country has failed you. Please, take me to my plane."

He started toward the door.

"Wren-san, wait."

Wren didn't. He banged on the metal door three times. The door opened and he started to walk through.

"I apologize," Yamaguchi shouted abruptly. "Wren-san, please."

Wren stopped. Turned.

Yamaguchi was on his feet now, looking distraught. Terror blurred into fury on his face, even as he struggled to control both. This was an international incident in the making, and he knew it. Japan ripping away the USA's fig leaf. He'd been sent to bottle it up, and he'd just made it worse.

Wren said nothing.

"It is not your fault," Yamaguchi went on, forcing a new way through. Sato's eyes bugged wide. "It is not your country's fault. The truth is, the fault lies with me. I did not support you sufficiently. I did not allow you access to crime scenes. I stood in your path for reasons of my own personal vanity. I did not want a foreigner to resolve this crime on our behalf. For this I apologize unreservedly."

Wren blinked. Now the pendulum was swinging further than he'd expected.

"Yamaguchi-san-"

"It is my shame," Yamaguchi insisted, and now he dropped to the floor. Wren couldn't believe it. On his knees, the older man bent over and prostrated himself completely: head to the concrete, arms spread out before him. "I must resign my commission. Wren-san, I hope you will forgive me."

Wren stared. The camera blinked. Sato snapped to his feet with a snarl, muttered something inaudible then pushed past Wren and out the open door. Wren was left reeling. The old man remained on the floor, totally prostrate.

"That's not necessary," he said. "I-"

A hand came on his arm.

"Well, you really screwed that up," said a quiet voice by his side.

Wren turned and recognized the face of the American ambassador to Japan. He was a handsome African American man, mid-fifties, dressed in an expensive gray suit with a tight mass of afro curls atop his head, and the dark dab of a soul patch beard under his bottom lip.

"Time to go, I think," he went on in a restrained New York accent, then nodded at Yamaguchi. "He won't stand up until you leave. It's a matter of lost honor. Best not to prolong the moment, agreed?"

Wren said nothing and strode away.

41

AMBASSADOR

The ambassador picked a room. Not his building, not his corridor, but nobody stopped him. It looked like another interrogation cell. He took the cop's seat and gestured for Wren to sit.

Wren sat. Everything had just shifted, and his head spun too fast to keep up with it.

"We need to talk," the ambassador said.

"We do," Wren agreed.

The ambassador took a moment. Wren recognized him only vaguely. He'd been in the briefing materials he'd read in the plane, but he didn't know the man's name. He could ask, but he didn't want to cede the initiative.

"The President is-"

"I don't care about the President."

That shut up the ambassador.

"And if I don't care about her, you can be sure I don't care about you," Wren went on, speaking as the words came. "I know what you're going to do, now. Try to pressure me. Lay down the law about my family, my citizenship, about not making a mess. But I just made a mess. You saw it. It's on video. That's after I killed nearly a dozen yakuza and tea-bagged Godzilla's head.

Just this second, I got a district chief of Japan's top intelligence agency to resign in disgrace, because he got in my way. You think I can't get an ambassador fired, too?"

The ambassador narrowed his eyes. Not intimidated, Wren noticed. Perhaps amused. "You're fiery. I expected that."

"Bullshit you did. Say something useful or I walk."

"OK," the ambassador said. He rubbed his hands thoughtfully. "Useful. Let me see."

Wren stood up.

"First, my name's Aloysius Gage. Call me Gage. Believe it or not, I've sat where you're sitting right now."

"I'm standing," Wren pointed out.

"At a crux point between two great nations," Gage went on, as if Wren hadn't spoken. "It tests our mettle. You just played your cards, and quite well, I have to say. But now you're committed. I don't doubt you'll see this through. But you just committed the US along with you."

"The US can go fish."

"We can help. Please. Sit down."

Wren didn't. "I haven't eaten since yesterday, Gage. I'm hungry. Get to it."

"Let's eat together. I can order-"

"No. Talk."

"Talk, he says," Gage muttered. "Ok. Man-to-man." He fixed Wren in his gaze. "What you just did will already be winging back to the President. She's going to be furious. Her first instinct will be to pull the trigger on her threat. Cut you off. It'll be bad, because it'll mean a public relations war with you. Messy. Even if she wins it, she's going to come out damaged, because you're a popular man in many quarters."

"Ten seconds."

"Her second instinct will be to double down on you. That means actually give you the support she should have given you at first. Bend arms here in Tokyo to win their support, too. This is by far the preferable option."

"And how does that help you? What's your angle?"

Gage snorted. "Cynical. But you're right. The spotlight on Japan puts the spotlight on me, so now we're all standing in your shadow. You do this thing right; I get covered in glory. You screw up; I go down with you. That's what you wanted, correct?"

"I don't care about you."

"Now I call bullshit. This whole thing was always precarious. At least now it's mutually assured destruction. So I'm incentivized to help you."

"So help."

Gage stood up. "I will. In-country CIA resources are now at your disposal. Potentially US military forces, too. I think you'll find the PSIA far more amenable, going forward. We can-"

"Do you know what an *akaname* is, Ambassador Gage?"

Gage frowned. Wren studied his eyes. He'd only just met the man, but it was enough to get a good read. The look on his face seemed like genuine puzzlement, not a fake front designed to put him off. "No. What is it?"

"What about guys in full scuba gear, swimming around in the sewers?"

"I haven't got the faintest-"

"Don't worry about it. Here's what I want. That punk Sato, deputy director, shipped a thousand miles away for the duration. His buddy Nakamura, too. Pull whatever strings it takes. I want Makoto Toyama as my liaison to the PSIA. I want sweeping raids on the yakuza who attacked us cleared in the next few hours; a joint operation between the US and the Japanese government. If you don't clear the raid, I'm going in on my own. We're going to clean sweep these bastards, whatever it takes."

Gage paled a little. "Christopher, I don't think you understand what you're asking. The-"

"Call me Wren."

"Fine, Wren. The yakuza are not some two-bit street corner gang. They're everywhere, with tendrils spread throughout Japanese society. They exist in a fragile balance with the government, who turn a blind eye to their activities in exchange for peace."

"Then it's time to open their eyes. The yakuza just attacked an American citizen with two dozen street soldiers, Gage. Soldiers packing military hardware. You said you wanted to be at a fulcrum point in history between two great powers? So let's work that lever.",

"But how? Where would we even start?"

"Kabuki-cho. That's their flagship money-maker, right? Start with the pachinko joints, then hit the brothels, love hotels, bars, whatever. Every operation is yakuza-led, I hear. Start busting down doors and locking up gangsters, pretty soon something will shake loose. You just ready an army."

"I don't think-"

"Don't think, Ambassador. Just do. And if I find out you've leaked this to anyone, then I'm coming for you next."

The man puffed himself up. This had clearly not gone the way he'd expected. "Are you threatening an American ambassador?"

"Of course I am. Now get to it. I expect you to have the first raids lined up by noon."

Gage stared. Wren strode to the door. No way he was going to sit around and wait any longer. The *akaname* were coming down today.

42

SUZUKI

Wren strode out of the office and down the corridor. At the end was a double door barred with a magnetic card lock. Wren had no card, but that didn't matter. He slammed a huge front kick square against the lock plate, unleashing a thundercrack and splitting the double door down the seam.

He emerged through the flapping doors into a large open-plan workspace. Analysts were seated at long rows of back-to-back desks, all now staring his way. At the head of each row sat a larger desk on a slightly raised podium, like the overseer's post in a factory. Wren swept his gaze left to right.

Five rows. Twenty analysts to a row, which made for one hundred total, plus five overseers. He didn't recognize any of them.

"I'm looking for Makoto Toyama," he shouted. Loud enough for everyone in the large space to hear. Nobody said a word.

"Makoto Toyama," he repeated. "Now."

At the head of the nearest row an old guy stood up. He looked a fair bit like Yamaguchi; mid-sixties, short white hair, wearing a clean gray suit cut from decent twill, bowed slightly by age. He raised calming hands to the analysts in his row and approached Wren.

Wren strode toward him. "Where is she?"

"Mr. Wren," the man said in accented English. "I am section chief Nobu Suzuki. It is a pleasure to-"

"It's not. Where's Makoto Toyama?"

Suzuki's calm demeanor didn't break. "Perhaps if we go to an interview room and discuss this privately, we could-"

"What's there to discuss? You tell me where she is. I go get her. It's as simple as that."

Suzuki just looked at him.

Wren felt his heart sinking. "She's not here."

"I am afraid not," Suzuki said. "After retrieval from the rooftop, she was taken to an off-site secure facility. This was considered safer."

"Safer how?"

"Safer for everyone. Mr. Wren." Suzuki lowered his voice. "You do not need me to tell you, the yakuza are a large organization in this country. They are powerful. And, like you, Agent Toyama is now a target."

"You brought me here."

Suzuki looked uncomfortable. "It is not my place to discuss this. But, as you are a foreigner, I will be direct. You are a special case, Mr. Wren. Your immediate repatriation to America would best satisfy the yakuza, or so it was believed. You did kill ten of their men."

Wren couldn't believe what he was hearing. "Satisfy the yakuza? They sent those ten men to kill me!"

"That is a very simple way to see it," Suzuki said softly. "The yakuza will not see it this way, I am certain, and balance is very important in Japan. Now your repatriation has failed, and this creates new imbalances. In the eyes of the yakuza, this imbalance must be corrected."

Wren stared at him. "You're saying the yakuza have called open season on me?"

"I do not understand 'open season.' But I believe, yes. On both you and Agent Toyama."

Wren gritted his teeth. This was a different country, after all. Things would be done differently. "So where's the secure facility? Put a call through and get her here. She's safer with me."

"I am afraid it is a silent operation. Extremely secure. No calls in, none out. But I will take you there."

"You?"

Suzuki drew himself up. "Yes, Mr. Wren. Now I will be even more direct. I am not entirely happy with the current state of balance in this city. Perhaps this is an opportunity to shift that balance."

"So let's go."

Suzuki nodded and strode toward the shattered doors. Wren followed. Twenty yards along the corridor lay a bank of elevators with no call button, only a magnetic swipe bar. Suzuki ran his keycard over it and the nearest set of doors chimed open.

"You think she's in danger there," Wren said, as the doors closed behind them.

"We should not speak freely here, Mr. Wren," Suzuki answered. The elevator started down. "There are likely listening devices."

Wren frowned. "Bugs in your own elevators?"

Suzuki met Wren's gaze. "Do you not have these in your CIA, also?"

"Probably."

"Yes. It is much the same here."

The ride down passed in awkward silence. The elevator hit basement-level and Suzuki led them out, striding swiftly over to a sleek silver Honda Civic Type R. "This is my personal vehicle. It is safe."

He dropped into the driving seat and Wren crammed himself into the passenger side. It was a tight fit. Suzuki revved the engine like a drag racer and spun out.

"As we were saying," he said calmly, speeding at twenty miles an hour around the parking lot. Wren pulled his seatbelt on. "There are many factions within the PSIA. I think you know now what kind of man Yamaguchi-san was. Also, the kind of men he surrounded himself with. These are not representative of Japan's best, Mr. Wren. Unfortunately, they are the majority."

They spun up a spiral ramp at twice the speed Wren would normally take it. "You're saying the PSIA's corrupt?"

Suzuki seemed to simmer for a moment, wrestling with something. The Civic breached the end of the spiral and shot down a straightaway toward the exit ramp. "What you are doing here, Mr. Wren, is unusual. Breaking procedure to gain results. Some in the PSIA welcome this change. Others despise it. At best, they are biased against a foreigner interfering. At worst, well..."

Suzuki was a master of leaving things unsaid. That didn't work for Wren.

"At best, they're *akaname*."

Suzuki frowned and turned to him, even as he hit the ramp up to the road hard enough to punch the Civic hard in the suspension. "*akaname*, what does this mean?"

"That's the right answer. Eyes on the road, please."

"I can drive this route in my sleep," Suzuki said, and spun hard right into traffic. "This is the correct expression, yes? My English teacher often uses it."

Wren resisted gripping the dashboard. "It's correct." Out the window he recognized the fringe buildings of Kabuki-cho. It was mid-morning, but the skies were dark and the district's neon lights were fuzzy through a drizzling mist of rain. "More rain. Where's the safe house?"

"It is rainy season. And ten minutes away."

A lot could happen in ten minutes. "I'm going to make some calls. Forgive me, but could you put the radio on?"

Suzuki turned to him and flashed a surprisingly dazzling smile. "I understand. Do you like jazz?"

"It'll do."

Suzuki hit the radio and syncopated piano trills spilled out through the car. Wren wasn't a fan, but it was good enough for covering sound. He brought up his phone, dialed the number for his hackers and pressed the handset to his ear. Almost instantly the line opened, and the first thing he heard was rattling keystrokes, hitting fast and hard like hail on a tin roof.

43

EVOLUTION

"Very busy here, Christopher," Hellion said in her brusque Bulgarian accent, the keys still flying in the background. "All night hack is coming to conclusion."

Wren's heart began to pound. "Good. Are you up to speed with everything that's going on here?"

"Last night you are attacked by yakuza, killing many, then arrested, now un-arrested. Yes, we are. Major international incident, President Ablas is furious, usual Christopher Wren behavior." Keys clattered. "Signal shows you are moving east in vehicle of PSIA section chief, Nobu Suzuki. Is this good idea?"

"The best I've got right now. I'm looking to liaise with Toyama; apparently, they sent her to a different location than me. A secure site."

"Interesting. We did not know this. We like her."

Wren swallowed a smile. "She's OK. Apparently, the yakuza have declared war on us both, so I need her where I can see her. I've declared war right back, with raids spinning up of PSIA, CIA and even military assets, if the ambassador comes through." He took a breath. " Now, tell me you're getting somewhere with the hack."

"Getting very far," she answered fast. "You want *akaname*? We are turning over stones with many cockroaches underneath. Very close now."

"How close?"

"I am attempting to pinpoint precise location. Data in booster box is rich."

Wren sat up in his seat, chanced a look at Suzuki, but there was no way he could hear over the flood of syncopated jazz. "Rich how?"

"B4cksl4cker," Hellion said. "Please explain this."

"Yes," came B4cksl4cker's voice, as the storm of keystrokes continued in the background. "Booster box had four lines, Christopher. This is two lines total, in and out. First line is easiest to hack. Prepare yourself for strange truth."

"I'm prepared. What is it?"

"This line carries new darknet."

Wren blinked. "What do you mean, a new darknet?"

"New. Not same as old. Completely different."

"Different how?"

"Physically. As you know, old darknet is transmitted on same data line as main Internet. Uses same undersea cables circling world, same servers, same protocols, same satellites, same coding language, same dictator countries offering data sanctuary for darknet activity: drugs, human trafficking, children. Usual horror show. Except we have been disrupting darknet and destroying data sanctuaries directly ever since Blue Fairy. This is Foundation key goal, of course. Many governments are doing this also. Darknet is being blocked with greater success than ever."

Wren took a moment to absorb that. He'd barely checked in on his hackers' progress for months. "OK. Rogers said something about this, too. Now you're saying this new line bypasses all that?"

"Yes, bypasses completely. Criminal services we could attack on old darknet, we cannot attack here. Child can be ordered, packaged like pizza, delivered to home of pervert. Death porn movies can be filmed and streamed on whim. Drugs are sent by aerial drone, terror plots exchanged by encrypted text message. Very bad, Christopher."

Wren gritted his teeth, heart pounding harder now. He pictured the leatherbound child in Kenji Ando's apartment, crawling on the floor, and rage tightened his knuckles.

"And this darknet's live now?"

"Yes, it is active. I have seen some of this content, Christopher. Death porn movies. Man named 'Ripper' in black mask; he tortures women. Each ends with same kill. They are slit open at middle. He calls this 'uncorking'."

Wren winced. "You watched that?"

"I did not want to. We were searching for location clues."

"And?"

"This 'Ripper' is active in Japan, we believe. Very large man, Christopher, taller than you. Could be yakuza. Could be involved in management here."

Wren gritted his teeth. He had no problem taking down very large men. Men like this 'Ripper', he'd even enjoy it.

"How widespread is their coverage?"

"This we do not know. Depends on reach of cables. Could be just under Tokyo. Could be all Japan, or all world. New undersea cables are also possible, Christopher. Ocean is big. Darknet value is in trillions. This is good investment."

Wren gazed out the window but saw nothing he recognized. Just tall buildings and faces passing in a blur of rain. "You're talking about a whole new Internet."

"Yes. Capable to rejoin main Internet when it wishes to. Bypass it when it wishes to."

"Is that even possible?"

"It is very possible, and very dangerous. Must be stopped."

Revelations spun through Wren's head. "No wonder the yakuza are after us. We just interrupted a potentially trillion-dollar operation. They're going to send everyone they can."

"Yes."

"And what about the second line? There were two lines, right? Is that a backup darknet, or something else?"

"Something else," B4cksl4cker said. "Different configuration, but we found very little data on this line. As for purpose, we do not know. Could be something very bad."

"Worse than a whole new darknet?"

"Yes. This is possible. But we will only be guessing."

"So guess."

The big hacker took a deep breath. "Very well. There is possibility that second line is new trunk route direct into everything. Power, water, gas, data, banks, money. All by direct connection, bypass all normal controls. This would explain how they flushed you and Agent Toyama, Christopher. Very fast control, instant response, nobody could see it happen or trackback method. This is because it can be linked directly through underground hardlines."

Wren's eyes widened. "Say again, B4cksl4cker. It sounds like you're saying this line could rewire a whole city. Is that right?"

"Yes, easily. It is thought experiment at this stage, Christopher. But if I am evil organization? Yes, I would do this. Begin with private darknet, run this for trillions until we reach certain point of capitalization. Then hit city, Internet with vast hack. Lock down everything. All computers, everywhere. City will stop. No light, no power, no money, no police, no sewers, no elections. This becomes chaos. Vast scale hostage situation. Blackmail is possibility at this point, like Blue Fairy attempted, but blackmail would not require second line. Second line opens up very new possibility."

Wren's heart began thumping harder still. Again they were talking about the Blue Fairy. "What possibility?"

"No need to blackmail to take control. Simply they take control. After hack, no one has access to money, essential services, election infrastructure. Second line gives this to *akaname*. They can control city, even country. This is new means of silent coup, Christopher. Data coup. *Akaname* call instant new election and replace leaders by manipulating information, vote counts, newspapers, police. Use powers of state to arrest anyone who resists, push them into prisons with no appeal. Manipulate banks to bankrupt enemies. Take control of laws, armies, weaponry. This is possible."

Wren reeled. Abruptly the seat felt unsteady beneath him. "That can't be possible."

"Is easy," B4cksl4cker said. "Like boiling frog. Warm, warm, warm, then suddenly frog dies. We are from Eastern bloc, Christopher. Many countries here, we experienced this world. Dictator controls everything. Gulag is constant threat. But can happen anywhere."

"But we're not frogs. This couldn't just happen without anyone noticing."

"Very correct," Hellion chimed in. "Let me ask simple question, Christopher. When tree falls in empty forest, do you know it makes sound?"

He said nothing for a moment. It was an old philosophical question. "I don't know. I believe it."

"This is power of current information state. Data is big. Nobody can understand it. Nobody can witness it. Elections. Social media. Criminal records. System is built on trust. Second cable can reroute all, invisibly. People will not know it has happened. They will be grateful Internet is back. New elections will be annoying, results may be frustrating, but what can they do? Destroy whole system? Those who attempt this, who mistrust, who protest, who attempt to fight, are easily separated and destroyed. New system takes control like cuckoo in the nest. There will be no way out."

Wren felt the world shifting around him. "You're talking about the complete and total overthrow of a civilization."

"Yes. Is possible. Many dictatorship countries now, darknet sanctuaries, run this way. There is no freedom. No dispute. No press. Second cable could bring this state on everywhere, all at once."

Wren didn't know what to say.

It felt like an evolution. He'd thought the Blue Fairy were flattened, but here the *akaname* were taking their work a step further. No attempt at blackmail was even necessary. With these new hard data lines, they could go for everything - enough to plunge the world into a new digital dark age, one from which there could be no escape.

His voice came out tight. "How long until they pull the trigger?"

"Could be today. Could be tomorrow. We do not know."

"How do I stop it?"

"Very difficult. How to stop cuckoo? Destroy eggs, Christopher. This means root out cables. Destroy data sanctuaries. Disrupt server farms that route new darknet. This is what we are hunting."

Wren grappled with that. "How long until we have a location?"

"Could be minutes, could be hour, perhaps two. Current estimate is somewhere in G-CANS flood surge system."

"G-CANS." Wren's eyes widened. "Toyama mentioned that. They're huge underground halls, to manage rainy season overflow."

"Vast," B4cksl4cker said. "As big as stadiums, and dozens of them."

Wren felt the pieces fall into place. "As soon as I secure Toyama, that's where I'm going. I'll slip in and tear it down while the raids above ground distract them."

"Yes. We will provide flash drive with self-executing cryptoworm virus. Easy to transport, will permanently lock all equipment connected to darknet. Also will collect data on second line. It must be inserted into root server, may take minutes."

Wren nodded. "Good. Get that drive to me."

"We will. Now we must focus."

The line died.

Wren felt the world tunneling down. Around Tokyo, maybe around the world, depraved *akaname* were getting their squalid desires delivered to their doorsteps right then; a multi-trillion-dollar industry getting served in 21st century style.

It was sickening. He hadn't expected any of this when he'd come out. Tokyo was only ever supposed to be a murder investigation. Not something larger, not something darker, and it set an old rage boiling.

His fists clasped tight. He'd killed hundreds of men like the *akaname* already, back when they were calling themselves the Blue Fairy and wearing Pinocchio masks.

He clearly hadn't killed enough of them.

Suzuki reached out and killed the jazz. "We are here," he said, and pulled sharply into a narrow side road leading up a hill. It looked like a residential district, flanked by five- and six-story apartment blocks with shallow balconies, all of them tall, thin and glistening with chrome highlights.

Wren's gaze was already locked on one of the buildings ahead.

"Stop the car. Do you have any weapons?"

"Weapons?" Suzuki asked, slamming on the brakes. "No."

Wren surged out of the vehicle, eyes roving through the rain.

One window on the third floor was shattered; a characteristic fracture pattern created by a small but powerful projectile. Like a bullet.

The *akaname* were already here.

44

TOYAMA

"Call the police," Wren barked at Suzuki, then sprinted over a low embankment through sodden green shrubs. He reached the side of the building and jumped, catching the bottom floor of the balcony overhead. He wrenched himself up to a balcony with two cute garden chairs squashed either side of a slim glass coffee table, climbed onto the railing then leaped up again, catching the third-floor balcony.

In seconds he was up alongside the smashed window. The balcony was spattered with glass. Wren pressed close to the wall and leaned in.

There were men's voices inside. Maybe three, just audible over the drumming of the rain. He scanned the balcony, but there was nothing he could use as a weapon. He'd have to improvise.

He slid under the shattered window, back to the wall, and edged up to the sliding door. No time to peek through. Instead he knocked three times on the glass.

The sound of conversation within died. Footsteps padded over within. The door slid open and a hand protruded outward. Wren noticed three things in three tenths of a second: the hand was missing its little finger at the knuckle, a well-known yakuza tell; it clutched a Smith and Wesson M&P pistol tightly, chambered for seventeen cartridges; the wrist was coated in swirling black tattoos.

Wren swung both hands up, one grasping the gun's frame and isolating the trigger, the other clutching the *akaname*'s wrist. He pulled hard and drove upward with his thighs at the same time, slamming his shoulder neatly into the guy's armpit like a dovetail joint, thrusting him into a judo throw.

The guy climbed and Wren spun. The gun slipped clear as the guy approached his zenith over the balcony railing and began his descent face first, letting out a fearsome cry.

Wren ducked back into cover as gunshots barked out, followed by a meaty crunch as the *akaname* hit the deck. Sparks clipped the railing. Wren checked the gun's slide and safety, took a step to the side and fired through the shattered window.

Both guys dropped, one with a burst head, the other thumped twice in the torso.

Wren sped in through the open door, kicking their weapons away. Dead and dead. In seconds he cleared the apartment. Two dead PSIA agents were stuffed into the box-like bathtub, their throats cut. That didn't explain the shattered window, but Wren figured that came down to Agent Toyama.

He flipped the top body in the tub, and found it had an empty shoulder holster. So Toyama had grabbed his weapon and put up a fight. The window had gotten shot out. He surveyed the wall and found several bullet holes. Someone must have put out a police call, but nobody had yet come.

Wren ducked over the bodies and patted them down. There were a few extra cartridges for the M&Ps. He slipped one of the guns into his back waistband, then dumped the other two and the extra cartridges into a plastic bag retrieved from the kitchen.

Just then a phone rang somewhere, muted.

Wren spun, searching for the source. It was chased by a knock on the door.

"Who is it?" he shouted.

"Suzuki," came the old guy's voice. "I think you'll want to answer this."

Wren opened the door, M&P up. Suzuki was standing in the doorway, holding a small, black, chiming Nokia.

"Tell me that's not yours," Wren said.

"It belonged to the dead man in the parking lot. I retrieved it."

Wren took it and hit answer. "Where is she?"

A second passed, then a deep, abrading voice with a slight Japanese intonation answered. "I take it my men are dead?"

Wren didn't recognize it. "These three are. Release Agent Toyama or I'm coming for more."

There was silence, followed by the sound of low chuckling. "We both know you will keep coming in either case. I look forward to it."

"If you harm her in any way, you'll die slowly."

"Then come quickly," answered the voice, all amusement gone. "Within the hour, or I will do to her what I've done to a hundred other women."

Wren's blood chilled. "And what's that?"

"Uncork them. You have no idea how devastating a single deep slice across the abdomen can be. All their lies come tumbling out. I will mail you the pieces, as you are so fond of her."

Wren grimaced. "Is that one of your new darknet services?"

"I'll make an exception for you. Little Red Riding Hood, come to Grandma's house so very far from home. You have no idea what you're toying with, and that amuses me."

"You'll like me even better in person," Wren said, tapping out an emergency order to Hellion and B4cksl4cker. "I'm the life and death of the party."

"Then come to us soon, Little Red. I don't know how long she will last."

The line clicked silent.

Wren was back in the room with two corpses and Suzuki,

who was turning pale. Fury bubbled inside him like a volcano readying to blow.

"Wren-san," Suzuki said.

"There are two dead agents in the bathtub," Wren said swiftly. "Can I take your car?"

Suzuki stared for a moment, then reached into his pocket and produced the keys.

"Thank you," Wren said, then swept up his plastic bag of guns and sped out into the hall.

"Hellion," he shouted into the phone.

"What is happening, Christopher? I am tracing vehicle from your location, but CCTV record is disappearing via ghosting protocol. Is this Makoto Toyama?"

Wren cursed. The ghost protocol was everywhere now, erasing forage in real time. "It's Toyama. I'm in pursuit."

"In Honda Civic? I will push call through vehicle. You do not have T-CAPS hands-free system installed, correct?"

"Put it through the dash." Wren hammered down the last of the stairs in the apartment block and emerged into the lot. The rain was coming down hard now. He raced for the Civic, its lights blinking as the doors unlocked and the engine engaged remotely. He dropped into the driver's seat and hit the gas.

"Where?" he shouted.

"South," came Hellion's voice through the car's speakers. "Three miles already, best guess. I am losing them, Christopher."

"So type faster," he grunted, and spun out.

45

GHOSTS

The Civic handled tight even on the rain-soaked street, hydroplaning in a wave as he skidded off the hill and back onto the main road.

"Elevated highway is best," Hellion said, keys hammering through the car's speakers. "Your next right."

Wren saw the signs overhead but couldn't read them. He was flying blind through the downpour, adrenaline jacking him higher. The turn onto another spiraling ramp appeared through the gray wall of rain, and he hit the handbrake and spun toward it. The Civic skidded but just about bit the road, sailing Wren across traffic and up the access route. He was closing in on eighty miles per hour as he shot out onto the walled highway, feeling like a ball in a pachinko machine.

Cars whipped by either side as he accelerated. A hundred. A hundred-twenty.

"Hellion!"

"I am tracking, Christopher. Footage is disappearing. This could be darknet in action. Substituting itself for real network. I cannot access fast enough."

"They're blinding us?"

"Ghost signals are spreading. I had panel van, clear trajectory, now it is gone."

Wren hit the wheel. "Last known location. Extrapolate. Where are you on the server farm?"

"Very close. This is correct general direction. G-CANS has many underground halls south of Shinjuku. Wait!"

"What?' Wren barked.

"I have them! ATM CCTV, they did not ghost it. I have clear view, Christopher! Vehicle has turned off highway, your next exit, approaching to, no. Stopped! I see them. Two figures, these are *akaname*, Christopher, in full equipment. This may be Makoto Toyama also, wrapped in bag of some kind."

Wren hit a hundred-ten miles an hour, racing up on the next exit. "Direct me."

"Yes, they are on side road, now opening up sewer grate. They are heading down, Christopher. Hurry!"

The exit came and Wren screamed onto it, taking the spiral descent so fast the civic edged up onto two wheels, sloughing up a wall of spray.

"Side road on right, before restaurant!" Hellion called, and Wren peeled across traffic and shot toward what looked to be another Jonathan's family restaurant, barely visible through the downpour.

The *akaname*'s panel van was there and unattended, rear doors hanging open. He killed the Civic and sprang out, readying his M&P pistol as he advanced on a pool of darker shadow in the middle of the road, signaling an open sewer drain.

Water poured down through the open cover. Wren brought up his cell phone flashlight and shone it down; the waterfall of rain run-off caught the light, splashing down off a metal ladder into darkness.

"I'm going down," he shouted, then stepped down onto the ladder and slid down the rails.

Instantly the sound of the storm shifted, from the drumbeat of rain on all sides to the splashing and churning of a surge flow below. A peal of gunfire cracked out ahead, briefly lighting the interior of a deep, broad sewer pipe. Ricochets chipped the walls, then Wren's feet hit the floor and splashed.

Water was everywhere and flowing fast. He spun, seeking the right direction, even as more bullets whipped in his direction. He buried the cellphone flashlight and pressed himself against the sewer's curving wall, straining to make sense of the chaotic helter-skelter of gunfire echoes. Hellion's garbled voice came through on the phone and he killed the call.

Only the weak gray light from above gave Wren any sense of his surroundings at all: the tunnel was a tight oval and looked much like the surge control tunnel in the dark sewer beneath Shinjuku, beyond the point where Kenji Ando was found. There were no lights, and the walkway beside the sewage channel was already submerged by several inches of fast-flowing water, as the deluge above filled Tokyo to the brim.

Another gunshot rang out, and this time Wren located the source and broke to his right, splashing wildly into the dark.

Everywhere was the sound of water tumbling down: from sewer pipes adjoining the walls, from run-offs either side, from manhole covers and drains in the road far above. Fat flows rinsed over Wren's head every few steps, constantly blocking his vision, but still he ran on.

He couldn't see them. Perhaps he could hear them, though; two men manhandling a strong, tall woman along a narrow, awkward walkway in wild conditions. Wren squinted his eyes shut against the constant downpour from above and raced after them, moving so fast he didn't notice the wall directly ahead until he ran into it at full tilt.

His roving arms hit first, buckling fast and bouncing his shoulders and head off the wall. His legs continued on, slotting through a waist-high opening then dropping. His body rotated backward as he fell; back striking the surface of the water and being carried by the flow, under the near-invisible archway and down through the air until-

A raging torrent of water ten feet down slapped into his back, and he submerged under the current. He flailed wildly, hands slapping at concrete and sliding on moss-slick walls, caught in the churn until his right hand snagged on a pipe and his forward roiling momentum halted.

He pulled, and in seconds was on his feet again, water rushing by at knee-level below, head bowed beneath the low ceiling, feeling a rumbling sense of dread fill him.

This was a lower flood surge tunnel. He turned, spraying the sopping walls with his cell phone light. The *akaname* must've come this way, but there was no telling which way they'd gone. Wren spun in both directions. Nearby hung the ladder leading back up to the tunnel above. It was hard to think in the rush of water, but with a fifty percent chance either way, he wasn't about to retreat now.

He picked a direction and ran; flashlight grabbing onto the curving walls to a depth of five feet out, water chuting past, feet dragging at the flow. Maybe a hundred yards he ran, ears keening for any unusual sound over the surge, trying to key in on the tunnel's ambient chaos and tune it out, until he felt something new.

Not the sound of footsteps or gunfire. This was a sharp, cold blast of wind in his back, like the cushion of air driven ahead of a subway train, and he knew exactly what it meant.

A flood surge was seconds away. The *akaname* had lured him in, racing with no way back, and now he was going to die.

Wren ran. With every passing second the cold blast grew sharper and stronger. Now he could hear the roar of countless tons of floodwater surging his way. It seemed the water underfoot drew back slightly, like the drawdown of an incoming tide sucking itself back off the beach, then just as he saw the dull glint of metal up ahead, it struck.

He leaped.

The surge hit like a freight train, blasting the air from his lungs. His legs were fired up against the ceiling, his body wrenched sideways and around, limbs smacking off concrete as the water was everywhere. He couldn't breathe, couldn't see, couldn't do anything but cling to the narrow sliver of metal protruding through the ceiling with all his strength.

Thirty seconds passed as the surge crescendoed and batted him side to side, a minute, then there was a slight slackening, and Wren finally dared release his left hand and reach up.

His palm found another rung. He grasped it tight and sent his right hand after it. It took fifteen rungs before he rose clear of the fizzing, frothing churn of water from below, and sucked in foul air. Ten more rungs and he emerged into another dark sewer.

He lurched out on his knees, the flow here nominal and inches deep only. The sound of the surge tunnel below still echoed up, like the cry of a lost river embedded in concrete. His cell phone light shed little light, but revealed another ladder nearby, leading up.

Wren made for it, before the *akaname* could send another flood surge his way. At the top of the ladder, he forced the manhole cover off the drain and emerged in the backend of the Jonathan's parking lot, shrouded in hammering rain.

He'd lost Makoto Toyama.

46

SACRIFICE

Wren stamped in the rain around the near-empty parking lot of the Jonathan's family restaurant, panting hard and trying to figure out what to do.

They had Toyama.

The rain poured over him in icy sheets. He was soaked to the skin, but he didn't care. Frustration bit into him like a buzzsaw.

He needed a destination, but he didn't have one.

He needed a way to pass unnoticed through the sewers without triggering another flood surge, but how? The rain was a lethal weapon in the *akaname*'s hands, and he'd just let them lure him into their dark realm, where he'd almost drowned for the second time.

There had to be a way through. He brought up his phone and dialed.

"Can you lock out their control of the flood surges, Hellion?" he shouted over the torrential rain. "You over-rode the Shinjuku controls to the G-CANS once already. Can't you do it again?"

"We are trying," came Hellion's harried voice, the sound of keys hammering in the background. "But we have only second-party access, or worse. *Akaname* have hard-wired network to sewer controls, which I cannot bypass. Perhaps this is linked to second line. I cannot stop surges."

Wren cursed loud and kicked through a deep puddle, throwing up a wall of water.

"We will have destination soon, Christopher. Find access, and you will have Toyama."

The line went quiet.

Find access. How was he supposed to find access?

He kept stamping around the lot, trying to think his way through the problem, but there were no answers. He couldn't help but picture Makoto Toyama on the *akaname* operating table, surrounded by rubber-skinned freaks. Laid out like a sacrifice on an altar, paying the price for his-

He stopped abruptly in his tracks. Rain slammed down on his head.

That was it.

He was back in the past, standing at the entrance to the Blue Fairy's temple, in the heart of their Pleasure Island tanker. A pyramid of negative space had been cut out of the shipping containers, leaving the structure all crude iron angles and rough ceiling joists. Tiers of seating had been cut out for the Pinocchios, looking down at the sacrificial altar at the center, where their greatest enemy ever was due to be vanquished.

Finally all the pieces fell into place.

'When did you give up on justice?' she'd asked, via the anonymous call on his first night in Tokyo.

Now he knew who she was, and knowing who she was opened up the door to 'how'.

He just needed to find her.

He lifted his phone again, tapped in another number and dialed. It was mid-morning in Tokyo, which made it late yesterday evening on the east coast of the US. The line picked up in seconds.

"Rogers."

"Sally, it's Wren," he shouted over the drumbeat of the rain.

"I need everything you've got on an old acquaintance of ours, as soon as you can. My partner here's in danger and Tokyo's about to erupt."

A second passed. "Boss. I heard about the diplomatic incident. I don't know if I can-"

"Remember the Blue Fairy, Sally?" Wren interrupted. "Remember how that felt, coming in hot for a highway landing on a busted private jet, hunted by everyone, so close to losing everything we valued in our country?" He took a breath. "I think we're there again, but this time it's worse. This time the Pinocchios are everywhere, operating right underneath our noses. If I don't act now, innocents are going to die, and we may never get a shot at them again."

There was a momentary silence. "Why are you talking about the Blue Fairy? I heard some yakuza took a run at you last night. What's the connection?"

"They just took another couple of runs," Wren said, talking a mile a minute. "They're working for, or they're part of, a new group called the *akaname*. I'm thinking they must've evolved out of the Blue Fairy, but with ambitions like nothing we've seen before. They're building a second darknet carried on their own secret optical fiber. We're talking about a mass cable-laying project spread throughout the sewers of Tokyo and most likely further afield, probably in the US too." He paused a second to let her absorb that. "I'll send what data I have on them, for your eyes only, but right now I need your help to locate this one person. Seconds count. Can you help me?"

This time the silence was the length of a single breath. They'd come a long way together, and trust counted for everything. "I'm on it. What do you need?"

He gave her the name. She didn't believe it.

"I'll get you what I can."

Within five minutes the first tranche of data came in; a firehose of shell corporations, dark money transfers and suspected assassinations from around the world. All the dead men were ex-Pinocchios. All the dark money flows served a single purpose. All the shell corporations pointed in one direction, confirming Wren's hope: the woman he'd spoken to on the phone was conducting her own secret war against the remnants of the Blue Fairy.

There was a phone number, too; a number through a number through a number, all backtraced across a dozen different shell corporations.

Wren stabbed it in and hit call. It rang three times then cut out. He went to dial it again, but his phone abruptly rang from an unidentified incoming line.

He answered.

"It's you."

She said nothing, but he could feel her presence carrying through the air. Overhead the first bolt of lightning lit up the sky, chased swiftly by an earthshaking roll of thunder.

"You engineered all this," he went on. "You lured me out here with dead *akaname*, set me up like bait. Now I'm on the edge of their server farm. Strikes on the yakuza are happening within the hour. I need safe passage through the sewers, and if you've got the means, now's the time to share it."

Still she said nothing. Another streak of lightning forked the sky, the thunder redoubled and the rain lashed down.

"They've got my partner," he shouted into the handset. "Give me what you've got or I'll hunt you down to get it."

"No need for that," she answered at last. "I'm right behind you."

Wren spun.

The lot was gray, the lights from inside the restaurant barely putting a dent in the thick pall of rain. He scanned the grayscale shadows rapidly, dismissing figures running to their cars, an old homeless guy shuffling through the rain, a young guy on his phone in the dry of his car.

Then he picked her out.

She stood in the rain between two vehicles, wearing a black

hoodie from which dyed black hair spilled out. There were the faint lines of tattoos on her cheeks, in the shape of Chinese pictographic writing. She wore black jeans bulked out with what had to be plate armor, along with a thick jacket obscuring who-knew-what. On her back hung a scabbard for a wooden kendo sword, but Wren had no doubt it contained a real blade.

The last time he'd seen her, she'd been standing over her would-be rapist in the belly of the Blue Fairy's tanker ship, holding a knife. That man's screams had echoed through the tanker's metal halls even as Wren had gone on his rampage against the rest of the Pinocchios.

Her first castration. He should have seen this coming.

Now she strode toward him.

"Mona Gebhart," he said. "Or should I say, Clara Baxter? First daughter of the Blue Fairy."

"Just call me Clara."

47

CLARA

Clara stopped three yards from Wren, her eyes burning with a fierce inner light. He'd seen that light many times before, in the eyes of men and women willing to die for their cause. He'd seen it in himself, back when vengeance had almost consumed him.

This woman looked like she'd been swallowed whole.

"I want in," she said.

Wren's mind ran a mile a minute. She was dangerous. Vengeance made you reckless and destructive, and he knew she didn't care about collateral damage. She was willing to do whatever it took to kill Pinocchios or *akaname*, while sacrificing anyone who got in her way.

But he needed her.

"Can you get me through the sewers, Clara? That's all that matters."

She inclined her head. "That depends."

He didn't have time to play games. "You must have a way. How else did you take Kenji Ando, or any of the six men you killed?"

Her dark eyes stared through him. "You don't know I killed anyone."

Wren's mind raced faster. "I know you. You're like me, only you're further gone. You'll never move on. Never forgive. You killed that Pinocchio on Pleasure Island, and now you're killing *akaname*, but how?" Fresh possibilities dumped into his head, bringing the only answer. "I walked every step of Kenji Ando's commute to work; there was unmodified CCTV everywhere. The only way you could've taken him was through the sewers; but the *akaname* didn't flood you, did they? There's only one possible reason for that." She said nothing. Wren made the final leap. "You've got one of their masks, haven't you?"

A long, horrible silence stretched out.

"I've got more than a mask," she said at last. "I've got two."

It felt like a pit opened up in Wren's stomach.

"We took them at great cost, along with two full suits," Clara went on. "You need both helmet and suit to evade their automatic defenses. Each helmet's got a magnetic RFID passkey built in, paired with the suit. Together they allow safe passage." She paused a moment. Lightning flashed overhead and thunder boomed. "If you want one set, then you share the location and we go together."

Wren stared at her. It could be a great deal, but she was a wild card, capable of disrupting everything on a whim.

"One condition. Our primary objective is to rescue Makoto Toyama and hack their servers. I need to back-trace the second line and shut down the darknet, Clara. Once that's done, you can kill as many *akaname* as you like. Break those terms and blow the mission, then I'll kill you myself. Do we have a deal?"

She stared. Wren stared back. He knew her kind of zealot. They only respected strength.

She stuck out her hand. "Deal."

Wren grabbed it and shook. "Deal. Now where are the masks?"

"Come with me."

She spun on her heel and stalked away through the rain.

A panel van was waiting in a neighboring lot. As they

approached, the side door slid open and a figure stepped out; short, stocky and bald, wearing shorts and a wifebeater and holding a length of something that could be a shotgun.

Wren pulled the M&P pistol.

"She's with me," Clara said.

"She?"

Clara strode over and Wren approached on full alert, wary of a trap. Close-up, in the faint gray light Wren realized the figure was a Japanese woman; one he vaguely recognized.

"I know you," he said, wracking his mind for how. "I've seen you before."

"Airport," she said flatly, her voice deep. "Kabuki-cho several times. I was one of a team following you."

She held the shotgun-shape up and pushed a button. A tall, wide umbrella shot out, cutting away the rain. Wren tucked the gun back into his waistband.

"I'd remember that bald head," he said. "You must've worn a wig."

"No wig. I dress as a monk and nobody looks twice. The name's Chaps. Now come in, you'll want comms."

He held up his phone. "I've got comms. All I need is the mask."

Chaps snorted. "That phone carries a signal a hundred yards underground? I don't think so."

Wren's eyes widened. "You can carry a signal in the sewers?"

"Of course we can. How else do you think we run kill-hits on these creeps? Come in and we'll sort you out."

Clara gestured him on. Wren debated it for a millisecond. Enter the truck, and he'd be at their mercy. But right now he was at the *akaname*'s mercy, and he liked his odds with Clara Baxter better.

He ducked his head and stepped in, and at once his jaw dropped.

The van's interior was hot, baked dry like the backwash off a 787 and crammed full of a custom-built array of computer cores.

They stood to either side of a narrow central aisle in tall shelf-like racks mounted to the van's walls, each blinking with red lights like the pulse of Tokyo by night. Front-to-back and back to-front, the van was ridiculously overclocked. Hellion and B4cksl4cker would have a field day.

Black cables ran like jungle vines along the ceiling, with the only break coming for two tiny workstations in the center, each in a tiny booth with a keyboard, mouse and a drop-down virtual-reality immersion helmet.

"You don't even have monitors," he muttered, as Clara hustled up and slid the door closed behind them.

"They take up too much space," Chaps said, squeezing her way down the narrow aisle. "Live in Japan for any length of time, and you'll get it. We're experts on storage. The VR rigs are better than monitors, anyway, like having a six-screen setup at sixty inches each."

The specs were lost on Wren. "What is all this, a server farm?"

"Something like that," she said, while Clara dug into a hatch under the front seats. "This is what it takes to ghost CCTV footage, and track the NBPs as far as we can, keeping ourselves beneath their radar." She tilted her head slightly. "You call them *akaname,* right?"

"Yes. You don't?"

She grunted. "I get it. The masks? They look like creepy *yokai* monsters. But no, we call them NBPs, New-Breed Pinocchios. Or just creeps. They call themselves 'Real Boys.'"

Wren stared. "They what?"

She shrugged. "It's the Pinocchio thing. They consider themselves Blue Fairy two-point-o. Pinocchio wanted to be a real boy, so that's what they've become." She shrugged. "They're creeps, any way you look at it. Now, you wanted comms?" She pulled out a tray built into the server racks, and from within plucked a familiar-looking earbud, which she handed to Wren. "Put it in now and it'll sync to the van's systems."

Wren studied the gray chunk of molded plastic. He recognized the model, but he'd never known one that could operate through a hundred yards of earth. "How does it sync up from underground?"

"The old-fashioned way," Chaps said, lifting a cable spool loaded with black line. "You carry this down with you, then it's transponder tabs dropped every hundred yards or at every bend in the route. The tabs are tiny and we have hundreds of them, so our practical range is largely unlimited."

Wren grunted. It was a simple but elegant solution; with only one flaw he could see. "And if the transponders get washed away in a flood surge?"

"They won't," said Clara. "Not with these."

Wren turned. She was kneeling behind a black plastic chest with the lid lying open. Glaring up from within were two *akaname* masks, laid on a bed of slick black wetsuit neoprene. In the van's bright lights, they were still grotesque, but the tech underlying their exaggerated features was clearer: the infrared goggles baked into those vacuous eyes; the long tongue-like rebreather pipe reaching down and back up into an oxygen tank; the slick, shiny skin of the masks' latex surface.

"Our prized possessions. One for you and one for me. Now where are the NBPs?"

Wren looked down at her, mind racing. She was clearly motivated, and competent too, but he was about to put both his and Makoto Toyama's life in her hands. Trusting her intentions was one thing. Trusting her abilities was another.

"How did you even get these?" he asked, then gestured around at the van and computer cores. "How long have you been building this operation?"

Clara looked like she was about to push back, then gave a small nod. "You don't trust me. I understand." She slammed the plastic case closed. "After Pleasure Island, I hunted Pinocchios down one-by-one for a time, just like you did. I got most of my twenty-seven kills in that period, and I built a small network of dedicated women, like Chaps here."

"OK. What brought you to Japan?"

"You already pulled my record with the CIA, correct? So you've seen the rabbit hole I went down. Every time I killed an ex-Pinocchio, they talked. There was something brewing out of Tokyo, they said. A new hope for men like them. I had no idea what it was, so I came out here, and I found the 'Real Boys'." She opened her mouth to go on, held it a second, then continued anyway. "The one thing you neglected in your investigation so far was the ties between the men I killed. I thought you'd catch on faster."

That threw Wren briefly off-track. "What ties, that they were all elites?"

"No. That they all had some substantial ties to China."

That took him by surprise. "What?"

She held up a hand and started counting off fingers. "Kenji Ando was in telecoms; he was making phone parts in Chinese factories and shipping them here. The judge, banker and government minister were all involved, in one way or another, with China's belt and road initiative. You've heard of it?"

Wren cast back through his memory. "Belt and road, you mean their global infrastructure project? What's that got to do with anything?"

"I had no idea until you uncovered their darknet line. Now I figure the NBPs are using belt and road as a cover operation." She paused a moment for him to catch up. "That kind of construction infrastructure kicks up a lot of noise, a lot of dust, a lot money. If they bribe the right minister, get a judge to sign off on the right law, get the right banker to obfuscate the funds, they can lay their darknet cable unseen, leaving the work itself to their local criminal partners. In Japan that's the yakuza, who handle almost all construction already. My guess is your *akaname* have been using this Chinese infrastructure push as a cover for laying their Japan darknet."

Wren stared. It was an immense conspiracy, but perhaps it made sense. "OK. What about the surgeon. The fifth elite you killed?"

"Him? He was a Pinocchio through and through, used to take underage sex holidays to underdeveloped Chinese border towns. The law gets real loose out on the Siberian edge of Western China."

"I've never been."

"You'd be busy," Clara said. "I sourced half my kills there. Now, keep up your end of the deal. Where are the *akaname* hiding?"

Wren looked at the gray plastic chunk in his hand, then slotted it into his ear. It chimed as it synced in with his phone, then again as it linked to the van.

"I'll make the call."

48

DESTINATION

Hellion answered before the line could even ring.

"Christopher, this is bad mistake," she said immediately. "This woman is wounded animal. Leave this van now."

Wren set his jaw. The sound in his ear was clear and sharp. Hellion must have hacked his phone to listening mode throughout. "There's no choice, Hellion. We need her. Now-"

"Does not matter. She is cutting off men's penises, Christopher! Also their testicles. Castration, this is called. Many times. This is very negative pattern, not good record for partner. Ms. Toyama had much greater respect for personal equipment of Christopher Wren. In fact-"

"Stop, Hellion. I'm doing this for Toyama. Now is not the time."

"It is always time," she blasted back. "Tell castrating bitch, do not attempt to castrate Christopher Wren, or I will-"

"Do you have the location for the *akaname*, Hellion, or not? I need to be there now. Everything else can come later."

There was silence for a second. Clara stared at Wren.

"Yes," Hellion said.

"Where?"

A moment passed. Wren knew enough that this meant Hellion was handing the phone over.

"We are just finalizing precise coordinates, but it is beneath National Stadium," came B4cksl4cker's deep voice. "This is very large sports facility, capacity sixty thousand, dates back to 1964 Olympics, but was rebuilt completely for 2021 Olympics. Several hundred million spent in that refurbishment, includes new deep G-CANS flood control system. *Akaname* server farms are in these chambers somewhere."

Wren looked at Clara, who shook her head. "There's nothing there. I've been everywhere underneath the National Stadium. It's a blank."

"Tell her there is something there," B4cksl4cker countered. "One hundred-megawatt server facility, enough to drive darknet across all Japan, disguised by sports stadium above. Very clever, probably secret access. We will guide you. I understand how psychopath killer missed it."

"All right," Wren steadied. "That's good news. Where is the National Stadium?"

"Very near, Christopher. South side of Shinjuku."

"Shinjuku," he muttered. Clara was already opening the sliding door. "We were right on top of them the whole time."

Chaps pushed past Wren. "We'll be there in fifteen minutes."

She stepped out into the rain. Clara slammed the door closed and opened the plastic chest again. The front door opened then the engine kicked into gear and the van jerked forward with a jerk.

Wren grabbed hold of the computer frames to keep from being tossed on his back.

"Both of these suits came from Japanese men," Clara said, holding up the masks. "Which means you're a foot too tall and a hundred-fifty pounds too heavy to fit comfortably. But you've had your Hep A vaccine shot, correct?"

Wren winced. "Yes."

"Don't worry," Clara said, stripping off her hoodie as the van picked up speed. "We'll wrap the rest of you in plastic. It's the only way Chaps fits. Only a little gets through."

Only a little. That was some consolation. She tossed a wetsuit and Wren caught it. It seemed as flimsy as a dishrag. The van cornered hard and he caught himself again on the computer racks. Clara was down to her bra already.

"You should strip every layer. Any clothes you're wearing now, you're not going to want to keep them after this."

Wren shrugged off his jacket and peeled away his soaking t-shirt.

In ten minutes he had the suit on. The feet were webbed and broadened like scuba fins; enough to allow for propulsion when submerged. It was stretched so tight around his chest, hips and thighs that it was almost cutting off blood circulation. His arms burst clear of it at the elbows, and they'd had to slit the suit at the calves to get his feet in.

Didn't matter.

"Here," said Clara, producing a roll of black plastic. Her suit fit her perfectly. She looked as oily and slick as the first *akaname* Wren had seen in the sewers. "Color's an important part of their alarm system. You could dress in yellow, too, as that's what sanitation workers wear, and they don't want their auto-flood defenses killing them constantly. It'd be suspicious. Otherwise it's the RFID tags."

She pulled a sheet of black plastic off the roll with a violent tearing sound, then ran a boxcutter down the edge.

"Right leg," she commanded.

Wren stuck it out. "I have to make some calls."

"You've got five minutes," Clara said, beginning to wrap Wren's leg. The plastic was adhesive backed, and he could already feel its industrial-level glue adhering to his leg hairs. Taking it off was not going to be pleasant.

He brought up his phone.

"Boss," came Rogers' harried voice. "What is happening over there? I'm showing dead bodies and-"

"I need you to run point on something for me, Sally," Wren said. "Can you do that?"

"Of course. What is it?"

"Yakuza raids. I'm about to go dark for a while, but the pieces are in place. Ambassador Gage is on board, he should be shaking up our forces. I've got a guy I trust in the PSIA, sub-section chief Suzuki. Get them both on the line and, with Ablas' blessing, this thing should be a go."

"Yakuza raids," Rogers repeated. "Because they've come at you twice, now?"

"They're at the heart of this, so I figure they've come at me four times now, maybe five, counting sewer surges. I just need you to push it through. Don't take no for an answer. Boots on the ground right now would have a real impact on our chances of surviving what's to come. Tell me you'll try."

"I'll lose my job over it if I have to, Chris. You're going operational? Good luck."

Wren took a second. That meant a lot. "Thanks, Sally."

He killed the line then dialed back to Hellion and B4cksl4cker.

"Yes, Christopher?" B4cksl4cker answered.

"The data cryptoworm, is it ready?"

"Yes, ready. It is simple program, less than one gigabyte, can transfer it now."

"How do I get it into their servers?"

"Flash drive will work, probably. Any access port. Potentially wireless access, also. If there is comms underground, we will be with you."

Wren grunted. "OK." He looked up. Clara was already at one of the tiny workstations, holding the VR unit above her head.

"Tell them to send it," she said.

"Sending," B4cksl4cker said. "Godspeed, Christopher."

49

MASK

The van rocked to a halt and Clara swept back the door. Outside, the rain was a barrier of sound and motion, cutting off anything beyond ten yards away.

"Here," Clara said, holding something toward him as he stepped out. It was a belt fastened with various pouches and the holster for what looked to be a large Bowie knife. "No guns down there, because they'll hear it. Sonic sensors are the third leg of their security system, so we can't talk either. Your earpiece has bone conduction, though, so you can subvocalize."

"Got it," Wren said, fastening the belt around his waist then drawing the knife. It was eighteen inches long, a consummate weapon with twelve inches of solid carbon steel, featuring a razor edge, a serrated back and a full-length tang. He re-holstered it then checked the pouches; each was stuffed with the small transponder tabs for extending their comms cover.

"Here," said Chaps, appearing through the rain behind Wren. "Tanks."

She was carrying twin large black oxygen tanks. He squatted and eased his arms through the shoulder loops. She pulled them tight then fastened the rig across his chest. They were heavy but easily manageable.

Through the drumming rain Wren could just make out the shadowy flank of what might be the National Stadium. "Is that it?" he asked.

"That's Yoyogi Hospital," Clara shouted. "We're still a mile away from the Stadium, due west; there's no way we can just walk up and drop down from so close. Now, time for the mask."

She held his out, then pulled her own down over her head. There were catches to fasten at the neckline, where the mask clamped down on an inner line of ribbing to make for an airtight, watertight seal. Wren watched carefully as she cinched them all, memorizing their locations. The ones in the back fell to Chaps to attach.

Wren pulled his mask over his head.

The contraption was heavy, unwieldy and too tight. He just pulled harder, until it slipped down his rain-slick temples and across his face. At first, he couldn't see anything, and worked to line up the eyeholes, augmented by infrared goggles, then it was as if the world beyond opened up.

The rain peeled away. Now he saw the dappled system of heat rising up off the hospital; some rooms hot, others cold. He turned and saw Chaps and Clara, who looked as if they were highlighted sprites inside a videogame. Clara had a blue box superimposed above her by some algorithm in the suit's AI, whereas Chaps had a red box.

"Blue's a friendly, red's the enemy," he muttered.

"Get used to subvocalizing while you're wearing the mask," came Clara's voice in his ear. Her tone had the trademark sibilance of a subvocal communication; relying on bone conduction to carry a whisper from the jawbone into the electrical pickup system.

"Roger that," Wren throat-whispered, and started feeling for the catches on his chest. He bolted the first few himself, then Chaps turned to him and expertly flicked the rest. "Where's the sewer access?"

"You're standing on it," Clara said. "An old river runs right under here, twinned with the main sewer for the hospital. We can drop down the drain, make our way east for a mile, and we should end up exactly where your hackers say the access point to the server array is."

Wren grunted.

"Here," said Chaps, lifting the long tongue-like rebreather tube from where it hung from his mask, and attached it to his tanks in back. "Turning on your canned air."

She flicked a switch, and there was a hiss followed by a deeper silence as the interior of the mask pressurized. The air tasted stale and metallic. Everything seemed slower and heavier. He went to practice pulling his knife under the new conditions. The mask was unwieldy and threw off his balance, and made looking down at his own body impossible. His gloved hand pawed at his waist three times, constricted by the tight neoprene and tacked-on plastic around his forearms, but on the fourth he found the knife and swung a few experimental waves through the air before him.

"Ready?" Clara asked.

"Let's go."

Chaps handed over something to Clara, which Wren figured had to be the cable spool, then set down on her knees with a length of metal to pry up a nearby drain cover. In the mask, Wren couldn't pick out the cover's contours; there was no heat differential at all. He could barely even hear anything, bar the drumming of rain and Clara's low breathing, picked up by the subvocal rig.

"I can't pick it out," he said. "Can I change the visual settings?"

"Ask the system," Clara answered. "Fifty percent infrared is a good overlay for these conditions. In full dark, you'll want to go one hundred."

"Fifty percent overlay," Wren subvocalized, and instantly his vision took on greater clarity. He could see the drain leading down, and the crowbar in Chaps' hands, as well as her orange glow and the red box around her still.

Just then there was a muffled clank and Chaps reared back. "It's open," she said. "Good luck!"

Pooling water in the hospital lot cascaded down the open drain.

"Hellion, B4cksl4cker, have you got the route ahead mapped," Wren asked.

"As much as possible, Christopher," Hellion answered in his ear. "We are with you."

"After you," Clara said.

Wren peered into the hole, then set his foot carefully through, found the first rung and began the descent.

50

DARK

The sewer was a simple tube barely five feet in diameter, forcing Wren into a low stoop as he touched down on the curving concrete base. A torrent of fast-flowing rainwater flowed halfway up his thighs, and there was no light but the faint rinse of gray from above.

"Seventy percent," he whispered, and the suit's AI accommodated the request, shifting the mix in his infrared goggles. The tunnel snapped into a sharper clarity ahead; a long geometric tunnel leading away in lightly contoured shades of gray.

Clara stepped down into the stream behind him, holding the cable spool.

"Check comms," she subvocalized.

"We hear you," B4cksl4cker said. "Proceed directly east."

"East is a go," said Wren, and started into the dark at a hunched-over run, half-carried along by the wastewater current.

"You should reach first descent in seven hundred yards," Hellion said.

"I'll drop transponders," Clara said in his ear. "If you see NBPs, take it easy. They don't know who we are; we'll show up as friendlies in their systems."

"Roger that," Wren said.

Every step carried him deeper into the dark. He scaled his vision back up to one hundred percent infrared, and the tunnel's pitch-black confines became a polygonal wireframe stretching to a vanishing point. His legs sloshed through the water and his hands patted the walls and ceiling, but they felt very distant, like the fins and engine of some deep-water submersible. The rhythmic suck of his breath isolated him. The mask cut him off, luring him into a kind of steady-state lope. This is what it felt like to be an *akaname*. he figured, removed from the real world and living by your own law.

"Here," came Hellion's voice in his head. "Down now, Christopher."

He stopped, momentarily confused. A hand came on his shoulder. "It's OK", came another voice. It took him a second to register it was Clara. "It happens to us all. The mask, the confines, it zones you out. But things are about to get real."

He turned to her. In the deep dark she burned like a Roman candle, haloed by a blocky blue box. Those big eyes, that lagging tongue. His hand instinctively went to his knife, but Clara caught him at the wrist, exerting just enough pressure to slow his reactions.

"It's OK, big guy, it's just me. Look past the mask."

Wren took a breath, then pulled his hand back. "Sorry."

"It happens. Now look down."

He looked down. The precise water-level was invisible via the infrared goggles, but he could feel it running around his thighs. He kept scanning below until he picked out the wireframe contours of the shaft leading directly down.

"Friction imparts a little heat to the walls," Clara whispered. "Enough to pick out the route. They say we're going down. I've never been this way; all records I've accessed show it's too narrow for human passage. We'll find out soon enough. Get ready to submerge."

He stared down into the shaft, some three feet across. It looked like the throat into an *akaname* underworld.

"Down some distance then south in narrow access chute," came Hellion's voice, slightly scratchy now with interference.

Clara slapped a transponder against the ceiling, then turned to Wren. "I can take lead," she offered.

Wren tried to shake off the strange sense of disconnection plaguing him. There was no time to waste.

"It's fine," he said, and dived headfirst into the shaft. His head and shoulders passed neatly into the gap, then the weight of his legs above drove him down. His hands found the ladder rungs and he pulled himself deeper rung by rung, kicking with his fins.

"That's a good motion," Clara said in his ear. "Look out for the surge chute to the Stadium's G-CANS, I'd estimate it's around thirty yards down."

Thirty yards was deep, and already Wren felt the pressure thickening around him; deep enough to suffer debilitating effects upon resurfacing. Microscopic bubbles of inert gas from the air tanks would begin compressing from his lungs into his blood and body. If he rose up again without taking enough time to decompress, those bubbles would burst out like fizz from a shaken soda bottle, spreading agonizingly through his skin, joints, lungs, muscles and brain.

The bends.

Dangerous. Lethal, if he went deep enough then came up too fast.

"Christopher, do you see access chute?' came Hellion's voice, very faintly now. "I think you are close."

"Not yet," he subvocalized back. The wireframe of the tunnel was growing faint, as the slowing flow of water reduced the temperature differential provided by friction. Perhaps that was a signal that several flows were about to meet. "I think-"

He stopped dead instantly, falling silent to hang upside down in the water and stare as a blazing orange figure emerged through the wall five yards below. It was facing upward and had the limpid round eyes, the lolling tongue and the sleek neoprene outline of an *akaname.*

Wren's heart jumped up into his mouth. The creature was circled with a blue box, marking it as a friendly, but it didn't feel friendly. The dark staff in its hands didn't feel friendly either. It was a shotgun-like shaft of some kind, silhouetted dark against the *akaname*'s hot body, swinging around now to point straight up at him, and what could that mean other then-

"Hug the wall!" Wren shouted, pushing off the ladder even as he kicked hard with both legs.

The bolt released invisibly from the *akaname*'s harpoon gun, shooting up toward Wren. He felt the faint displacement in the water then the slicing pain as it glanced off his trailing left calf.

Another seven yards. Clara shouted something from behind, but Wren had no time to help her. All that mattered was reaching the *akaname* before he could reload. Wren kicked with all his strength and pulled down hard on the rungs, closing the yards in seconds, just fast enough that he managed to get his fingertips on the harpoon gun's tip in time to push it sideways.

The bolt fired off with an audible jolt and a compaction of the deep water, whipping past Wren's shoulder and away up the shaft. Without thinking Wren grasped the gun and tugged with his left hand, even as he brought his right hand down in an almighty punch.

It struck the *akaname*'s face mask with no power at all; the water robbing it of any momentum. By then the figure had released the gun and wriggled in the water, pulling out the pale orange blade of a long knife, drawn from a holster kept tight against the body.

Wren stared like this was happening to someone else. The knife came in for his forearm, and he only jerked to action at the last moment, but not fast enough. The blade bounced off his reinforced plastic forearms and the tip sank into his bicep. He let out a cry then grabbed the handle. The *akaname* wasted no time, kicking up from below to use his whole weight to drive the knife in deeper.

Wren shoved sideways at the same time, and the blade sheared off the side of Wren's arm and the *akaname* rocketed past him, knocking Wren spinning into the wall. His head clanked off the ladder and his body spun off-kilter in ways he hadn't anticipated for. While he'd spent plenty of time underwater, he had no experience of underwater combat. He tried to get a purchase on the ladder with his feet but his rotation pulled them off, then he tried to push off the facing wall to reorient himself, but by then the *akaname* was coming back toward him.

Just then a tremendous impact thumped into Wren's lower back. He looked down and saw the hot orange tip of a harpoon bolt emerging just above his right hip.

He'd been shot from below; a through-and-through.

The first *akaname*'s knife came in from above. Wren did his best to blank out the sudden pain from his belly and finally found his footing on the ladder. This time he caught the incoming *akaname* by the wrist, and this time he had the leverage.

The figure's wrist was thin and fragile; Wren squeezed with both hands and wrenched it sideways. The *akaname*'s shriek carried even through the water. Wren wasn't done though, and twisted in the water as hard as he could, thrashing like a rolling alligator to drag his prey with him.

He completed the underwater pirouette just in time for the *akaname*'s body to absorb the thunk of another harpoon bolt. The razor-sharp tip speared out through its chest, unleashing a plume of hot blood that clouded Wren's vision.

He kicked at the water, propelling forward by feel. There was hardly any sound and only the rush of his own breathing in his ears as he pushed the dying *akaname* ahead like a shield. One more bolt buried itself in the body, then Wren shoved it aside and met the second *akaname* head on.

This one hovered just inside the chute heading south, harpoon gun forgotten and drifting away, with a long knife blade now dancing out to replace it.

Wren couldn't stop his own momentum; all he could do was rely on his instincts and hope they carried underwater, as he pulled his own long Bowie knife from its holster.

The *akaname* sent out a swipe, but Wren managed to bat it away and lanced out with his own blade. The *akaname* retreated swiftly back into the narrow chute like a squid coiling amongst the rocks, its goggling eyes leering out from its perch.

Wren kicked off the shaft's wall to fire himself like a torpedo into the chute, knife out like the nose of a sawtooth shark. The *akaname* backpedaled desperately, but the chute was barely two feet wide, not wide enough to turn around in and get any real purchase on the water. Wren hit and pushed the blade through the *akaname*'s guard and steadily into his chest.

The figure kicked and roiled, but there was nowhere to go. Wren kept driving forward with his fins, driving the *akaname* backward at the point of the blade, so his own dead weight in the water drove it home until it punched through ribs and bisected the heart.

The *akaname* stilled.

Wren let go of his dead body and managed to holster his knife. He felt giddy and lightweight in the crushing force of water all around.

"Clara?" he subvocalized, but there was no response. "Hellion?"

Nothing came back. He pushed himself back along the chute, what felt like a very long way until he found himself back in the vertical shaft. The body he'd used as a shield was already some fifty feet down, flushed by the flow of water, its hot orange glow becoming a distant star. He looked upward, trying to pick out some trace of Clara, but she was gone.

Maybe she'd been hit by the first bolt; maybe flushed in another direction by an unexpected flow of water.

"Hellion!" he shouted.

Nothing came back through the suit but static. He pawed at his belt and managed to uncap the snaps, releasing a flurry of tiny transponder tabs. They blinked and spread but did nothing for the signal.

He was alone.

He contemplated going after Clara but dismissed that thought swiftly. The harpoon bolt through his belly had just put a tight clock on this operation. Take too long swimming along blind channels searching for her body, and he'd die of blood loss before he ever made it to the server room.

He had to hope Clara Baxter would survive on her own, as she had countless times before. Instead he clapped his hand to the wound. The water was a murky orange with the heat of his blood. The bolt ended in a three-cornered star of razor-sharp edges; slitting runs in his thick gloves as he probed. He reached around to his back and felt the slim flights of the harpoon bolt, extending some ten inches from above his right kidney. He considered tugging it free, but that would just open up the wound. At the same time, he couldn't keep swimming through narrow tunnels with a ten-inch bolt sticking out of his back.

He got both hands on the shaft where it emerged out of his back. If it was metal, this was hopeless. If it was wood or some kind of carbon fiber, then maybe…

He wrenched with both hands. Something in the bolt's shaft fractured like an *akaname* wrist, even as fresh pain lit through his belly. He gasped in stale air from the tanks, then made one more jerk to finish the job, breaking the shaft off just above his back.

A gray wave of unconsciousness swamped up toward him, but he pushed back. He had to stay awake or he'd certainly die down here. Makoto Toyama would die down here.

He turned his gaze back to the chute. Even now the harpoon gun, barely visible by the heat it still carried on its grip and shaft, was scraping along the lower edge in the current, about to fall off and sink down the shaft.

Wren snatched it just in time. He kicked into the chute until he found the floating body, retrieved three bolts from a snug quiver down its back, then loaded the gun and finned further into the darkness.

51

G-CANS

The tight chute stretched on for hundreds of yards, with no side channels, no shafts up or down, nothing. Wren had no map. He kept periodically trying a subvocal call to Hellion or Clara, but nothing returned, so he kept on finning forward, until after some four hundred yards he reached a four-way intersection.

One shaft cut straight through up and down, one slanted away up to the northwest, one slanted down to the southeast. They were all equally narrow, and at the edges Wren could feel the component mechanisms for retractable barriers. Clearly these chutes were designed with flood controls in mind; some could be opened, others closed, and the overflow redirected safely.

All four gates hung open. Perhaps that was something to be glad of. But it still left him with only four choices, with nothing on the comms.

He drew the map of his route so far in his head. His starting point had been Yoyogi Hospital, a mile due west of the National Stadium. The first tunnel had carried him seven hundred yards, call it close to half a mile, directly east. Then he'd dropped down and taken the chute south by some four hundred yards.

That suggested he needed to bear northwest. The closest

chute was heading southeast, but that was still the wrong direction. Maybe up or down were the right choices, but how much time did he have to waste in experimentation? Already the dizziness was getting worse. The world took on a silvery hue around him. He'd lost perhaps a quarter gallon of blood so far. The constricting neoprene was actually some help with that, forcing more of his blood back to the core, as was the cold water and the pressure.

The moment he stepped out of the water, though, the clock would pick up speed.

But which way?

For seconds he hung in the void of cross channels, buffeted by water flows from each direction tugging him sideways, up and down, until he realized the answer.

The *akaname* would tell him the direction.

He cast his mind back over what Clara had told him; the steps necessary to trigger an *akaname* security response. One was color. One was noise.

He had nothing colorful, but noise he could do.

He slid back into the chute he'd come from, laying his body as flat as he could manage so his heat signature was screened, while still maintaining an eyeline along all four other routes leading away. He took a deep breath, then a prompt came from the harpoon bolt emerging from his belly, scraping along the chute's concrete floor.

The roar of pain burst from his lungs and Wren made no effort to hold it back. He didn't use words, it was just inchoate sound which churned within the mask, pummeling his ears. His stomach burned as his lungs heaved. He kept shouting until his head swam with gray, then he stopped and sucked more stale air, counting the seconds.

A minute ticked by. More. It was hard to keep track in the *akaname*'s gray netherworld.

Then he saw something. A flash of heat encircled in a distant blue box, approaching from the tunnel slanting southeast and down. Wren tucked himself as far back into the chute as he could, waiting for first one, then two, then three figures to swim up the surge shaft. They all had the dark shafts of harpoon guns held across their bodies.

There was little sound and barely any extraneous motion. They moved smoothly and efficiently, as if they'd been born to the sewer pipes, every stroke leading them forward in synchrony. Wren's heart hammered in his chest, and he watched until he felt sure they'd see his glow spreading through the water; fifteen yards, ten yards. At that range he could hardly miss, and pushed the harpoon gun's tip over the edge of the chute, lining up the shot to fire.

The gun made a faint click in his hands as the bolt deployed. Water displaced, then there was a thunk, and Wren was already in motion, pulling and pushing himself out of the chute, across the shaft and hard down at the three panicking figures in the tunnel.

Wren saw he'd caught the first full in the face, the bolt shearing through the mask and back into his brain, killing him instantly. The others were struggling to get around him, or to turn around and flee.

There would be no escape from this, though.

Their own harpoon guns discharged harmlessly into the water. Caught in a roiling panic. Wren reached the dead body and pushed through, dragging the corpse back so he could squeeze past. His harpoon tip scraped off the wall again, flushing up another surge of immobilizing gray, but the adrenaline was pumping too hard now and beat it back.

They were backing away, glowing red *akaname* eyes wide, pushing off and against each other, their harpoon rifles forgotten. Then Wren was upon them.

The Bowie knife darted and slit; into the limpid left eyehole of the first, down to sever his rebreather tongue then up beneath his rib cage to finish the job. He bled out and died like chum in the water, and Wren scraped by him too, to the last. This one had his knife up, even made a game try to charge Wren, but Wren caught him by the throat, impaled the oncoming wrist with his open blade, then left the Bowie hanging while he proceeded to unmask the figure with his bare hands.

The mask's cinches ripped loose under Wren's prodigious strength, and the false face peeled back, revealing a tattooed yakuza male beneath that Wren thought he recognized. The guy from the pachinko parlor.

His hot, bright eyes opened wide and he clutched at his throat, sucking water instead of air, unmindful of the Bowie knife shredding his chest through his own wrist. Wren wasted no time to watch him die; he simply pulled the knife free, forced a path past the man as he convulsed and swam on.

The chute continued southeast and down for several hundred yards, then swerved due east, then hit a T-intersection with a vertical shaft. This time Wren rolled the dice and went straight up. It rose some twenty yards then surfaced into another five-foot wide round tunnel. This one was completely filled with water, but it ran east-west.

Wren broke east and swam as hard as he could. A hundred yards. Two hundred. He had to be closing on the Stadium now. If only he could-

"Christopher, answer please, Christopher!"

He gasped in his suit.

"Hellion!"

Her gasp rang through his head. "Christopher, you are alive! This is wonderful. Where are you?"

"A round tunnel that's got to be due west of the Stadium. Not far now. Can you direct me?'

"Yes, one moment Christopher. This is chaos, now."

"What happened? I lost Clara and then I lost comms."

"*akaname* came for Chaps, Christopher. I am sorry, she is gone. Entire comms array is destroyed. Somehow, they had warning where you will enter from. I am piggyback on multiple systems currently, including subway Wi-Fi booster. Fact you can hear me at all tells me-" keys flew, which made for a surreal sound deep underwater, "you are in secret overflow tunnel near Oedo line. Very deep line, very new, also excellent cover for laying cable. Christopher, you must continue one hundred yards, then climb up. From all data, this will lead you to secret server facility."

"Roger that," Wren said, filing away the apparent betrayal and loss of Chaps for later. "It's good to hear your voice, Hellion."

"And yours, Christopher, even if you are stubborn man sometimes. I said this was sewer side mission.""

Wren barked a laugh that surprised him. "Hellion."

"Yes, it is I. You are almost there, Christopher. Keep pushing. Yakuza strike is in full action now. This should help. But you may run out of-"

The signal died and her voice was lost in a haze of static. He kept trying as he swam on, but she didn't come back. Still, it was enough to buoy Wren on. In moments he spotted the shaft leading upward. It was filled with water too, and he kicked off the floor and shot up its spacious three-feet wide expanse. There were ladder rungs and he tugged on them, kicking with his fins, rising far too fast but there was nothing he could do about that but try to outrace the bends, until-

His head broke through the surface. He saw hot lights, the vector shape of some kind of dome, but little else.

"Thirty percent infrared," he said, and the mask adjusted immediately, overlaying the lights and vectors atop something he hadn't expected, but perhaps should have.

It wasn't another sewer or tunnel, though Wren had no doubt he was still at least fifty yards underground. Instead it looked like a moon pool chamber; an open surface of flat water around him, bounded by low retaining walls either side and all encircled by a pressurized metal dome studded with bright white lights.

He'd seen moon pools before in marine research stations and vessels, as well as on drill ships and oil platforms. Their pressurized nature kept the water from flooding up into the space, and allowed scuba divers easy access to the waters below, without facing the onslaught of ocean tides.

It was the perfect entrance route for the *akaname*. Now he'd cut infrared, Wren picked out the thick orange cable darknet leading out of the water alongside him. It headed across the floor and out of the chamber through the wall, beside which hung a large metal pressure door.

Wren pulled himself out of the pool. His body felt too heavy, the air tanks threatening to drag him back into the water, but he didn't shrug them off. He might need them. Instead he just reached round to his back, where he'd stowed an M&P pistol in a carefully wrapped and duct-taped bag in one of his large utility belt pockets.

The thick fingers of the gloved wetsuit barely fit through the trigger. He glanced at the harpoon bolt emerging from his belly, then regretted it. It looked bad. The neoprene was glossy with his blood. He strode toward the door, already feeling the dizziness and nausea of early-onset bends, even in this pressurized chamber.

Bubbles of inert gases were even now diffusing out of his tissues and trying to burst their way out through his joints, his skin, his nerves, and it was only going to get worse

There was nothing else for it, though. The door had a wheel, and he spun it hard. His belly throbbed. The door cracked open. Wren stepped through into a dark airlock, where a pair of tattooed man were just suiting up into their *akaname* gear.

Wren was on them before they could disentangle themselves from the suits. One he stabbed in the throat with the Bowie knife, and the other he held fixated with the M&P.

"Where is Makoto Toyama?" he said, as slowly and clearly as he could.

The man stared, eyes whipping to something on the floor, then he went for it.

Wren kicked him in the face, dropped an elbow into his back then finished him off with a knife thrust that severed his spine.

Wren took a breath. The small airlock space spun. It was glass-walled, had to be triple-thick and reinforced to withstand the pressure, but would allow anyone outside to check anyone coming in now.

He could see nothing beyond. Whatever kind of room it was, it was pitch black.

"Infrared eighty percent," Wren said, and instantly the room beyond snapped into thermal relief. There were no people, as far as he could see, but there were computers. Dozens of them, stretching away in rows, all the screens dead and only faintly lit by low red emergency lights. Not the server racks, he figured, but the control room for monitoring the new darknet line, the second line, maybe checking sensors and CCTV throughout the sewer system, and controlling the flood surges directly.

The door was right there. A red light blared above it, and it took Wren a long second to figure out what that meant. But of course. You couldn't open the inner door without first sealing the metal door to the moon pool, or the whole facility would flood from below.

He shifted back to the metal door. Every movement came slow and heavy now. He felt drained and weak; that was both the oncoming bends and the loss of blood. He slammed the metal door closed and spun the wheel until it locked. A few seconds passed, then the red light above the inner door switched off and a green one lit up.

He stepped up and put his hand on the handle. No time even to take off his *akaname* gear. He knew that as soon as he opened the pressure door the bends symptoms would come on thick and fast. He just had to find Toyama and hack the servers before it got so bad that all he could do was scream.

The handle turned. The door opened. The real agony began.

52

AGONY

Wind hissed out of the pressurized air lock as it equalized to the other side, and Wren's head instantly felt like it was clamped in a vise. Every part of his body screamed out for relief from the pain as the gases inside tried to tear him apart.

His joints seized and threatened to lock up. He felt sick and gagged. His first step barely landed, and he had to catch himself on the glass wall, but even that touch to his skin felt like blisters bursting. Breathing came hard, there was a gray tinge pressing around the edges of his vision and he wanted nothing more than to rip the mask and suit off.

But he didn't. The suit's compression might be the only thing keeping him alive, and the mask threw a few seconds of confusion his way whenever a fresh *akaname* saw him.

He staggered on, every step a further lurch into pain. He found his left hand clutched protectively around the bolt in his belly, while the M&P shuddered at his side; it would have dropped if not for the thick gloves caught in the trigger guard.

The control deck of dead computer screens passed by on his right. There was a door leading in, but he ignored it; Hellion and

B4cksl4cker had been very clear. He had to plug directly into the servers.

Stairs lay ahead, switch backing upwards. He took them, managed five then teetered. He couldn't get his left arm up in time but did manage to redirect his fall and avoid slamming the harpoon bolt into the stairs. His body slapped down on his left side and his head cracked off concrete, only slightly protected by the mask.

Inside the suit he grunted as the bubbles ran over his skin like a sharp-booted army of cockroaches. He shuddered and braced himself for another push back to his feet.

Then they were there.

Three figures. Men in business suits. Their faces were a blur, but they weren't *akaname*, at least not on the outside. One was Japanese, maybe yakuza with a trademark topknot man bun, while the other two were something else. Tall. White. Maybe American.

They seemed as surprised as Wren was.

"What the hell happened to this guy?" one of the Americans asked.

Wren shot him first, or tried to. It was hard to raise the S&P high enough, and instead he spun the guy with a shoulder shot. He rolled back, but the other two didn't stop. The second American swiftly pulled a gun. The yakuza pulled a sword out of nowhere and brought it flashing down.

Wren's brain jammed up. No way he could swing the gun in time to catch both. He had to pick one, and his stuttering brain made the choice for him; he could live without a limb, maybe, but a bullet could kill him clean.

The S&P discharged with a roar, and this time Wren's aim was luckier; the American's head popped like a soap bubble and he fell flat back. The sword came on though, arcing like a maul to split Wren like a cord of wood, until something too fast to see happened.

It seemed like a beam of silver light, shooting into the frame of Wren's vision and somehow deflecting the yakuza's blade before it cleaved down into Wren's outstretched palm. There was an almighty clang, followed by the arrival of someone new.

Another *akaname*.

Wren stared as the new figure stood over him, spinning a long curved blade so fast it made Wren's head throb. A katana.

The Japanese guy shouted an attack cry and lashed out. The new *akaname* leaped further into the fray. Wren entered a slow-motion slide backwards down the stairs, trying to make sense of what he was seeing. The sword was familiar, maybe something about the way the *akaname* moved, but he couldn't place it. Two steps slid by, three, and he struggled to half his steady descent.

The yakuza stabbed out three lightning thrusts with his blade, while the *akaname* blocked and riposted smoothly. It didn't make sense. To confuse things further, the *akaname* seemed to have a harpoon bolt sticking out of its shoulder. Had Wren done that? What was going on?

Five steps, now, and picking up speed. He thrashed for a railing but there was none. The gun was useless in his hand, preventing him from properly stopping his tumble. The yakuza redoubled his attack, this time focusing on the *akaname*'s right side, realizing the weakness.

The *akaname* defended slowly, barely managing to send the blade glancing away, and taking a cut across the triceps as payment.

Then Wren heard her. Maybe she'd been talking the whole time, her voice a sibilance in his ear that was swallowed up and overawed by the nausea.

"Help me."

It was Clara Baxter!

The yakuza was coming in hard. The *akaname*'s katana was gone. It was so fast Wren hadn't seen it happen. She was defenseless. The yakuza thrust his blade out, a heart shot, and only stopped when Wren's bullet ripped through his rib cage.

In the right side, out the left and ricocheting leftover

momentum out in a rattle up the stairs. Blood spurted, the yakuza spun and his sword fell, then he coughed blood. He turned, eyes focusing on Wren, and managed a few words in Japanese before he fell and slid down the stairs.

Wren's descent was sped by the discharge of his M&P, so he came to rest at the bottom of the stairs, looking into the yakuza's eyes as he died.

Then the *akaname* was there, hoisting him up.

"I thought that was you," came Clara's voice in his ear. Her *akaname* expression didn't shift in the slightest. As impersonal as a phone call. "That ridiculous swagger."

Wren coughed. "It's the bends."

"We've all got the bends," Clara said.

"And a new piercing."

She laughed, dropping down the steps to stand over him. "I'm thinking of getting mine removed."

He raised his hand to her, realized he was pointing the gun at her, then offered the other hand. "It suits you," he gasped. "Mine, though, is a real drag. I feel like I've been hooked by some giant fisherman."

She grabbed his hand with her left hand and hauled. "We're both falling apart. I thought I was dead."

Wren finally regained his feet. Silver lights flashed behind his eyes. "You came in through the moon pool?" he managed.

"Right behind you. Same for the sewers. I followed the trail of blood."

Wren grunted, trying to push through the pain. "I'm sorry. I thought you were flushed away."

"I was. This hit," she nodded at the bolt protruding from her chest, "knocked me out cold for five minutes. I came to half a mile away. Close enough that my basic comms heard them killing Chaps."

That reminder dumped a fresh swell of adrenaline into Wren's system. He straightened up. "I'm sorry. We need to finish this."

"Agreed."

She spun her katana and took a step up, then almost fell. Wren held out his hand. She stared at it for a moment, seemed to undergo some complex calculation. Wren knew it wasn't easy. She wasn't the kind of person to ask for help. Neither was Wren. But maybe, together…

She took it. Wren steadied her as much as she steadied him. With the blade in her left hand and the M&P in his right, they tackled the stairs together.

53

RIPPER

The stairs gave way to a corridor lined with white vinyl. Harsh fluorescent lights flooded the space from above. Basic, simple, practical. Two directions, left and right.

"I'll go-" Wren began, but Clara cut him off.

"We go together."

He grunted, and they hobbled right. A guy sped from a room on the left, discharging his own pistol wildly. Wren caught him center mass, knocking him into a spin, and Clara finished him with a single decapitating stroke. His head bounced along the corridor, still spinning like a top.

The room he'd emerged from looked like a security bay. There were a dozen monitors showing various CCTV feeds: many of white-lined corridors, one of the moon pool, one of the corridor outside with a spreading red stain, one of what looked to be a vast server array, and one of Makoto Toyama.

Wren's heart boomed. Toyama was dressed in a white surgical gown, gagged and bound in the corner of a white room, with a tall Japanese man holding her from behind. He had one thick arm wrapped around her neck, the other held a bloodied scalpel to her stomach as he dragged her toward the door.

A red mist descended on Wren. Everything else disappeared.

"I have to-" he began, turning to Clara, but the mounting fury in her eyes stopped him cold.

"I know. Let's go."

They went on together.

The pain in his middle receded. The nausea and agony of the bends faded back. His stride evened out as his body surged with a final burst of adrenaline.

Figures appeared ahead of him. They fired and Wren fired back. Clara spun, taking off limbs and hacking through heads. The M&P clicked empty, and he scavenged more magazines. Perhaps he glimpsed the server racks through a window, but he didn't care.

All that mattered was Toyama.

Doors opened in every white-lined corridor they passed down. Men emerged like cockroaches from under a rock. Yakuza. *Akaname*. NBPs. 'Real Boys'.

Wren's gun bucked in his fist. Clara spun and sliced. He didn't feel the kills. Nothing seemed to matter. He'd kill a thousand just to-

Then Toyama was there.

It was abrupt, staggering out through a door that Wren was too bleary-eyed to even see, with the big man close behind. They were just ten yards away. Now blood was trailing down from Toyama's stomach, where the scalpel blade touched her skin.

Everything stopped.

Toyama was kicking and scrabbling like a woman possessed. Tall, beautiful, righteous Toyama, fighting this giant man with everything she had.

But the man was a monster; easily 6'5", with steroid-induced muscles bulging through an all-black suit. His forehead jutted forward like a caveman, but his eyes told the whole story.

He was a killer. He'd killed before. He'd kill again.

"Do it!" Toyama shouted.

Wren fired.

Not at the head. A shot to the head could lead to random

neurons firing as the brain disengaged, which could lead to a single fatal twitch of the hand holding the scalpel, which could gut Toyama like a fish.

Better to take out the machinery that could deliver the fatal blow.

Two bullets blasted through the big man's right elbow, shredding muscle, bone and tendons in a spray of organic shrapnel and blood. The arm holding the scalpel began its inexorable drop, just as Wren's trigger finger pulled an empty click from the M&P's mechanism.

Out of bullets.

The big man roared but didn't over-react; he didn't step out from behind the cover Toyama provided, and his left hand clamped tight around her windpipe. Wren had nothing, no way to stop a man of his strength from ripping her throat out in the time it would take him to close the ten-yard gap.

Good thing Clara was already moving at a sprint. Her katana swept back then plunged forward with precise aim, the blade shooting through the big man's head like meat for the grill; in through the left eye, out through the back of his head.

He jerked back, yanking the blade from Clara's hand, but miraculously did not drop immediately to the floor. Toyama fell to her knees, choking for breath through her damaged throat. Clara lunged for the hilt of her sword as the big man staggered like a drunk, pawing wildly at the blade jutting from his face with his good left hand.

Clara closed the gap again and yanked on the hilt, but the blade was stuck; wedged through the thick bone plate at the back of his skull, and all she succeeded in doing was dragging him onto her.

His left fist swung in a massive haymaker blow that nearly took off her head. She was flung left into the wall, where she struck and collapsed and did not get up.

Then Wren was there. The M&P was forgotten, so instead he sank the Bowie knife with all his flagging strength into the gap inside the big man's right clavicle. It sank deep, but too far from the heart to achieve a killing blow, and now the dying beast spun on Wren.

Both arms flailed wide and he clamped down around him in a huge bear hug. His right arm sagged at the elbow and was weakened at the shoulder, but he more than made up for that by closing his grip with his good left hand and slamming Wren in.

Instantly he felt the crush. The gray walls rose up. His arms were pinned by his side and his ribs were already creaking with the pressure. The big man was minutes from death, and all Wren had to do was tweak the sword in his skull or tug on the knife in his chest, but he couldn't move his arms an inch.

The gray walls of unconsciousness rose up. Toyama was gasping. Clara was out for the count. It fell to Wren, and now he was going to die in the embrace of this pin-cushioned freak.

"Uncork ... you..." he hissed in Wren's ear as he squeezed. Three-hundred-plus pounds of solid mass on a 6' 5" frame could smother even a man of Wren's size. He couldn't get a breath in. He couldn't do anything but strain helplessly away.

Then he remembered the big man's threat. The big man's name.

The Ripper.

And he understood what had to happen next.

He managed to get his arms up enough to grip the Ripper's back and hold him tight. He managed to get his right leg up enough to kick off the nearby wall, propelling them both backward in an ugly clinch.

Wren's back slammed into the wall. The harpoon bolt through his middle jammed hard and pushed through his body, thrusting the razor-sharp tip a good few inches into the Ripper's belly.

His eyes flared wide.

The pain for Wren was indescribable.

"Uncork this," he whispered in the dying man's ear, then

threw everything he had into a propulsive twist, forcing the harpoon's tip to unzip a deep line across the big man's stomach.

The Ripper sucked in a startled breath, and stepped back, and for a moment everything held still as gravity found its new balance. Then the contents of his abdominal cavity cascaded to the ground like filth in a sewer drop.

This time he fell and was dead before he hit the ground.

Wren dropped to his knees, vision dimming. Blood was everywhere. He'd come uncorked, too, and the flow was picking up. He sagged to his side, aware that he'd just sacrificed the mission for a woman, and now they were all going to die.

Then Toyama was there. Looming over him in her bloodied white surgical gown, moving swiftly and smoothly, pressing one hand hard against the wound in his belly.

"This is going to hurt," she said in a hoarse whisper, then wrapped one hand around the bolt in his belly and ripped it the rest of the way out.

He roared. She followed up by snatching up a gun, discharging it three times down the corridor, then pressing the baking hot muzzle directly against his wound.

The pain punched him down into the dark.

54

FARM

Wren saw the farm.

It wasn't the way he'd left it, though. The bodies of X fanatics weren't garlanded across the clearing like bunting after a party. There was no blood. The cabin still stood, exactly as he'd built it. The skies were blue and the forest was green, and the peaceful silence was the most beautiful thing he'd ever experienced.

Until a noise disrupted it all.

His son, Jake, came bursting through the undergrowth and out into the clearing. He was riding a BMX bike and laughing hard. His daughter Quinn followed.

A race.

Wren saw himself from the outside, standing at the edge of the clearing where the finished brick pizza oven stood. Now the air hung with the scent of sizzling cheese and crisping pepperoni. The kids raced each other around a fire Wren had set for s'mores later that evening; when the sun dropped down and they wrapped up in sleeping bags and watched shooting stars streak across the night sky.

"Chris!" someone called, but it was a distant voice coming

from very far away. Wren went to scoop out the crunchy pizza from the oven but-

"Chris, you have to wake up!"

He came back to himself in the white corridor, upright and hanging with his arms slung over the shoulders of two figures, one all in black, the other all in white. Everything hurt and there was a roar of water all around. He could just pick out a flood tide rising up his body. His waist, his stomach, his chest. Someone was shouting, and finally he caught out the words.

"You have to climb, Chris!"

He turned. It was Toyama. She was right there, holding him up. She steered his chin around, redirecting his gaze to the ladder right in front of him, stretching up.

"You have to climb," she repeated. "The *akaname* are flooding the facility!"

The words made little sense to Wren. He turned the other way and saw the figure all in black. He could see her face, now, with the mask stripped away. The whole right side was black with bruising from the Ripper's punch, her right eye was solid red with ruptured blood vessels, but otherwise she looked OK.

Clara Baxter.

"They blew up the moon pool," she shouted over the chaos of thrashing water. "The pressure's tanking everywhere and this is the only way. We climb or we die."

She took Wren's right hand and put it on the ladder rungs. Every movement burned.

"Flash... drive," he managed to whisper.

"Toyama handled it. Now climb or we all die!"

He didn't have anything left in him. Not blood, not energy, not adrenaline.

"Now!" she ordered.

He closed his fist around the rung and climbed.

It climb stretched on forever. Throughout the two women steered and guided him. At the top he collapsed, and they slung him over their shoulders again and hobbled on. The water kept chasing. Wren thought about forgotten underground rivers, and *yokai* monsters lurking in the dark, and a second secret darknet streaming filth into depraved minds.

Finally, a door opened somewhere, and they burst onto a brightly lit subway station filled with cheering people, all waving the colors of their football team.

Wren dropped to the floor. A train rushed in, pushing a cushion of warm air ahead of it. Toyama went for the nearest phone. Clara started yelling for a doctor. Then Wren was back on the farm, and the days just stretched on and on, filled with fun adventures as he scooped for crystals in the creek with his kids, and raced bikes along the trails, and rumbled away on hayrides that went on long into the night…

55

SYMMETRY

Wren came to in a low-lit, cavernous metal space, surrounded by the deep grumble of overpowered engines. The air smelled of gun-oil and jet fuel, suggesting a large military transport plane, maybe a Hercules. He was laid flat on his back on a gurney, which clanked and jostled against its restraints as they passed through patches of turbulence.

Everything ached, from the top of his scalp down to the tips of his toes. That was the remnant of the bends, he figured. His stomach was a numb black hole; probably they had him on a spinal block, or the pain of his injuries would be overwhelming.

Long minutes passed as he lay still, remembering flashes: a paramedic crew putting emergency staples into his stomach and back right there on the train platform, tubing a flow of blood packs direct into his aortal artery, and even hitting him with a crash cart when his heart flagged out.

Toyama had been there throughout. Not Clara Baxter, though. He smiled at the memory of her receding back on the train platform; the anti-*akaname* returning to the sewers she'd came from. She'd saved his life, this time. They'd saved each other. But it wasn't her style to hang around. Besides, she had her own crew to think of now.

Chaps was dead. Maybe others; Wren had no way of knowing.

After that they'd transported him up from the train station and into a waiting ambulance, where the real work began; fresh blood and pre-emptive antibiotics were pumped into him, followed by a full-body iodine rinse to combat the gray water he'd been submerged within, the they wheeled him into surgery.

He sank in and out of consciousness in the hours that followed, laid up in a dark ward. At times Toyama was there; she had bandaging on her stomach, but otherwise she looked well.

"The whole complex is underwater," she said quietly. "But it's OK, Chris. I inserted the flash drive. I got everything!"

He didn't try to say anything. Just mustering the wind to speak brought the gray walls of unconsciousness rising up again.

"It was encrypted, but your hackers did an end-run and the whole thing's opened up. Raids are already happening! Suzuki-san, he's now taken over from Yamaguchi, he's leading the arrests. We're getting the ringleaders, Chris; soon we'll have them all and we'll start working on all the lower tiers. It'll be hundreds; the biggest yakuza bust in Japan's history. It's a huge win!"

He drifted back under before he could say anything.

Wren tilted his head to look around the Hercules. There were several medical stands holding half-full blood and plasma bags, all tubed into him. Looking down at his own body, he saw the metal structure of a traction rig, likely bolted to his pelvis, to prevent any movement tearing the delicate sutures inside his belly.

Across the way two figures dressed in military medical fatigues were slumped in the webbing against the side wall, asleep.

"Hey," he whisper-shouted, his voice coming out hoarse and painful. "Hey!"

One of the surgeons shifted. His eyes opened on Wren and widened wide. He extricated himself from the webbing and hurried over, talking in low tones.

"Corporal, how are you awake? We gave you enough tranquilizers to dose a horse."

"I have … a fast constitution," Wren whispered. Just saying that much left him breathless and panting.

The surgeon surveyed him swiftly and professionally; checking his readouts on a monitor, the levels in his blood bags and inspecting the traction rig around.

"Everything looks OK. How do you feel?"

"Like I got … my guts spiked."

The surgeon nodded. "It'll get worse. What you did, it's...." He trailed off. "It might interest you to know, another few minutes in that water and you'd have fallen into irreparable sepsis. The Japanese team did incredible work to flush your whole system. They built a solid foundation for us to work with."

"Thank you," he whispered. "We going ... home?"

"Back to the US, Sir? Yes, Sir!"

Wren cursed low. He hadn't wanted that, though he understood why they'd done it. He hadn't even had a chance to say goodbye.

"Can you ... get me a ... phone?"

The man stared. "Sir, you're in no condition to-"

"Phone," Wren insisted. "That's an … order. In the ... nicest way."

The surgeon considered for a second, then shrugged and dropped a hand into his pocket and came out with a curved Samsung cell phone. "This is my personal cell phone. We're not supposed to, but it'll be my honor. Number?"

Wren recited the number. The surgeon dialled and it went through. The line rang twice then hung up.

Wren frowned. There was something strange about the ring tone; like an echo.

"Try again," he whispered.

The surgeon hit redial. This time there was only one ring before the hang-up, and there was definitely an echo.

Then a touch came on his shoulder.

He looked up, and saw dark eyes framed by dark hair, looking down. For a moment he thought he had to be hallucinating, but the details were too realistic; she was clearly exhausted, with slumping shoulders and red-rimmed eyes, but there was a clear resolve in the set of her jaw that made her more beautiful than ever.

"Toyama?" he croaked.

She smiled. "Hey, Chris. I thought someone better escort you home."

His lips cracked in an involuntary smile. "You're on the plane."

She smiled right back. "I'm on the plane."

He couldn't quite believe it, and didn't know what to say. "Very gentlemanly ... of you. But ... how?"

She squeezed his shoulder. "I hammered some nails. I had to. You risked a lot for me." Her smile quirked guilily. "But I'll be honest, those nails weren't exactly procedure, and my presence here may not be entirely approved."

"Wait. You're saying ... you're a stowaway?"

Toyama just shrugged, and this time Wren let out a single rasp of laughter. It ached right down to his belly, but it was worth it. There was something about this woman.

"They must know ... you're on board ... now."

Her smile spread. "They do. I'm in big trouble, apparently. Ordered to get right back on the next plane to Tokyo."

Wren could only admire the symmetry. At the start, she'd been the one saying those words to him.

"Stay," he said.

The word came unbidden. He hadn't meant to say it and it surprised even him.

"Come see ... the farm," he followed up. "You'll love it."

She gazed at him for a long moment, then she leaned in closer, until her dark eyes filled his vision.

"OK," she whispered, and leaned in for a kiss.

FROM THE AUTHOR

Thank you for reading Never Forgive! I hope you loved Wren's first overseas adventure. I lived in Tokyo, Japan, for 10 years, and while I didn't bring down an evil underground cartel during that time, I did visit many of the same places Wren did. I can highly recommend a visit.

I'd also like to recommend something new and exciting: Girl Zero - the first book in the Clara Baxter thrillers.

Zero carries her own dark secrets and grudges, offering a glimpse into a world where assassins lurk around every corner, family must be fought for at all costs, and criminal organizations reign supreme.

Or at least, they think they do...

You don't need to read Girl Zero to enjoy Wren's next adventure - War of Choice, set in Ukraine just as the war begins - but it will certainly deepen the experience.

\- Mike

ALSO BY MIKE GRIST

Christopher Wren (thrillers)

Saint Justice

No Mercy

Make Them Pay

False Flag

Firestorm

Enemy of the People

Backlash

Never Forgive

War of Choice

Hammer of God

Girl Zero (thrillers)

Girl Zero

Zero Day

Kill Zero

The Last Mayor (post-apocalypse)

The Last

The Lost

The Least

The Loss

The List

The Laws

The Lash

The Lies

The Light

Printed in Great Britain
by Amazon

61170217R00180